AN
OKTOBERFEST
DEATH

Melody and Justin —
   It was wonderful meeting
you at the Kiefer party! Here's
another murder mystery to keep you
in that frame of mind. Thanks for
ordering.   Prost!
                    Tom
www.thomasjmillerauthor.com

@thomasjmillerauthor

AN
OKTOBERFEST
DEATH

A BETHANY R. JUDGE MYSTERY

Thomas J. Miller

iUniverse

AN OKTOBERFEST DEATH
A BETHANY R. JUDGE MYSTERY

iUniverse books may be ordered through booksellers or by contacting:

iUniverse
1663 Liberty Drive
Bloomington, IN 47403
www.iuniverse.com
844-349-9409

ISBN: 978-1-5320-8796-7 (sc)
ISBN: 978-1-5320-8795-0 (e)

Library of Congress Control Number: 2020917580

Print information available on the last page.

iUniverse rev. date: 09/17/2020

For my wife, Tamara.
Thank you for your endless love and support.

CHAPTER 1

A LATE-NIGHT TRAIN

They left the station punctually at 22:00, marking another success in on-time departures for the German rail system. Night had fallen heavily over the city, but as they continued into the countryside, the darkness thickened, leaving little to see out the train's large windows. He looked at the American again and briefly shook his head. She had been so proud of herself, of her visit to the Oktoberfest. For the first twenty minutes of the train ride, she had ranted like a drunken lunatic, repeating over and over that this was the best experience of her drinking career. She had made claims he couldn't quite understand. Of being a beer expert. What did she call it? A Master Cicerone? His English was good, but he didn't understand those words. When he had a chance, he'd have to look it up. But not tonight. No, he had other work to complete.

Her breathing had settled, suggesting that severe inebriation had given way to a deep, drunken slumber. Morning, he knew from experience, was not something this stranger should look forward to. A smart woman would serve herself a beer for breakfast.

He smiled thinly, admiring her passion. He could respect it. Who didn't take pride in their profession? He certainly held himself to high standards. He was certain she did the same for herself.

It was odd, though. She had said something else between her slurred words. About being a cop. Okay, not exactly that. More like an ex-cop. From Buffalo, New York. That had given him reason to raise his eyebrows, maybe even reveal his pleasant surprise in the corners of his eyes. He was very good at not showing emotions, at remaining detached, but he knew Buffalo a bit, back from the time he had slipped across the Peace Bridge for a job down in Cleveland. It had been simple to sneak into America. But ever since then, nothing had been very easy.

Except maybe tonight. Yes, tonight—this was working out just fine.

She called herself Bethany Judge. Bethany R. Judge, to be exact. And she said some German woman she met in baggage claim at the airport that morning had just come up with the neatest nickname for her: Beer Judge. A little play on Bethany—her mom had called her Bee—plus her middle initial and last name. Bee R. Judge. Beer Judge. He shook his head again. Women were hard to understand sometimes, regardless of their nationality.

And now, with this new career as a beer expert, she had to come to Munich to try the real stuff, the true Oktoberfest beer. Not the questionable versions they were producing back in America. He appreciated that comment the moment she said it. Sure, he had tried some decent examples of Oktoberfest beers in the United States, but it was nothing compared to what the Munich breweries created. The flavor, the freshness—Munich's beers were incomparable.

The man across from Bethany also slept, a light snore rising from deep in his throat. He had watched this rotund middle-aged German kindly and gently help Bethany through Munich's Hauptbahnhof, the main train station. Bethany had been a mess, stumbling her way to the train, hanging onto to his shoulder. She had called him Hans, thanked him even, and poor Hans had needed to suffer through the criticism of his two friends. They had wanted Hans to abandon Bethany on the train, to get back to the Oktoberfest. Hans had insisted against it, saying this was the gentlemanly thing to do.

Jake and Uli—those were Hans's friends. He had watched them together at the Oktoberfest and then as they had helped Bethany out of the beer tent, down to the U-Bahn, and over to the Hauptbahnhof. He had wondered a little about their intentions, listening closely as they yelled at each other, putting faces to the names. They worked together at the brewery, the Augustiner Bräu, and had been at the Oktoberfest that day. It was their day off; the whole brewery was closed so the workers could enjoy a day at the Wies'n, as the Oktoberfest was known in Munich. And Jake had simply bumped into Bethany, met her randomly. Jake had realized that she was an American, like him, and alone. So Jake had invited her to join them.

And now they were on this train together. Hans, Bethany, and him. The trip would be short, but even shorter for some. He reached into his pocket, feeling the knife. Thoughts drifted through his mind as he recalled the day. Had he made any mistakes, let himself be identified? Would someone come for him when the job was done? He closed his eyes, thinking through every step, every moment. In the back of his mind, knowing what was to come, he pondered the kindness of strangers and the dangers of traveling alone. Bethany Judge might have considered these things before her visit to Munich.

He had waited to board the train, given it until the last moments before the whistle blew and the doors slid shut. He had felt the need to create the perception of chance, of hurrying to not miss the late-night train. That kind of thing happened often enough, even in a country renowned for the punctuality of its trains. Humans—even Germans—had the tendency to push their luck to the last second. Even Jake and Uli had yelled at him to hurry as he sprinted down the platform. The fools. Yes, the ruse had felt complete.

He had jumped onboard, three cars distant from where Hans and Bethany sat. As the train had lurched, beginning its departure from the station, he had moved easily in their direction, his body swaying with the rhythm of the train's motion. His eyes had passed over every passenger, measuring his or her demeanor. Did the person seem nervous? Agitated? Was there any reason he or she would interfere with his mission?

He had passed plenty of open seats and many available cabins, feigning a search for a reserved seat. He had kept moving, each car feeling as though it stretched to eternity, his own anxiety growing. He knew they were onboard; he had heard Jake and Uli cursing Hans, telling him to just leave her behind. They had only wanted to get back to the Oktoberfest. But Hans had insisted, had claimed it was his duty. And begrudgingly, his friends had fetched some bottles of Helles beer from a nearby shop, something to keep Hans occupied during the long trip down to Garmisch. That was where they were going—an overnight round trip to the small town at the foothills of the Alps. The train ride, he would learn moments later from Bethany's intoxicated ramblings, was a hell of a lot less expensive than a Munich hotel during the Oktoberfest.

He had to admire their loyalty. Jake and Uli didn't get Hans bottles of Spaten or Paulaner, or Hacker-Pschorr or Löwenbräu. No, it had to be the Helles from their brewery, the place they all worked together, the famous Augustiner Bräu. He smiled. They had passed the brewery moments after the train left the station. It stood just a short distance off the main tracks on Landsbergerstrasse. The monks who had founded the brewery nearly seven hundred years ago— could they even have imagined the quality of the beer that would be made today? Guessed that the Oktoberfest would have started as a wedding festival in 1810 and grown into a modern international phenomenon? Predicted their ancient brewery would hold the reason behind what he had to do tonight?

Then he had found them, alone, just the two of them in a second-class cabin. Bethany was a waterfall of loud inebriated words. Hans sat across from her, looking both amused and bored, his mustache tinted with the hint of beer foam. Someone needed to hand him a napkin.

With a deep breath and a quick pull on the sliding door, he had opened the cabin. Hans had looked his way.

"Tickets?" Hans had asked.

"No, no," he had said, shaking his head. "Is a space free?"

Hans had motioned to the seat beside Bethany.

"Thank you," he had said, thinking that he'd rather sit beside an attractive lady than a fat man well along the path to killing himself.

Hans's breath reeked of beer and Snus; the aroma filled the cabin. He had wondered how Hans could even taste his beer, filling his nostrils with that horrible snorted tobacco. That stuff was a certain path to an early grave.

Not that Hans would live long enough to suffer that miserable fate.

He had spent the first thirty minutes of the journey listening to Bethany's ceaseless chatter. He kind of enjoyed it, actually, if only as an opportunity to practice his English skills. Speaking, reading, writing, and listening were all different talents when it came to foreign languages. He needed to take advantage of all opportunities, especially when he could pick up little intricacies of a local accent. Bethany sounded like a typical Buffalonian, just like the ones he had met when he crossed over from Canada for that Cleveland job. They had been helpful fellas, very nice guys. Too bad they had sounded so stupid.

With that thought, he had smiled at the silent joke. It was an unfair characterization, he knew, but hardly different than what students of German said about the Bavarian accent. Or the Austrian accent. Yes, those southern dialects were far different than the polished, clipped Hochdeutsch taught in schools. More primal, like a song that blended all the languages of Europe. Perhaps that was why Germany's greatest leader had risen from the tiny Austrian town of Braunau am Inn. He had spoken the languages of eternity.

Bethany had tired finally, the effects of too much alcohol bringing weight into her arms and legs. Dropping to her seat, she had exhaled loudly. He knew he wasn't a good audience, and he regretted that slightly. Some of what she had talked about might have been interesting on another day, in a different life. But today, quite frankly, he just needed her to shut up and sleep.

As if on cue, Bethany had allowed her eyes to flutter closed. Her breathing slowed and her body relaxed, the rocking of the train encouraging her to rest. The ride to Garmisch would not be long—just a couple of hours—and then would come the unpleasant wait in the station for the train back to Munich. He wondered how many hours that might be.

Hans had stood at that moment, pulling a thin blanket from the rack above Bethany's head. "It isn't much," Hans had said, his voice a whisper as he draped it across Bethany's body, "but it will keep the drafts away." Hans then plopped back into the seat across from Bethany, shivering slightly as he reached into his pocket and removed a small bottle opener.

He had watched Hans pop the lid from the bottle and then blow away the thin vapors that rose over the lip of the glass rim. He appreciated how brewery workers allowed their bottles to warm in their hands, usually for at least a few minutes. It improved the flavor, they claimed. Beer tasted better when it wasn't so cold, they said. It made sense, of course. The palate could not experience the malt and the hops when it was practically frozen.

Hans had kept to that tradition. It had taken a while—one hundred seconds to be exact—but finally Hans took his first swallow, letting the liquid wash over his teeth and tongue in soft, bubbly waves. He'd felt grateful when Hans stifled the belch that would naturally follow. Who could fight the carbonation in beer when they took a mouthful like that? A moment later his gratitude had been converted to repulsion when Hans released a long stream of rank breath. His job was getting easier by the moment.

He had looked at his watch—22:35. They would be to Garmisch before midnight. He needed to get this done quickly.

His eyes had eased mostly shut as he feigned an effort at sleep. He had watched Hans through his eyelashes, and soon, Hans drifted into an uncomfortable semisleep, disturbed only by the occasional motion of his hand lifting the bottle to his lips.

The conductor had passed through at 22:45, sliding open the glass door and requesting tickets. Wearily, he had sat forward and produced a ticket. Hans had done the same for himself and then dug into Bethany's front pocket, removing a train pass. The conductor had punched holes through each ticket, a silent frown fixed to his lips. He had looked at Bethany, his eyes sending a warning.

"Don't worry," Hans had said, "she was sick back at the Hauptbahnhof."

The conductor had closed the door and was gone. Hans had finished his first beer and fumbled with the second but then stopped. Setting both bottles on the floor between his feet, Hans had settled back into the corner against the window. It had taken only a few brief moments before deep breaths signaled the start of sleep. The beginning of the end.

His eyes opened. Everything was ready. He could account for each moment. There had been no mistakes. The time was now.

His hand was squeezing the knife's handle. If he could see his knuckles, he was certain they would be white. He focused on his breath, trying to relax. There was no reason to be tense now. Hans was asleep, unable to defend himself. This would be quick and merciful.

He looked at the beer bottles on the floor. They were still braced firmly between Hans's feet. Maybe a drink would be the quickest way to get his emotions under control. He shook his head, knowing better than that. Beer clouded his mind and slowed his reactions, and if he moved them, Hans would probably wake. That would change everything.

But afterward, that full beer would be there just for him.

He checked his watch and then leaned for a view out the cabin window. The lights of Garmisch brightened the horizon. They would arrive at the station in minutes.

Squealing brakes slowed the train as it approached its destination. The stranger's body swayed, and he bumped gently against Bethany. She moaned, still deep in sleep. With a quick motion, he drew a long knife from his coat pocket. The silver blade cast a dull reflection of the cabin light. He stood and lunged at Hans with a powerful jab, the knife sinking into the side of Hans's throat. Hans threw open his eyes and tried to jerk back in surprise, unable to make a sound. In one sweeping motion, he twisted the knife and ripped forward, severing Hans's esophagus and carotid artery. A brilliant stream of blood burst across the cabin, covering Bethany's sleeping form. Hans gurgled, his face contorted with confusion until he tipped sideways, eyes frozen in death, not making another sound.

Quickly he whirled to face Bethany. He held the knife inches from her cheek, ready to plunge it through the sleeping woman's eye.

"Hey," he said, "*wach auf*!" Wake up!

Bethany breathed deeply, unconscious, oblivious to the scene around her. He pondered this woman's fate for one short moment, deciding on the spot not to degenerate into the mode of a cold-blooded killer. The dead man—he served a purpose. This American, this beer expert, an ex-cop—it was probably a big mistake if he took her life. He wiped the blade clean on the seat and returned it to his pocket.

With a sudden brightening outside and a final lurch of the brakes, the train came to rest in the Garmisch station. A loud, long hiss escaped into the cool evening, and a smattering of passengers quickly disembarked. He was among them, leaving a dead body and a sleeping woman behind in the cabin. Sipping on an Augustiner Helles, he disappeared in the direction of the distant mountains.

Hangovers had become fuzzy memories relegated to the faded past—as a beer expert, she had learned the art of moderation—but this morning, Bethany Judge had the pleasure of revisiting the morning-after trio of nausea, headaches, and uncertainty over what she had done the night before. In truth, her misery wasn't too bad;

all she needed to do was not move. Sitting still on the little stool in the stark white office was tolerable. Her muddled brain hoped for just a little time to recover before the next round of questions began. That and some water.

The commotion on the train had registered with her vaguely, enough to wake her when a young Teutonic doctor reached under Bethany's shirt and pressed a stethoscope against her chest. Bethany had pried open her eyes, mumbling drunken words that made no sense, even in English. Moments later, the doctor had left the cabin and Bethany drifted back to sleep, not remembering anything until two oversized men pulled her out of the green-and-white Volkswagen police car and locked her in this room.

And what had they told her since? Bethany squeezed her temples, trying to collect her thoughts. Forgetting where she was for a moment, she decided to stand and pace the room. Maybe that would help. But instantly she lurched leftward, knocking against a chair. It skittered across the room and crashed against the white brick wall. Bethany sat again. Immediately, a feeling of panic drained into her bones.

"Gotta get control," she whispered, again squeezing her head between her hands. "Pull it together—that's all."

The sound of a key in the lock caught Bethany's attention. She slowly raised her head, squinting as the door swung open on silent hinges. A young officer stood in the doorway, his green uniform neatly pressed and his lean, round face tipped to the side as he read from the clipboard in his hand. He rubbed his chin, pursing his cherry-red lips, his left eyebrow rising at each piece of interesting information. Finally, he looked at Bethany and stepped into the room.

"Bethany Judge," he said agreeably, reaching for the chair near the wall.

"Some water, please," said Bethany.

"Yes, of course," the German officer said in near-perfect British English. He stepped back into the hallway, calling out in a deep baritone. Another policeman arrived a few moments later, carrying a bottle of water.

"Thank you," Bethany said, swallowing her first cautious sip. The water was sharp on her tongue.

"It's carbonated. I'm sorry. That's the only good water we had available."

"It's fine. Tap water would have been fine."

"Germans don't drink tap water, Ms. Judge. But, of course, you probably wouldn't know that."

"First time in Germany," Bethany said, drinking again. "Well, actually, I was here as a kid with my parents. To visit the Oktoberfest then as well."

She closed her eyes, trying to block the memory. Bethany could almost smell the bratwurst and beer from that visit, could practically feel the Oktoberfest beer Fräuleins pressing their breasts against her back, leaning across the table to serve her father those liters of golden brew. The clarity of that distant past was entirely her father's fault. He had dragged the young Bethany and her mother from beer hall to beer hall, from sausage stand to sausage stand, each day of the three-week festival until Bethany's clearest memory was the sad eyes of the beer ladies pitying the young girl's upbringing.

"You came on holiday?" the German officer asked. "To visit the Oktoberfest again?"

"To see the Oktoberfest, yes. That was all."

"And yet you're traveling on a train?"

"I couldn't find a hotel room in Munich."

"Ah, yes. That's quite a creative solution. But now you get mixed up in such an awful thing. I'm truly sorry about it."

"And I don't know anything. I really don't remember anything. I was at the Oktoberfest. Now I'm here in …"

"Garmisch," the officer said.

"Garmisch, right," Bethany said, nodding, as recollection from the previous day returned to her clouded mind. "The ticket cost fourteen euros. Ninety-minute train ride one way. I bought it when

I first got to the main train station. After I stored my luggage. Before I went to the Oktoberfest. The train was a place to sleep. It seemed like a good idea when I couldn't find a hotel."

"A creative solution," the officer said again.

"And I met this American. Jake. Jake Stoddard, I think, was his name. He works at one of the breweries in Munich. Took me with him to the beer tent. We joined a table with a bunch of his coworkers and some of their wives. The brewery was closed for the day so they could all visit the Oktoberfest. They had free beer tickets for themselves and shared a bunch with me. Too many, to be honest."

"And now here you are in Garmisch, covered with blood."

Bethany shrugged. "I have no idea how I even got to the train station. I drank too much and blacked out."

Tapping the clipboard, the officer scanned the notes once more. "I read here that you're also a police officer?" he said.

"In Buffalo, New York. That's right," Bethany said. "I'm retired now."

The officer raised his eyebrows, observing her brown hair and eyes, slightly crooked teeth, and broad, flat nose. He looked down at his clipboard. "One hundred sixty-seven centimeters? You are taller than most women I know. And forty-two years old?" He looked up at Bethany. "Retired? So young? Well, regardless, you do understand the position I am in?"

"Most absolutely, yes. And I'm willing to cooperate in any way I can once I stop feeling like crap. Too much beer and jet lag make for a bad combination."

"Yes." The officer laughed. "You may have done better to just sleep last night, catch up on your rest, before tackling the Oktoberfest."

Bethany refused to be offended by the suggestion of irresponsibility. She merely grunted.

"I've never been known for making the best decisions," she said. "That's part of the reputation I live with."

"Yes, yes. We have learned about you after some research and phone calls, but it does seem a coincidence that bad luck always follows the same person. Wouldn't you agree?"

"Oh, I don't believe too much in the virtues of coincidence. Perhaps I'm subconsciously looking for trouble and for that reason find myself in the middle of it."

Bethany closed her eyes. She knew his clipboard would not reveal her entire story. He could not know that she had never been of great importance in law enforcement circles, regardless of her remarkable aptitude for the job. Troubled as a youth after years of moving from St. Louis to Memphis to Cincinnati to Cleveland and, finally, to Buffalo, she had achieved nothing in life except her police badge and a sense of duty that belied her tattered childhood.

Raised beneath the zealousness of an alcoholic carpenter father and an overtly religious homemaking mother, she was prone to angry outbursts even during her moments of greatest fortune. These had been enough to hold her career in check, even as her reputation for excellence quickly outpaced her. Bethany blamed her problems on boredom or a subconscious anger that her job, no matter its importance, hardly helped the community she served. Whether Bethany Judge secretly despised her own career, none of her colleagues really knew. Bethany didn't know either; she took things as they were and shrugged away expectations. It was, after all, just a job.

"Subconsciously looking," the German officer said, pondering the thought. "Yes, I could believe that. Others are going to have a much harder time, though. Like the newspapers. They'll paint you as a cold-blooded drunk, traveling overseas to commit a random murder. You visit the Oktoberfest, drink until rage overcomes you, board the train, and do the crime. Only you fall unconscious—an unexpected twist to your plan. That's how you're apprehended."

"And you believe this story?"

The officer shook his head. "Not a word of it, but still, we're searching the tracks for a weapon you, or the murderer, may have dumped."

"May I ask two questions?"

"Ja, klar."

"What is your name?"

"*Polizeihauptkommissar* Fritz Weyermann," he said. "My rank is roughly the equivalent of detective in your country." He leaned across the table, shaking Bethany's hand.

"It's quite an honor, Detective Weyermann, though I'm sorry about the circumstances."

"We feel the same way on all accounts. And your second question?"

"Yes. This person who was murdered. Anyone special?"

Weyermann lifted the paper on the clipboard and removed a photograph from underneath. He slid it across the table, watching Bethany's face.

"From Munich. He had a wife and children, I believe. We are trying to contact them at this moment."

Terror rushed through Bethany as the moment of recognition struck. Hadn't she met this man the evening before, if only briefly, at the Oktoberfest? Yes, absolutely, but they hadn't really spoken. This man—Hans, wasn't it?—he couldn't even speak English. Why the hell would they have been together on the train to Garmisch?

"Ever seen the man?" asked Weyermann.

Bethany pushed the picture across the table, nodding. "Briefly. At the Oktoberfest. He was one of the Germans from the brewery ..." Her words trailed off.

"Was there any reason he would travel with you? Anything you can remember that put him on that train?"

Bethany shook her head, her eyes on the photograph.

"We're going to look into this closely, Ms. Judge. You understand. I'm sorry for the inconvenience to you, of course. This may just be an unfortunate set of circumstances that has you tangled in the middle."

"Oh, the webs we weave," said Bethany. "Please, don't feel bad about doing your job. When luck decides to turn against me, I find hard work is the best way to handle my disappointment. Perhaps in this instance I can make up my indiscretion to God."

"Indiscretion?" Weyermann's eyebrow arched again.

"Overdrinking, Detective. Just overdrinking. I'm a Master Cicerone, a certified beer expert—not just an ex-cop—and my enthusiasm for the Oktoberfest got the best of me. I should have known better."

"Perhaps though it appears God may be watching out for you as well. It seems a friend of yours is waiting in the front lobby."

"A friend?" Bethany asked, surprised, trying to understand the improbable chance that she would have an ally in this southern German town. Then it struck her. "You mean Louis?"

"Yes, that was the name he gave. Last name Frey. An American as well."

"I can't believe it!" said Bethany, brightening.

Now she remembered. Her friend Louis Frey had joined the military after high school and never looked back, eventually being stationed with the US Army Area Support Team in Garmisch. The fuzzy memory came back: The Oktoberfest band playing the "Chicken Dance." Hugging and laughter. Long lines at the restroom. And writing Louis a text explaining her plans to board a train that evening. She'd be in Garmisch about midnight. Was he still around? The details of the text were fuzzy—she hadn't even been sure his number was right—but it had obviously worked.

"He is still here!" Bethany said. "When can I see him?"

"The good news, Ms. Judge, is that we are processing your release right now. We can't hold you, but we do ask that you remain available for further questioning. This means that you don't leave the country, understand?"

"Of course."

"Once the paperwork is finished, you may go. I'll send my assistant down to retrieve you."

"Thank you, Detective." Bethany smiled and again shook the detective's hand.

"I do have one more question," said Weyermann.

"Anything."

"The man in this picture. You have no idea why he was on the train with you?"

"Not at all. I barely knew him. And I can't remember most of the night, to be honest."

The German officer tapped the clipboard with his pen. "It's just curious, really. A very curious thing that the two of you should be together in the same cabin. He is murdered and you are left alone."

"I can't explain it. I'm sorry."

"In due time, we shall understand more, but isn't that always the trouble with police work? So many questions and so few answers!"

"I will do my best to help, Detective."

"Of that I am certain! Thank you, Ms. Judge. I'll be in contact soon."

"Thank you," said Bethany, but already Detective Weyermann had pulled the door closed.

Footsteps retreated down the hallway and soon fell silent. Bethany settled into the chair again, sighing as a wave of nausea swept over her. Another drink of water removed the pasty dryness from her mouth, but it could not erase the lingering question of how and why Hans had been murdered.

"Inches away," Bethany whispered, taking another sip. "Only inches away and I missed it all."

CHAPTER 2

AN OLD FRIEND

"Don't take this the wrong way, but you've really gotten yourself into a hell of a mess," said Louis Frey.

Bethany Judge flashed her old friend a cold glance. She had known Louis Frey since high school. They had always been good buddies—"drinking pals" was probably the best way to define the relationship—but Louis had never been the shallow type. Even after they went their separate ways, the two had remained in contact, if only on occasion because of the distance between them. Louis was the faithful type, committed to God and country more than any man Bethany had ever known. That quality had helped him reach the rank of major in the US Army. People found that they could trust him, that he had a remarkable knack for leading even when a situation looked bad. Bethany hoped that leadership would poke its head out right about now.

"It's not too often that a pretty lady arrives in Europe and winds up on a train with a dead guy and all in less than twenty-four hours."

"I didn't plan for that to happen," said Bethany, half smiling at the small compliment.

"No, of course not. But there must be something behind it. Some reason."

Bethany covered her face and spoke quietly into her hands. "I met the guy at the Oktoberfest."

"What!"

"We had drinks together—that's all." She quickly rehashed the story for Louis. "I had to get out of Buffalo. I left my husband a few months back, retired from the force. And, in the process, became a Master Cicerone. That's a certified beer expert. The Oktoberfest seemed like the perfect vacation. The fest of all festivals!

"And then the weirdest shit started to happen," she continued. "I meet this lady at the baggage carousel. She's German. From Munich, actually. But more than that, she's a German professor from back in New York. I'm pretty sure she said Columbia University. Something like that. Anyway, she said she had come back to Munich for a research sabbatical. And then she starts warning me about the dangers of the Oktoberfest—the strength of the beer, mostly. And she gave me some tips about storing my bags at the main train station and booking a ticket to Garmisch to save money on a hotel room.

"And the bags are taking forever, so we are having a nice chat. She even commented that we might have to fill out lost baggage reports. I suggested that we meet while I'm in Munich, maybe at the Oktoberfest. She says it is impossible, the event is too massive for that, but perhaps a stroll some morning and a cup of coffee would work. I agree, and she takes out a pen and pink sticky note from her purse. Then I look up and see this guy. He's wearing a black overcoat and standing about thirty yards away. He's just staring at us, watching. You get a vibe, you know? When you've been a cop, you just get that sense something is wrong. Even in Munich, something felt off."

Bethany swallowed hard. "And she was clever. Figured out my full name could be converted into a cute little nickname—Beer Judge. Get it? From Bethany R. Judge?"

Louis smiled, nodding. "That's rather cute," he said. "And creative, especially for a German professor."

"We parted ways shortly after that," Bethany continued. "Our bags finally arrived. She walked off in the direction of the guy that had been watching us. I caught a train to downtown Munich and did what she told me. Locked up my bags. Bought the ticket to Garmisch. And then I'm walking into the Oktoberfest and this American guy grabs me by the arm. Jake Stoddard was his name; I'm sure of that. Said he works at a brewery in Munich. He takes me to that brewery's beer tent and introduces me to his coworkers. It all seemed legit. We had a great time. They gave me plenty of free beer. And the guy on the train? You know, the dead one? He was from the brewery too. One of this Jake guy's better friends, as I remember it. They all worked together in a specific part of the brewery."

"This is incredible!" Louis suddenly said. "You meet this American guy, he introduces you to his German friends, and one of those guys ends up on the train with you! Obviously, he's alive when the conductor comes through to check tickets, which means he got murdered in the last hour before the train actually arrived in Garmisch."

"And I would guess he had a round-trip ticket to Munich," Bethany said. "The brewery was open the next day; I remember they told me that. Who knows how the hell they work after drinking like that. But they will be looking for him at the brewery. If not today, then definitely tomorrow."

"You think he rode to Garmisch to watch over you? Because you were so drunk?"

Bethany shrugged. "I'm pretty sure I told them my plans. It appears so, yes. I can't think of any other reason."

"A kind-hearted German helping an American he barely knows? I've lived in this country long enough to know that doesn't make sense."

"I thought the same thing. When the police showed me his photo, I could hardly believe it. And they said he has a wife and family. I feel just terrible."

Louis reached over and squeezed Bethany's shoulder. "He made his own choices. What about the other people you met? Friends of his, you said?"

"Coworkers, sure," said Bethany. "They all worked together at the Augustiner Bräu in Munich, if memory serves me right."

"And this American you mentioned. He brought you all together?"

"Jake Stoddard. That's right. He told me the whole story of how he came to Germany, studied brewing. A young guy but quite friendly. He had all kinds of free beer to hand out. I couldn't just walk away."

Louis sniffed loudly. "You would have been better off to do so. But right now I'd say we have bigger problems than a few too many beers."

"At least we have his name. Assuming it is really his name, of course. If he does work at the brewery, I doubt they have many other Americans working there."

Bethany sat back and sighed, shaking her head in bewilderment.

"Look," said Louis, "I'm just wondering here—you know, to get everything out in the open—but have you done anything recently, or sometime back, that may have led to this? Maybe a mistaken identity or something?"

"You think they wanted to kill me but made a mistake?"

"It's possible. Don't you think?"

"Anything's possible when you speculate, but that's a big mistake, killing a guy when you're after a woman."

"Bee, listen, we have nothing now. A dead guy, the name of some American, and a brewery where we might be able to find him. That's all. Otherwise, we need to figure out how you fit in."

"Maybe just by coincidence," said Bethany, hating that word as soon as she said it.

"That's possible, though someone once said coincidence is a way for God to remind you he's there while still remaining a mystery."

"What the hell is that supposed to mean?"

Louis grinned. "I don't know. You're the gal who fell into the middle of a crime, remember? You're the one who needs to figure out where you fit in. Me? I'm just hoping to be of assistance."

"Great," said Bethany, her voice laced with sarcasm. "Thanks."

"My pleasure. Now, is there any reason for you to be involved with this?"

"My record is clean, Louis, honestly. The only connections I have to Germany are two trips to the Oktoberfest and the Bayer aspirin in my medicine cabinet."

Bethany glanced down at herself, contemplating the image she conveyed. Even stained with blood, her clothing screamed American casualness. Maybe even more so. A woman of modest upbringing, she had no cause to dress otherwise. It was only her second time overseas, and besides, everyone she had ever known believed in the virtues of blue jeans and T-shirts. She had nothing to prove to anyone.

Only her old police badge had given her reason to feel more special than others she met. Even Louis. She imagined it, tucked away safely in the bottom of her black carry-on, now locked away safely in Munich's main train station. The badge had always been her pride, something that made her feel important, and for reasons she could never quite explain, she always refused to just leave it at home. Even now, with early retirement behind her, she felt herself an officer of the law. Her badge made that connection, no matter that she was thousands of miles from home.

"Okay, so we figure the hit was on the German guy," Louis said, breaking her reverie. "They left you alive for what reason?"

"Because I was drunk and unconscious. I posed no threat to them getting caught."

"My thoughts exactly. There was a reason to kill that man—something we still don't know about. Once we get up to Munich and find that American, we might be able to answer that question."

"Look here, Louis. You don't want to meddle in this. You have a great career going, right here in Germany for that matter. If you start nosing around with a suspected murderer, your superiors might think twice about future promotions."

"You know what, Bee? A career creates a very predictable life. Wake, work, eat, sleep, repeat the next day. I enjoy the recognition for my little successes, but my career isn't my life. You're my friend, you're in trouble, and you can count on my help, regardless of what happens to me or my job."

Bethany smiled. "Okay, I appreciate that. And I couldn't ask for a better ally. I just don't want you languishing in some thatch-roofed house in Malaysia five years from now, counting out rations for the troops."

"That can only happen if you're guilty, and I don't believe that to be the case. All we're looking to do is clear your name. We'll be fine."

Bethany shook her head doubtfully. "It's easy to step on toes during an investigation like this, Louis. Probably even easier to do so in foreign country. People aren't going to want to listen to us, and they sure aren't going to want to talk."

"We'll do our best. Maybe we'll get lucky and the cops will figure it out first."

Bethany smiled again, though deep in her gut she lacked any sensation of cheer. It reminded her of her miserable existence as a cop, always wearing a veneer of optimism but never truly believing it. Her mind drifted back to Buffalo, where race relations had declined and financial troubles plagued the city that had once been one of America's finest. She thought of the long nights stuck prowling the streets, alone in her cruiser because of cutbacks. Sometimes she was handpicked to raid crack houses in the particularly dangerous parts of the city. All those memories, even in Munich, had become the tattoo she wore on her soul.

The evening of her second day in Germany had turned crisp. As Bethany walked with Louis, they discussed how they might proceed, and she tried to ponder how dramatically her life had changed in the last twenty-four hours. Here she was, traveling for the first time in her adult life, and she couldn't even do it right, not without chaos.

She never liked Buffalo enough to not travel; it was simply that her husband had made it impossible. He was a total asshole, the type who believed a move from Niagara Falls to Buffalo was equivalent to a transnational relocation, and the sort who jabbed at his wife's every fault and shared that criticism with friends. To her own great surprise, Bethany had awakened one day to discover she had suffered enough. With the divorce final and her superiors hoping Bethany might finally change her ways, she had hit the retirement button and spent her free time studying the exciting world of craft beer. She had worked through four levels of education to earn her Master Cicerone certificate and immediately purchased a flight to Munich when she passed the final exam.

"That's the Zugspitze," Louis said, pointing up, way up toward a glacial area, a well-known ski area and Germany's highest point. Bethany glanced at the distant peaks, not impressed. Her problems dwarfed the soaring mountains that stretched southward into the starlit sky.

Bethany found her judgment clouded, perhaps as much the result of drinking as from a lack of sleep, culture shock, and the surprise from her sudden predicament. She closed her eyes, feeling the bad memories bubble to the surface, clenching her jaw to force them away. Not everyone lived life like Buffalo gang members. Especially not in Europe. There were plenty of other, finer people in the world. But Bethany had seen the shit—the real shit—and here it was again. She was in the middle of it. She had built her career on the belief that things could get better. She just had to give more, dig deeper as a cop and a community advocate. Things would eventually improve. And then came the day when it was obvious they would not. Not in Buffalo. Not in her marriage. But maybe if she tried, they might in her own life. Bethany opened her eyes and sighed. Did she care too much now?

They strolled along a row of low-hanging trees, a thick bed of wet leaves swallowing the sounds of their footsteps. Above them, limbs drooped wearily, tired after a season of slow growth, their final burdens awaiting the chance to flutter heavily to the ground. Bethany breathed in the thick perfumed air. *Only inches away,* she reminded herself, shivering at the thought as it danced through her mind.

Over the course of her career, danger had been a constant companion. Hardly a day had passed without Bethany landing in front of something deadly—a bullet, a knife, or an accidental contact with meth. And never had the idea of death bothered her. But this time had been different. Alcohol had overtaken her. Only the mercy of a murderer had spared her life. Death, Bethany admitted to herself, had taken another pass.

Louis led the way into a local café. Bethany noted his silence, aware that it was a reflection of her taciturnity. They took their seats at a small round table just big enough for the two of them to eat a meal and have a drink. The restaurant was roomy and bright. High ceilings created an airy, relaxed environment. Servers moved sullenly between tables, plates of food and mugs of beer gripped in their strong hands. After settling comfortably into her chair, Bethany glanced around at the surrounding group of diners, noting the homogenous collection of white skin she would have expected to find in a place like southern Germany. At all the tables, well-dressed men and women leaned toward each other, their voices lowered to whispers. Bethany looked down at her clothing and, for the first time in her life, felt underdressed.

Their server approached, requesting a drink order. Bethany waved away the suggestion of a beer. Coffee was never her first choice, but it was the beverage she needed right now, something to give her ailing body a little lift. Several sips of the viscous brown liquid did precisely that. Though she remained tired when the last drops of the first cup disappeared past her lips, a slight tensing of her muscles indicated the caffeine was doing its work.

For an appetizer, Louis ordered Wurstsalat—sausage salad—a dish consisting of cucumbers and hot dog slices swimming in a bowl of vinegar, oil, and spices. Bethany grimaced at the unsavory combination, but her stomach's grumbling forced the first bite; subsequent mouthfuls came because the dish was delicious. They finished just as the main course arrived. Her Wiener schnitzel was unlike any back in Buffalo. The side dish of Rotkraut especially complemented the juicy cut of breaded veal.

Bethany dabbed a napkin to the corner of her mouth, relaxing slightly as the heavy food churned in her stomach. She considered her situation for a moment. In truth, there was nothing to be worried about. She certainly hadn't killed the man. She also was a victim, nearly as dead as the body they had found beside her. And if she had been killed, the police wouldn't have any information to work with, would they? Still, the thought of even being involved in this fiasco raised her blood pressure. She hadn't flown across the ocean for this.

No, this was supposed to be an escape. A new beginning. A complete reset from the past she had lived until the moment she stepped onboard the plane to Munich. Perhaps she secretly despised her former life, her old career. None of her colleagues could have known. Bethany hadn't known either; in fact, she never thought about her professional errors, her missed chances, or her stagnant salary. She was too proud a woman to indulge herself with self-pity. She took things as they were and shrugged away expectations. It had been, after all, just a job.

But this was her future.

A couple across the room stood to leave, and their movement caught Bethany's attention. She turned her head, glancing toward them in a casual sort of way, not really focused on them or anything around them. Her eyes happened to flash across someone seated behind them, a face that seemed oddly familiar. A man. Bethany looked back quickly, alarm bells ringing in her head, but already the man had stood and turned toward the door, pulling on a black overcoat as he stepped outside into the cold Bavarian night. Bethany watched for a moment longer, a lingering suspicion squeezing the muscles in her throat. It didn't make sense, of course. She ran through a mental inventory of faces. The ones from the Oktoberfest were fuzzy at best. From what she could recall, this guy was nobody she had met. A doppelgänger—that was all. He probably resembled someone she had busted back in Buffalo.

Bethany reached across the table and patted Louis's hand reassuringly. He had seen her sudden change in demeanor and had followed her gaze across the room, craning his neck to look out the window. The person who had caught Bethany's attention was already gone. She shook her head, sensing that something about it didn't smell right.

"Do you have a pen?" Bethany asked. "And something to write on?"

Louis pulled a piece of paper and a pen from the small leather bag he wore slung over his left shoulder.

"Write this in German," she instructed, and she quickly dictated her request.

They finished dinner. Louis paid with crisp new euros and tucked the piece of paper, with words scribbled on it in German, between the bills: "The customer near the kitchen, seated alone, wearing a black overcoat when he left. Can you get me his name?" Underneath, he had written his name and cell phone number.

The following morning, they stood at the train station with tickets in hand for the earliest ride back north. Bethany sipped on a steaming coffee, wishing now for a beer. At least Louis had found her some new clothes the night before. Small victories, she supposed. She watched Louis lean with his back against a wall, casually flipping through the day's issue of Munich's largest newspaper, *Die Süddeutsche Zeitung*. He was looking for a story about the murder. There was plenty of boring copy about Bavarian politics; the American president; and Bayern Munich, the professional soccer team. But the only news concerning the train incident was near the back of the first section, and even that only mentioned a memorial in the Augustiner Bräu beer tent at the Oktoberfest the next night.

"We're going to stop there tomorrow," Louis said. "That will be our first order of business. If there's ever a chance we'll find this American you were talking about, this is it."

"I hope I can recognize him," Bethany said. "So much of the night is fuzzy. I didn't even think to take pictures."

"Don't worry about that," Louis said. "There can't be many Americans working at that brewery. If he's there, he'll be easy to find. I feel good about our chances."

"Anything else about the police investigation in the paper?" Bethany asked.

Louis shook his head. "That bothers me some. Either this means very little to them, or they are keeping things low profile for now."

"The police warned me that the press would come after me. Paint me as a cold-hearted killer."

Louis folded the paper closed. "None of it makes any sense," he said, putting his hand on Bethany's shoulder. "Let's get to the train. It will be leaving soon."

Their train departed punctually, with Bethany and Louis onboard. Bethany made no comments as they left the station, preferring silence to the uncomfortable thought that her previous passage over these rails had been disastrous. Ten minutes into the ride, Bethany eased into the corner of her seat, resting her head against the wall. Her eyes were so heavy and the sound of the train on the tracks so rhythmic. A little more rest would help, she decided, drifting toward sleep. She noticed Louis's heavy breathing and grinned, knowing he had already surrendered to exhaustion. She relaxed, but her mind suddenly jolted awake with the sound of someone walking past their cabin, a black overcoat swishing against the door.

I should lock that, Bethany thought behind closed eyelids. *Wouldn't that be something if someone murdered us on* this *train? Perhaps a Jack the Ripper on the Munich-Garmisch line? Hmm, I wonder if anyone has considered that. Probably not.*

* * *

Herta Stocker perched on the edge of a chair in the small Munich apartment she called home, tapping quickly on the keyboard, her fingers mere flashes as they hammered out another page of her latest manuscript. She spread her legs wide for balance, arching her naked toes against a soft Afghan rug. Her breasts heaved and fell with each breath, her black lace bra perfectly matching the delicate panties she wore. She was alone, fixated on her work, completely unconcerned with the sultry appearance she would convey if some stranger walked into the room. There was no reason for her to feel self-conscious, of course. She was a professor of German languages and literatures— *Frau Professorin* in her native language. This was her office; this was how she worked. Comfort mixed with a little touch of sexiness had been one of her secrets to success.

The loud buzzing from the phone smashed her creative sprint. She shook her head with annoyance, clicked the save icon, and stood. She raised a cramped hand to the receiver, flexing it twice before lifting the phone from the hook.

"Stocker," she said.

Her secretary spoke. "Your friend is on his way to Munich."

"Is that so?" said Herta, pausing to light a cigarette. "Is he coming in by train? Did he say if we should expect him sometime this morning?"

The morning train, Frau Professorin. That is correct."

"Excellent," she said. "I so much desire to hear from him. He must have had a wonderfully exciting little journey, even if it was quite short. Those mountain towns can be quite beautiful this time of year."

"Shall I meet him at the station?"

"He'd probably prefer for me to come down, wouldn't he? Yes, it's far more exciting when a lady shows up to sweep you away. Oh, dearest, I'm quite sorry."

"That's quite okay, Frau Professorin."

"It's that I meant to say a lady of authority, you understand."

"Of course."

"Sometimes I forget myself when I have been writing," said Herta. "I come across as quite the bitch, I know, and for that I truly apologize. Please, buy yourself a nice lunch today. It's my treat. Just send me the bill, and I'll take care of it. Meanwhile, I'll go to the Hauptbahnhof. I think he shall be pleasantly surprised, don't you?"

"Absolutely, Frau Professorin."

She dressed quickly and rushed out the door. The cold September air slapped her skin and chilled her lungs; she had to twice stop to catch her breath as she hurried to the nearby bus stop. With winter coming soon, she had to wonder why she didn't take her sabbaticals in a warmer climate, maybe Florida or the Canary Islands. This was a stupid question, of course. She had every reason to be in Munich. This morning's surprise meeting topped her list.

The dash inside Munich's main train station was blissfully short. On the way back, she decided the underground would be the more comfortable way to travel. Once inside the building, she was pleased to see she had beaten the train's arrival by a full fifteen minutes. Two espressos passed the time and then a quick trip to the restroom before the train chugged into the station. Herta stood on the platform, glancing anxiously back and forth.

She heard suddenly the raspy whisper of Christian Scheubel in her ear. "Herta, go!" he said. His strong hand squeezed her elbow. "Don't look back. Just keep walking out the front door."

"But the U-Bahn!"

"We'll take the bus! We'll walk to the other side of Munich if we need to! And keep your voice down!"

They charged out the front doors, crossing Bahnhofsplatz and continuing straight toward Karlsplatz. Christian remained silent, his grip on her elbow still firm, his other arm now wrapped tightly around her waist. He guided Herta down Herzog-Wilhelm-Strasse, turning left down Herzogspitalstrasse. They slipped through the front doors of a church. Only after they disappeared into a shadowy corner did he speak again.

"You were foolish to come to the train station!" Christian said, his voice barely a whisper.

"I wanted to see you, to congratulate you."

"Then you should have waited. As long as I was on that train, returning from doing my work, I might have been being watched. You could have compromised yourself."

"Then you should have walked past!"

"I couldn't. They were coming out behind me."

"Who?"

"Two Americans. One of them—she was in the cabin when I completed my task."

"And you—" She paused, lowering her voice. "And you didn't kill her?"

"She was unconscious, completely drunk. Our target had decided to watch over her or some sort of silliness like that."

"So she doesn't know you then. Or does she?"

"She might. She was conscious for a while on the train, talking nonstop. A drunken fool. And I was sitting beside her the whole time. But even on the train, I thought I recognized her. It has bothered me ever since I let her live. After the police released her, I decided to follow her a little while, just to see if something jogged my memory. Nothing happened until I got off the train and saw you."

"Me?"

"Yes, you. Remember the American you met at the airport? The one with whom you had the friendly conversation?"

"Yes. I think so, yes," she said, recognition dawning. "She was the woman on the train?"

"That's right, and she might have told you everything that happened if she had seen you."

Herta grimaced. "That would have been an uncomfortable situation."

"Do you know anything about this woman? Is she a threat?"

29

Herta shook her head, trying to recall their interaction at the airport. "She called herself a beer expert, whatever that means. And an ex-cop," she said.

"Anything else? Something personal."

"Divorced. Generally unhappy. She was looking for companionship—that much I could tell. I thought it was odd, to be honest, that she was traveling here alone solely for a visit to the Oktoberfest. She said some things about being a beer expert and having some type of certification. People like her bounce around to every new brewery in America, and now they come to Munich thinking they have discovered something new. They seem not to know about the German Purity Law of 1516 or that beer has been the fabric of our society for centuries. Perhaps they should see us as the promised land, not some amusement park."

Christian glanced about for anyone who might be eavesdropping. "How do you figure she got together with our man?" he asked.

"Pure chance, I have to believe. She didn't even know Munich. Didn't even have a hotel room. The train ride was just a place to sleep. It was my idea. Christian, I think you're making too much out of this."

Herta paused for a moment, centering her mind on Christian and his concerns. She had allowed her thoughts to get scattered by this surprising turn of events. She watched Christian run a hand through his thick blond hair, blinking heavily to shake some of the exhaustion from his mind. She knew him well, knew that he was being paranoid and overly cautious. He might want to toss the American aside as a simple coincidence and forget about this whole fiasco, but he was a perfectionist, not the type who left a loose end that might hurt him later. Now, having spared the American's life, Christian could not assume the best, could not lower his guard. Not when the operation was just beginning.

"We'd be fools to not stay on top of this," he said. "She brought another American with her back to Munich. That hardly sounds like someone who has no idea what she is doing."

"Oh, Christian," she said, smiling kindly, "your cautious nature is such an asset to the organization. It has been instrumental in our success."

"I failed myself on the train. My human nature prevented me from extinguishing the threat then. Now, quite honestly, killing her would be a big mistake."

"The police would see the connection," she said.

"Exactly. So we only watch her for now. If necessary—"

"If necessary, we'll worry about that later. Right now, shouldn't we retreat to my apartment? I certainly believe we'll be safe there for the evening." She smiled, knowing her suggestion sounded like the perfect way for Christian to forget his worries, at least for a little while.

"I can't help but think there's a reason she came back. And with a companion, for that matter. The police down there must want her around, don't you think?"

"They'll find her when they need her," Herta said. "This American is just coming back for more of what the Oktoberfest offers. Even a bad night—a really bad night—isn't enough to keep her from going back. I warned her about that, I seem to remember."

"You think this is nothing to worry about?"

"Nothing at all." She laughed. "Of course, I'm nothing more than a professor. What the hell do I know about intrigue like this? Perhaps she watched you the entire time, playing possum, and now she's coming back for revenge!"

"That's exactly what I don't want to hear!" said Christian, wrapping an arm around Herta's neck. "We need less doom and gloom coming out of that pretty little mouth."

"And what instead? Some gasps of pleasure? Maybe some oohs and aahs?"

Christian pulled her toward the door. "Let's catch the U-Bahn," he said. "This isn't the type of thing to discuss in a church."

* * *

Bethany Judge lifted her coffee. This was her fourth cup of the day, and a touch of heartburn had taken hold, probably from the strength of the European blends. The discomfort was mild but noticeable. Right now, a cold glass of water would have been great, if only the Germans served something besides the damned carbonated stuff.

Louis Frey had left her alone in this restaurant. There were errands to run, he had said, and they were best done quickly, inconspicuously. A suspected murderer was certain to attract some attention. Together, they had decided Bethany would keep a low profile and wait until the memorial service the following night.

So far, Bethany had managed to keep her frustration in check, but a wave of coffee-induced jitters and a general feeling of helplessness drove her out of the café, where on the next street corner she found the latest copy of an English-language newspaper. She scanned the headlines, reading nothing of great interest. Back home in America, everything was the same, at least on the surface. Democrats and Republicans were squabbling ahead of the upcoming elections. More troops were dead in the endless war in Afghanistan. The economy was still booming, and the stock market kept climbing. Yes, the world still turned, despite her personal crisis.

The world of sports was equally boring. Too early in the football season to give a damn, and already the New York Yankees had fallen out of playoff contention. She flipped to the arts section, allowing her gaze to float slowly over the miscellaneous items that normally held no interest for her whatsoever. She couldn't read this crap. Who had time for it? A musical about a Founding Father? Who gave a shit about that? And a new book about the struggles of women in America? She sighed. Those authors had no idea what struggle meant, not until they spent the day with a female cop in Buffalo.

Suddenly, Bethany gasped, her eyes freezing on a photograph. It was her, undoubtedly. The hair and the not-so-unattractive facial features, the strong gaze that dramatized the power of her feminine physique. She was pushing through a tight crowd in the photograph, her jaw locked with determination. Bethany glanced down and read the caption: "Herta Stocker, professor of German literature at Columbia University, emerges from a lecture marred with controversy as demonstrators protest her pro-Nazi sentiments."

"Pro-Nazi?" said Bethany under her breath, surprised at this bit of sensationalism.

Certainly, even during their brief meeting at the airport, the professor had not come across as an extremist. Quite the opposite, in fact. Prim and proper, perhaps leaning a bit toward the boring professional type. Bethany scratched her head and checked the photograph once again, trying to find something to disprove the claims of her identity. Yes, it was her. Even so, it was tough to imagine how the lady in the airport might share political inclinations with the likes of Adolf Hitler and Germany's latest version of the far right. She hurried back to the café, where Louis met her three hours later.

"You're certain it's her?"

"Yes," said Bethany. "The photo is a good depiction of the woman I met. Besides, Herta Stocker isn't a common name."

"True enough, though I'm rather surprised to hear that academics are running around spewing right-wing rhetoric. Last I heard the big problem with universities—especially in America—is that they're too liberal."

"I wouldn't know," said Bethany. "The funny thing is we talked about love."

"Love?" Louis asked.

"Well, divorce, really," Bethany said. "I told her about my recent retirement, my second career as a beer expert. And that I recently divorced. She came back at me with a quote about love. Made me look it up on my phone, actually."

Bethany scanned her phone briefly, searching her history.

"Here it is," she said. "Goethe. I guess he's a famous German author. 'Love is an ideal thing, marriage a real thing; a confusion of the real with the ideal never goes unpunished.' That's the quote she shared. Just pulled it out of the air, *poof*! Memorized, perfect for the moment. Kind of strange now that I think about it."

Louis scratched his chin, thinking. "And yet the paper suggests we have some German completely insensitive to the unique cultural institution of political correctness in America. Maybe she gives a different slant on German history. Maybe on German writers. I don't know, but I'm betting she got steamrollered at the university level. That's why she's back here."

"A witch trial type of thing?"

"Americans have been good at that for centuries," said Louis. "I wouldn't let a little newspaper story stop you from visiting her."

"Yeah, well, if I get a chance. Things aren't looking so great right now."

"That shouldn't matter. In a few days we'll have some answers. You'll deserve a break. Call her then."

"Good idea," said Bethany. "Yes, I'll do that exactly. Thank you, Louis."

The thought was enough to lift her spirits. Bethany let her hand drift into her pocket, where she felt the piece of paper with Herta Stocker's name and number. She could almost feel the coolness in the baggage claim area of Munich's airport, September's damp air reaching silent tendrils through the massive building. She remembered the loud buzzing that had signaled the start of the baggage carousel, all the black suitcases looking the same. And then the sudden sensation when Herta had eased against her, her gaze fixated on the passing luggage, her creamy cheeks and black eyes offsetting sharply against her straight blond hair. It was a look Bethany had never seen before. Bethany had guessed her age to be around forty, thin lines reaching from eyes to temples the betrayers of a fading youth.

Presumably, the information she had given Bethany was correct. It would be a shame to get excited about a second meeting only to discover she had been duped. She couldn't be sure, of course, and decided on the spot that optimism was the best policy. With all the other crap she had to deal with, the hope of seeing Herta again at least gave her reason to look ahead to the next day, and the one after that.

The evening temperature had fallen as a southern wind carried a chill off the distant, windswept mountain peaks. Louis Frey buttoned his jacket and continued walking past the darkened storefronts. Munich was such a foreign place to him, much larger than the alpine village he had come to call home. Even so, the stroll was pleasurable, if only because it gave him a chance to clear his head. He had not learned anything new that could help his friend; their first day together had been a complete failure in terms of intelligence gathering, and he could not help but wonder if his sincerest efforts would end in vain.

His thoughts drifted back to high school, to the girl he had known. Bethany had been a trusted friend, and now, with hindsight, he wondered why he hadn't felt a deeper attraction toward her. Perhaps it was the coarseness of her upbringing, the unpredictability she had derived from both her parents. Bethany could be a volcano, that was certain, always primed to erupt at the most inopportune times. Mount Saint Judge he had called her, both as a jab and a compliment. But if he was being honest with himself, in his heart, he loved her. And he would do whatever was required of him to help her.

He crossed the Marienplatz, with the famous Glockenspiel towering idly above him. During the day, tourists crowded this square, waiting for the moment when the bells struck and the little figurines performed their mechanical dance. But not tonight. The sound of cold wind filled the silence, hushing even the noise of his footsteps. Eleven fifteen. Maybe a quick beer and then back to the hotel they had found out near the old Olympic village. The last thing he wanted was to miss the last U-Bahn of the night.

He walked beneath an archway and past the front door to Munich's toy museum. Following a road to the right, he found himself in the middle of the Viktualienmarkt, the medieval city market. This was a bustling place during the day, filled with hundreds of shoppers, fruit and sausage stands, a place to buy mulled wine, a little beer garden. Tonight, not a single person shared the cobblestones with Louis. Funny, he thought, with the Oktoberfest still going on. In a city like Munich, someone should at least be out window-shopping. Perhaps the weather kept city folks inside.

Or maybe during the annual beer festival the city closed down at night, he reasoned. That would keep away the drunks, get them back home at a reasonable hour. He listened for the sound of a nearby bar and decided his search was in vain. Turning back, he soon arrived at the stairway to the underground train. He descended and had just reached the platform when his cell phone rang.

"Frey," he said.

"Silva Wolf here," the voice said, barely discernible.

"Yes. This is Louis Frey."

The woman spoke in German. "I'm the waitress from the café in Garmisch. The one you left the note for. I don't know if I should be calling about this or not."

"You know the person I asked about?" said Louis, his own German laced with a thick Bavarian accent.

"Not exactly. I've seen him only once before, several months ago."

"Just a moment!"

Louis held a hand over the phone as his train arrived in a rush of noise. The doors slid open, and he entered, sitting alone inside the quiet, empty cabin.

"Hello? Sorry. You had seen him before?"

"A group of men. They had dinner at our café once."

"And he was there?"

"Yes."

"What was this group? Did it have a name?"

"I don't know. There were ten men, maybe. Of all different ages."

"And what, something about them was suspicious?"

36

"No. Yes. I don't know. Perhaps. I hadn't really thought about it, quite honestly, but I recognized him right away. His eyes, you know, and his handsome face."

"Do you know his name?"

"I'm sorry, no."

The connection worsened. Louis strained to hear.

"What was that?"

"I said no, I don't know his name."

"Is there anything else? Like what they were meeting about."

"All kinds of crazy stuff, but mostly—"

Suddenly, her voice vanished. Louis yelled twice into the phone, asking her to stay on the phone or call back in a few minutes. The train reached the Olympic Village fifteen minutes later, and Louis sprinted upstairs. Outside, he tried calling back several times, but she never answered. After twenty minutes, his bus arrived. Dejected, Louis rode the next ten minutes, wondering what, if anything, the informant might have told him. If she didn't call back or answer his calls, perhaps he would return to Garmisch. But first, they would see tomorrow what this American brewer could contribute to their investigation.

CHAPTER 3

FRIEND AND ENEMY

The Oktoberfest was exactly as Bethany had left it. Loud polka music blew through the packed tents. Heat rose in silent waves from the thousands of bodies, some seated, many dancing, others stalking the aisles for a place to sit. Sober but with growing desire for a drink, Bethany felt a pulse of revulsion shoot through her stomach, a sudden jolt brought by the sight of a Bavarian man, his embarrassed wife holding his hand, the front of his lederhosen hanging open, exposing himself and urinating a clear stream onto the beer tent's floor. A semicircle of curious onlookers gathered to watch the spectacle. Before he finished, security rushed in to whisk him away. The man laughed and garbled drunkenly. His wife glowed bright crimson, her stoic face otherwise not disapproving.

Bethany now recognized how foolish she had been, drinking to excess. Despite this, a nagging urge begged her to touch her lips to a glass of brew. But it couldn't be. Especially if she wanted to make some headway in the tragedy that had unfolded around her.

Bethany settled herself on the edge of a wooden bench. She shifted uncomfortably, attempting to shake off a stabbing splinter that poked through her jeans. Unsuccessful, she stood and, after ten frustrating minutes, sheepishly discovered the culprit in her left rear pocket—a tiny, sharp piece of metal that had somehow made Bethany's pants its home. She removed it, wrapped it in a tissue, and stuffed it absently into her front pocket.

Her head moved back and forth, to find some amusement in the frenetic activity, for one, and for another, to spot anyone familiar walking past. Already she was at a disadvantage, having drunk away most of the memory that might have allowed her to remember the faces of the German men whose table she had shared. The tent was more than filled to capacity, and immediately Bethany believed only good fortune would make their evening a success. She knew Louis was prowling the crowd, invisible to Bethany, trying to dig up something through direct reconnaissance.

Bethany rose and left the tent, walking the trampled path to buy herself a cup of coffee. Fatigue urged her to sit and relax, but she hurried to drink the scalding liquid, knowing Louis would be angry at her for leaving her post. She returned to find her seat taken—not a huge surprise. Moments later, Louis burst through the crowd and grabbed Bethany's hand, a look of excitement creasing his eyes. They dove hurriedly toward the back corner of the tent. Bursting from the sea of bodies, they arrived at a table of fifteen men, all sitting quietly, all with beer mugs at their lips. Bethany danced her gaze across the faces in front of her, a prayer of recognition chanting silently through her mind. To not pinpoint a person from the other night was her greatest fear right now. A cop of her caliber would never live down a failure of that magnitude. At the far end of the table, shrouded in dim light, a figure rose.

Bethany gave Louis a nudge. "Back there," she said. "That's one of them."

The man advanced, speaking in English. "You're back? One night at the Oktoberfest wasn't enough? Perhaps you were expecting more free beer?"

"No beer," said Louis. "We're looking for an American. I'm assuming you're him."

"I'm Jake Stoddard, yeah. Who are you?"

"Louis Frey. You remember Bethany."

"She was the reason Hans got on that train. Stupid drunk, this lady."

"Look. Let's not make this personal, all right? It's a tragedy. We can all admit that. But it isn't Bee's fault."

"Sure. We know that," said Jake. "It's just difficult. Life sometimes throws you a curveball, you know? We're still trying to understand why Hans took a swing—that's all."

"I was right there, Jake. On the train. He was murdered beside me. I was covered with his blood."

Jake shook his head. "And you didn't see anything?"

"I first awoke in the police station."

"Otherwise, she was passed out," said Louis. "She remembers nothing after some time in the evening here with you. The police are keeping quiet with their investigation, probably because Bethany is a suspect. We're trying to clear her name. Independently."

"Shit," Jake said, turning away from Bethany and Louis to rest his hands on the table. Stretching down both sides of the table, his coworkers stared blankly, some playing cards, others inhaling small piles of snuff up their noses. "I wonder sometimes if they even care that he's dead," he said absently. "Without the free beer, would any of them have shown up at all?"

Jake drummed his fingers and sighed, turning to glance quickly back and forth at Bethany and Louis. "Let's get out of here," he said, rising and moving toward the nearest exit. "For the first time in my life, I don't want to be in a beer tent."

Louis and Bethany followed. Bethany was pleased to be in the outside air, where the aroma of fresh pretzels and roasted chicken swirled through the cauldron of amusement park rides, stale beer, and occasional wafts of vomit. They walked away from the festival, putting some distance between themselves and the noise.

Ahead, towering over the Oktoberfest like an omnipresent mother, was an immense iron-cast statue, a Germanic version of an Amazonian warrior, a symbol of pure strength and power.

"They call her Bavaria." said Jake, sighing with admiration as he looked up her height. "She's the patron saint of this German state."

"Kind of like the Statue of Liberty?" asked Bethany.

"I guess that's a good comparison. Bavaria was built between 1844 and 1850. The largest statue of its kind at the time, I think somewhere close to one hundred feet tall."

The three climbed, passing through Bavaria's shadow and coming to the front pillars of the Ruhmeshalle—Munich's Hall of Fame. Jake stopped and looked around, satisfied with the small crowd milling about the old building and statue.

"I know what I said back there, but this is tough for the men at the brewery," he said finally. "I feel defeated. Frustrated. And wondering how having you two involved will help with the situation."

"We understand that," said Louis. "All we want to do is help you, the men at the brewery, and Bee."

"But it's not just that Hans died, you understand? There's a feeling, kind of what you might call a superstition, that bad fortune is hanging over the brewery. Three weeks ago, one of the men—an Indian guy who had studied brewing here and was about ready to go home for a job—fell into a piece of machinery. Whack! It ripped off both his legs. He bled to death in minutes."

"Jesus!" said Bethany.

"Yeah, and two months ago, we were cleaning the cellars. We spray the walls, you know, to kill the mold and other bacteria. It's a lime-based mixture. Dangerous stuff. So one of our most experienced guys, he's there first thing in the morning mixing up a batch in this old bathtub, right? Somehow, he slips and falls into the tub. We didn't know where he was all morning. Only after using the solution did we find some of his clothing in the bottom of that bathtub. The police did an investigation. Ends up he had dissolved in the stuff. We had sprayed him all over the walls."

"Oh God!"

41

"I'm not surprised, you know. I'm not surprised that the other guys are just sitting there drinking beer. It's like they're waiting for their turn to die."

"I can't say I blame them," said Bethany. "Three deaths like that? We'd be falling apart at the precinct!"

"Precinct?"

"I told you I'm an ex-cop, didn't I? In Buffalo?"

"You might have. Who knows? That's a good thing for us, though. The cop thing."

Bethany shrugged. "It was a job. And Louis is an army major stationed in Garmisch."

"I'm helping however I can," said Louis. "I have connections. I speak the language."

"Yeah, that always helps. Two of us speaking German. That might dig up more answers." Jake paused, and Bethany found herself watching him, observing his behavior.

Jake's eyes passed warily over the dozens of men and women that loitered near them, appearing to fix momentarily on each face. She imagined him running each person through a mental catalog, perhaps hoping to see a face he'd recognize from the night Hans was killed. People, she thought, could always be recognized. Even the best disguise couldn't eliminate the core characteristics, those special attributes that made each person unique.

"So where do we start?" said Bethany. "With your coworkers perhaps? The people in the brewery who knew Hans?"

Jake bridled. "I don't know what that would accomplish. I was at the train station. Uli was there too. Neither of us saw anything suspicious. Just people, like what we have here. Hans got on the train with you, and that was that. Two hours later, he's dead."

"But someone had to board the train in Munich, don't you think?"

"Possibly, or on a station somewhere in between. But what do you expect? That we find every person on that train and question them? We should leave that to the police."

They discussed their options further. The late-afternoon sun slowly dropped to the horizon, the evening chill biting at their skin. Nothing offered much hope. Their choices were limited to discovering if Hans might have had any enemies. Bethany doubted very much that the investigation would yield much, but she knew the next obvious step was to arrange for interviews with the brewery workers.

"Can we get those set up?" she asked. "Hopefully soon, before the shock of all this wears off."

"I doubt they'll agree to the imposition," Jake said. "But what the hell, right? It never hurts to ask."

They started back to the Oktoberfest, descending the stairs past Bavaria. Bethany listened to Louis ask Jake about his life in Germany, and soon the two were chatting like long-lost friends. Mostly they discussed life in this odd southern state that nuzzled the Alps, owned dozens of unintelligible dialects, and had raised Adolf Hitler to power. Jake spoke of how the city had been destroyed during the war. Technology had brought a new boom to the region. Business was great. Louis described the other end of that spectrum, as one of the last remnants of the American occupying force. In his mind, the mission had grown vague, each day becoming more dissatisfying than the last. He longed to feel like a soldier again, not just a marginalized babysitter told to sit in the corner and watch.

Bethany felt swallowed by the deepening darkness as evening turned to night. She looked to the Oktoberfest's brilliantly illuminated roller coasters and the fake elaborately erected haunted houses. She knew these were sources of fun. Of entertainment. But she could not separate the screams she heard from the thought of terror and death. None of these thousands of loitering drunks could even imagine how horribly a person's life could end.

The sounds of a lively polka rose above the din, brightening the dark mood that had descended upon Bethany. They entered the Augustiner Bräu beer tent from the side, through an entrance where servers milled about near an oversized wooden keg, collecting full mugs to carry to their tables. Bethany watched Jake throw a charming smile at a young blond-haired beauty. He leaned in close and kissed her shoulder. She giggled, blushing on the cheeks and eyebrows. Jake lifted three full liter glasses and handed one each to Bethany and Louis. He kissed the girl again, and the trio scooted toward the stage, where the band had taken up a new tune.

"The Chicken Dance!" yelled Jake. "It's an Oktoberfest classic, just like that John Denver song. You know. 'Take me home, country roads, to the place I belong!'"

"Really?" said Bethany.

"I'm telling you guys—the Germans are a strange people!"

Louis laughed. "Tell me about it! I've lived here long enough to not be bothered by this type of weirdness anymore."

They knocked their mugs together, toasting their partnership. Louis and Jake drank deeply. Bethany watched, hesitating before taking a long, satisfying gulp. She washed her eyes over the two new friends, studying them, wondering what the hell any of this might mean and where it might lead. Perhaps they would start their interviews as soon as tomorrow. She swallowed, hoping she would remember to stop after this next liter.

"Come with me," Jake said suddenly, leading them to a distant corner.

Uli sat there alone, his latest liter nearly empty.

"Sure. Of course I'll meet with them," Uli said after Jake asked the question. "I'll do anything to find out who killed Hans. Tell them to come at nine thirty, after we finish our morning break. By then I'll have worked off some of tonight's beers, and we'll have most of the day's work done. I'll give them whatever information I can."

"You'll be there tomorrow, right? No oversleeping or anything?"

"There's always that chance, I suppose," Uli said. "This was my fifth liter. But I rarely miss work because of drinking. Besides, when there's something important to do, I usually wake up just fine."

Jake looked over his shoulder. Louis nodded.

"We'll be there," Louis said.

He translated for Bethany, and she gave a quick thumbs-up, a thin and appreciative smile on her lips. She could only hope for the best, sensing that Uli's battered liver and beer-soaked brain would push him to an early grave. If he gave them anything, it would probably be a headache.

"Have another," said Jake to Uli. He waved down a waitress and patted his friend's shoulder.

Bethany thought back to her first night at the Oktoberfest, to the night of too many beers. Perhaps it was brewery culture, but why would he encourage Uli to have another liter? Was Jake hoping Uli would not show up in the morning? She took a long drink, the beer cutting through the dryness that had settled in her throat, a sure sign that something was not right. She drank again. And then a third time, the warmth inside the tent folding around her like a blanket.

CHAPTER 4

DANGEROUS PLANS

"You look absolutely delicious, my dear," said Herta Stocker, running her hand over Christian Scheubel's mountainous bicep. "You've certainly taken good care of yourself while I've been gone. Perhaps there's a new gym in the city? Or maybe you have some machines in your apartment now? That would make exercise much easier, I suppose. Not having to drive or take the bus across town just to get your heart pumping. Anyway, I hope you're coming by it honestly. You know, not taking steroids or some of those other enhancement drugs that are out there these days. Either you have the genetics or you don't, that's what I say. Believe me, I haven't paid a dime for this body, other than some serious sweat at the gym. And everything I pack is just what God gave me, or perhaps I should say what he gave my body the ability to do. You'll agree there's purity to the Aryan bloodline that can't be denied. We should really strive to keep it that way. Perhaps issue a manifesto. Yes, that's something our people would like to see. It would show our leadership, don't you think? Our willingness to take up a cause and push it forward?"

Herta stood, her naked body still glistening with a thin sheen of sweat. Her apartment was small—functional but quite small—and warmed up quickly when she had guests. Especially when they decided to practice the art of Aryan procreation.

She touched the manuscript on her desk. This was her latest creation, perhaps her professional masterpiece. It explained everything. The history of the movement. Her ancestral heritage, which made her leadership undeniable. The vision for the future that would soon begin. She could almost feel herself seated in her chair, the words of the manuscript flowing through her fingers as if by divine intervention. Lovemaking had felt good, but getting back to work would feel even better.

"I think we should be careful what sorts of causes we choose to back at this time," said Christian, pulling a tight cotton shirt over his head. "It's the type of thing that catches the attention of people who normally wouldn't care about us, and it's also something that might anger some small contingent in the organization. We should let it go until we have the power. Practice the party tenet of doing no harm to ourselves until we gain enough seats in parliament to make the changes we desire. Then you may reign as you wish."

"You're correct, of course," said Herta, beaming brightly at her young attendant. "Yes, it's such a pleasure to have you around. There's nothing like being kept to an even keel, don't you think? If it's not one thing, it's another. Always pushing and pulling me around from thought to thought. I find it impossible sometimes to stay focused on the mission."

Christian smiled softly. "I try to do my duty all the time. The movement is my life. You are everything that we someday will be. I shall not waver."

"You are the most remarkable young man," said Herta. "So absolutely different than the American boys who attend the university. Even in New York City, where you'd think they would be open to radical ideas."

"The Americans are sated with their belief in wealth. That someday they all shall be rich."

"It is the beauty of capitalism. An impossible dream, yes, but beautiful still. And seductive. To live in that society, even I felt the tug. But imagine being raised there! Surrounded by it wherever you go! Their brains are shriveled, weak little things. They no longer can see the more profound conflicts of life."

"But why should they? Is it worth it to them?"

"Is it worth it? Look at yourself, Christian! Look at the person you've become. You are a young, intelligent man with wonderful political and economic sense. You discern the complexities of this world perhaps better than anyone inside the movement. And yet you also understand the simple brutality of life. You take it when necessary. You give it when you can. There is wonderful power in that, I think." She threw her hands above her head. "Life and death, Christian! You destroyed life on the train, and now you shall help give life back to Germany! To Europe! Pity those who stand in our way, who try to obstruct us! And pity those liberal capitalists who shed tears over the system we destroy!" She lowered her voice again. "We shall reclaim the Europe of old, and our spoils shall be shared. Yes, that is the dream."

"But I ask again, why should the average American care?"

Herta laughed. She bent to pick up her panties. Putting them on would mean she was getting back to work. Leaving them off meant she might succumb to further seduction. She could see Christian's muscles through the white T-shirt, could almost feel her hands on his skin. She clenched the panties, struggling with a decision.

"You're right again, of course," she said. "Why should they? There's an ocean between us! Centuries have cleaved our worlds apart, despite the shared blood."

"I've always believed that," said Christian. "Exactly that. They should be considered our enemies. Look! They fought us in two wars! Our alliance today is only a convenience."

"And obsolete at that, ever since the collapse of the Soviet Union." Herta frowned, watching Christian draw black pants over his legs and button them at the waist. She stared at the bulge in his pants, at the thing she had just witnessed in person a few moments earlier. What made him more desirable now that he was getting dressed? Why did going back to work on her manuscript now seem like a bad idea? She noticed suddenly that Christian was smiling.

"Do you find something humorous?" said Herta.

"I was just thinking of your books."

"You disapprove of them, I suppose. Everyone seems to frown on books these days, as if spending the time to sit down and write out your thoughts isn't modern enough. I think most people prefer the quick sound bites, the tweets, the stuff the editors have already dissected and decided is most palatable or conveys the message they want to send. Yes. Well, my goal is to transmit what I have to say, Christian. When the time comes, I want people to read my ideas in full. To study them.

"Think of it like this," she continued. "Television is so ephemeral. Movies and videos are so fleeting. Today, we're inundated with images, so we tend to simply ignore them all, don't we? The message needs to be so bold, too bold, really, to be safe for us to use. But a book—that's the modern equivalent of flying under the radar, isn't it? Only the intellectuals will raise their hackles at our message, and you can rest assured that nobody will read their complaints buried in the back sections of *Die Süddeutsche Zeitung*. But we shall make an impact, Christian, and with that, our future is secured."

"But you must admit books seem so anachronistic," Christian said. "For such a modern woman, I mean. And for such a modern movement."

"Don't be mistaken, my dear. Our movement is rooted in the past. Germany has had its successes, but it can never forget its history. We must draw upon it, create our strength in it. It shall shine forth from us like a beacon."

"I tell the truth," Christian said, "it's hard for me to contain my excitement sometimes, for the things yet to come."

"That's quite understandable, I assure you. There was seldom a day in America when I didn't think of the fatherland. You can only imagine my pleasure when my sabbatical was approved."

Herta's mind drifted back to her first day in New York City. She had walked from Times Square to Wall Street, capturing all the sights. And especially that moment when she finally could see the Statue of Liberty. There was no need to visit Ellis Island; a view from afar had satisfied her curiosity. She had pondered the majestic beauty of Bavaria versus America's unique symbol of freedom. As she had soaked in the sight, she had wondered about all the Germans who had fled the fatherland in search of something they believed this new country possessed. She could not blame them. All humans suffered from the yearning for something more, from an eternal feeling that what we were given was never enough. Her grandfather Otto had exploited it. She would make use of it. There was no stronger weapon in her arsenal.

"Even without the sabbatical you would have needed to come anyway!" said Christian.

"Yes, of course, but this attracts so much less attention, doesn't it? And already I'm gaining a bit of a reputation back in America. The sabbatical lets me leave under the guise of research. We can operate unobstructed now."

"And now is imperative. We must act with precision."

"Of course, the irony of it all," Herta said. "We wait for years. We pine for everything, and suddenly it's a stone's throw away. But then again, there are no guarantees, are there? Not until we have everything securely under our control."

Herta looked at Christian, admitting he had never quite been able to conceive of broad plans the way she could. His strength was in the implementation of her grandiose designs. And that strength was undeniable. He had never failed her.

"But of course," she continued, "you do have the situation under control, I'm certain. You have executed my strategy with the utmost precision."

"Do you doubt that?"

"Not at all, not after learning of the steps you took to eliminate the enemy. What a wonderful way to arrive back home! I knew it was your handiwork the moment I read the man's name in the newspaper. And his place of employment, of course."

"I worry, though."

"Really? About what? Certainly not that you have done the wrong thing."

"No, not at all. It's just that things have gotten sloppy, haven't they? These deaths will not be seen as mere coincidence."

"You shouldn't worry," she said, smiling at him. "We're going to begin moving fast now."

Christian left the small room and entered the kitchen. Yes, Herta had a keen mind. What a wonderful woman, so powerful and filled with a deep sense of purpose. That was the type of lady he preferred, if given the choice, and Herta possessed those qualities in spades, even if she was a bit too old for his tastes. Even so, she was a wonderful lover, and already this morning he felt the heavy weight of drowsiness from their endless lovemaking. Memories of her sweat-slicked body gave him a reason to grin into his glass of orange juice. The control she exercised over him, drawing from his body a power not even he knew he possessed.

There was something wonderful here, something beyond the magnificent dreams they shared for Germany. He would die for Herta Stocker and knew she would do the same for him. That commitment came as a natural part of her personality, while he had needed to develop his passion over years of struggling through hard, thankless work. Then there was the day his father had lost his business, and with it all the family's money, all because of this new breed of capitalism, all because of the push to globalism.

When his father committed suicide, Christian never looked back. But how he longed sometimes to be like Herta, to have the passion pulsing through him, in a bloodline that extended back through the ages to the men who had so nearly perfected the German nation. He barely dared to think it, so titillating was the thought. In her nose and eyes he could see the relationship most closely; even some of her mannerisms were similar, but these, he decided, might easily have been learned. He wondered whether anyone might have noticed, suspected her lineage. Lately, with her face splattered all over the news, it seemed likely a connection would arise in somebody's mind. People would be amazed, wouldn't they, to learn there was a descendent? And they'd be shocked to learn of the secrets that remained to be revealed, even to this day.

Yes, he was so close to the greatness that *was* and part of the greatness that *would be*. Herta connected it all, his lover, his leader. With their bond, Christian knew they were undefeatable.

"So what do you have there?" asked Herta when Christian finished in the kitchen. "Something interesting?"

"Oh, yes. This is a fascinating little piece of technology," he said. "Security for our movement."

"These are the things I trust to you." Herta smiled, touching his cheek. "So what is that then?"

"A GPS monitor. You remember our American from the train? I had one of our men track her. Seems she was at the Oktoberfest again last night. Now she's out near the Olympiazentrum, probably in a hotel room."

"Smart," Herta said "Who knows, right? She did refer to herself as a former police officer."

Christian nodded, raising an eyebrow. "I've had that concern, yes. We'll keep an eye on her. And don't worry, Herta. There are men on the ground nearby. They will note any aberration in the signal. If she does something we don't like, they will act accordingly."

Herta sat back, visibly relaxing. "Ah, to be surrounded by so much competence," she said. "You have no idea, Christian, how much strength it gives me to forge ahead. There's something Wagnerian there, don't you think, as if I am the libretto and you are the score that binds the whole movement together. So powerful, so much life and emotion. Already I look at you and see the face of a statesman. And you enjoy it, don't you, controlling the bodies and minds of your men?"

"You make it seem perverse."

"Do I? You're mistaken, for I cherish that exact thing. Knowing my army of loyalists will follow me to their death. Knowing all of Germany will bow at my feet. Knowing the world will someday tremble at my power. That is the essence of my being. And I absolutely do not find that perverse."

She sighed, looking deeply into Christian's eyes. "Our men out there —the ones doing your bidding—they are our little ants, aren't they? They contribute to the cause, but they aren't the leader, the queen. We must give them that, Christian, or they shall go lost. Do you understand? Even in the fatherland our sated masses fall victim to the temptations of money, toys, and travel."

"So we connect to something deeper? Their spiritual desire?"

"Yes, that's it," she said, pausing to jot a note in the margin of her manuscript. "A spiritual desire. We must be something for everyone, the next great Roman Catholic Church, answering every human frailty with a better alternative. Look at the men who do your bidding. Already we have succeeded with them."

"But an entire country is something different."

"The concept is the same. Don't convince yourself otherwise. To have one person or millions of people love you is all a question of marketing, in your face yet subtle. Like cooking a frog. Try to throw a frog into boiling water and the poor creature will fight you like mad. But turn the heat up slowly and it will boil to death. Turning up the heat too quickly—impatience—is what destroyed our movement in the past." She paused and then said, "This is not a mistake we shall repeat."

53

CHAPTER 5

CLUES AND CONFUSION

The Augustiner Bräu was busy in the morning. Workers zipped about on forklifts and buzzed around in trucks, some picking up shipments of bottled beer and kegs, others delivering empty bottles to be washed, delabeled, and reused. Sounds of the ceaseless activity echoed off the old brown brick buildings. Horns honked, motors revved, bottles rattled, kegs clanked. To the average observer, the scene was filled with a sense of warmth, the air practically heating amid the action. The brewery employees were dressed in their standard issue royal blue overalls and jackets. Despite the open courtyard and their exposure to the brisk fall air, they worked with purpose, as if desperate to forget their hangovers from yesterday's Oktoberfest.

It was, Bethany had thought as they walked across the brewery grounds to the malthouse, probably the same as any other day. Except not so much for Uli, who now sat before them, cringing in the silence. He obviously did not like being scrutinized.

"You knew Hans quite well?" said Louis, his first question lowering the tension in the room.

Bethany couldn't understand the German that rolled so easily off Louis's tongue, but she marveled at his impeccable accent. She was amazed that he could so easily shift from German to English to explain to her the interrogation and then back again to delve deeper with the subject of his questioning. Their high school hadn't offered German, just the standard French and Spanish classes that everyone loathed, so Louis had picked up this language skill sometime after graduation. She wondered if perhaps she had a similar linguistic talent locked away inside her. A talent like the "super taster" palate her Cicerone instructor had said she possessed. That surprising attribute had made it easy for Bethany to discern different beer styles, different malt and hop profiles, and especially beer flaws. It had made becoming a Master Cicerone one of the easiest tasks she had ever accomplished.

"Yes, of course," answered Uli, his German laced with a thick Bavarian accent. "We had worked together for years."

Bethany brought her mind back to the moment, trying to concentrate when she couldn't understand everything being said. She stood quietly in the corner, the blank concrete walls in the large room giving no visual cues to hold her focus. Louis and Uli sat at a long table littered with old newspapers. Morning sunshine fought through a single yellowed window, washing the room with an opaque glow. Uli ran a hand through his damp hair. He was sweating despite the lingering chill in the air.

"For years?" Louis frowned.

"Absolutely! Why? Had you heard something else? It would have been a mistake—or a lie! That's a fact."

"No, that's not it. I believe you. It just seems strange—that's all. Hans is your friend, yet you allow him to ride a train to Garmisch with some stranger?"

"He was an adult! He insisted! We told him to just leave her. We had the Oktoberfest to get back to. But Hans wanted to be the nice guy. See what that got him!" Uli raised his finger. "And I called his wife. He asked me to do that, you know! I called his wife after we left the train station. She was none too happy, I'll tell you. She slammed the phone down in my ear."

"Had he done this type of thing before? Stayed out all night, I mean?"

"Sure, yes. We knew all the late-night bars. There are places in Munich too where you can drink all night, if you know where to look."

"Any chance he had debts? Maybe made some enemies through gambling or something like that?"

"Hans had no problems with that, at least as far as I know. We drank together. We complained about our job. A normal friendship. Very German."

"There has been a barrage of strange things happening with your coworkers, hasn't there? There were two other deaths that preceded this whole incident, I'm told. That must be an awful thing to have lived through, three deaths so quickly in succession. And each of them so tragic."

"It has been terrible," said Uli. "We expect to grow old with these people, retire together. It's hard to imagine they are all dead, let alone how they all died."

"That will come slowly," said Louis, trying to be patient.

"That's what the psychologists say. Or they warn me that I'm—what's the word? Sublimating my memories. It depends on the psychologist I visit. You understand? The brewery has offered professional services to everyone in the malthouse. Since Hans died, I've had two appointments already."

"And you've received two different diagnoses?"

"Two different *suggestions*," said Uli. "Psychologists don't offer much more than suggestions."

"I take it you don't like them."

"They offer me little. I'm simpleminded. I find no use in exploring my emotions. Just let me get back to work. That's what I say."

"But you went to them, didn't you? It wasn't like you were forced. It suggests you have something to say or perhaps need to hear something. Perhaps to assuage some guilt? I'm thinking something is bothering you up here." Louis pressed his index fingers into his temples, his tone turning from patience to aggression.

This was the Louis that Bethany remembered. Her ears perked up, and she leaned forward, wishing she could understand the words pouring from his mouth.

"But I doubt it is survivor guilt. And I don't think it is general despondency. You call yourself a simple man. I doubt that. You can hold back from us if you like, but rest assured the police will get what they need later. Either way is fine by us."

"There's nothing, I tell you. Nothing at all."

"I think he's stonewalling," Louis said, turning to speak to Bethany in English. "He's claiming there is nothing between them beyond the fact that they were friends. Drinking buddies is probably the better description. He said Hans had no enemies, at least that he was aware of."

Bethany clicked her tongue. "It's tough to interrogate someone when you don't speak their language. I did that a couple of times with Hispanics in Buffalo, and if I learned anything from that experience it is to watch body language. This guy is giving off nothing bad, other than the fact, maybe, that he's nervous just being here. I'd take what he says at face value, Louis. Don't dig deeper than need be. We move on, right?"

"This is just way too cut-and-dried. We have nothing to look at. I don't like that, Bee. It makes me feel like we're getting jerked around."

"Maybe, sure. I can't really know because of the language barrier. Imagine being able to do only half your job."

"I'm giving you the best I can."

"Don't worry, Louis. I know that." Bethany sighed, searching for an idea. "Ask him about all three guys—the three from the brewery that have died recently. Any connection there?" She paused. "Did they work together regularly or maybe spend time together after work?"

"You think the other two weren't accidents?"

Bethany rubbed her forehead, thinking, trying to draw from her experiences as a Buffalo cop. There were always connections, especially when so many bodies were piling up in the same place. An accident, well, that was just what it was. But a series of accidents? Bethany shook her head. She was not a believer in coincidences.

"It's a shot in the dark—that's all," she said. "Who knows? I'm just trying to break something loose."

Louis switched back to German, posing the question.

Uli furrowed his brow, wrestling with his thoughts. "I don't think there's anything special to say," he said. "We all rotate through the brewery. For cross-training, to remain strong in our skills. I'm up in the kilning room right now. Next month I'll move down to the malting cellars."

Louis passed the information to Bethany. A thought flashed behind her eyes. They had walked into the malthouse just minutes earlier for this meeting with Uli, passing the brewhouse, the fermentation cellars, and the bottling plant along the way. There were so many places to work inside a brewery, especially one this large. And each area held its own unique risks. But a modern brewery with its own malthouse? Bethany was certain this was a rarity. She had noticed the ancient conveyer system designed to transport the fresh grain from truck to malthouse storage. And Uli was right. There would be a room to soak the grain. Then space to malt the grains. Then a way to transport the grain to be dried. So many moving parts. So many risks.

Bethany crossed the room to address Uli directly. "Where were the three working at the time of their deaths? To what part of the brewery were they assigned?"

Quickly Louis translated.

"Um, the, uh, the malt cellars," Uli said, flustered by Bethany's sudden questioning. "Yes. Shadeesh fell into the grain transporter and had his legs severed. Franz was cleaning the lower floors when we found him in that bathtub. And Hans had just started this fall's first batch of malted barley when the thing on the train happened."

"Who is down there now? In the malt cellar?"

Uli took a moment to ponder his response and then said, "Jake, I think. Look, there's nothing special about the work down there. You run the machines in the morning. The ones that turn the malt. Afternoons you help where you are needed. When the malting is done and the grain needs to be moved, we work together to get it into the grain transporter. That's it."

"Is Jake downstairs now?" Bethany asked.

"Maybe. We just finished our break. If he's working in the cellars, it's quite possible."

Bethany took a chair. Quietly she spoke to Louis, trying to put her thoughts in order. "Jake told us three people had died at the brewery. But he didn't say they all worked in the same part of the facility. And when they're assigned to the malthouse on a rotating basis but all die consecutively?"

Louis nodded. "Something is seriously wrong."

"We need to warn Jake. And tell Uli not to take work in the malthouse. At least not until we clear this up."

"No, no!" protested Uli after Louis explained. "You have this all wrong. You are quite mistaken! They were accidents. That's all. Hans didn't even die here, and as for the other two, well, what can I say? The brewery is a dangerous place! If you don't pay attention, *whack*! Every day you must pay careful attention."

A sound caught Bethany's attention. She could hear someone walking, nearing the green wooden door at the front of the room. She whirled, suddenly aware that Uli could be the next target. She scanned the concrete walls. No pictures, no beer mugs—nothing had been hung that she could use in a fight. She drew her hands into fists, not the best weapons of choice but the only ones available in the nearly empty room. Bethany braced as the metal door handle turned, squeaking slightly, revealing its age. Slowly, the door eased open upon rusted hinges.

A solitary figure entered. He was slightly stooped over, with rounded shoulders and thinning brown hair. His black-framed glasses sat low on the bridge of his nose. Blackened pores covered his cheeks, creating a raccoon-like appearance. He focused on a sheath of papers in his hands and startled when Louis spoke.

"Who are you?" Louis said.

"What? I am the supervisor of this facility! Why, I should ask the same question of you!" He looked at Uli. "Who are these people, Uli?"

"They are investigating Hans's death, Herr Steingarten. They are asking me a few questions—that's all."

Herr Steingarten studied Louis and Bethany, his piercing blue eyes sparkling with a youthful spirit. Bethany could guess what was going through his mind: this was an odd sort of thing, these two strangers. Perhaps he was weighing in his mind whether he should call the front office. Bethany glanced at Uli. He didn't appear to mind being questioned, it seemed, though the sweat stains in his armpits did suggest nervousness. But who wouldn't be scared, right? Three people had died, one of them Uli's close friend. Herr Steingarten probably felt similar angst. Bethany looked back at Herr Steingarten, wishing again that she could speak German.

Herr Steingarten simply smiled. "My office is back there," he said, pointing the papers in his hand toward the back of the room. "That door to the left of the window. I trust I will not be interrupting you."

Louis looked at Bethany, visibly relaxing. Bethany felt her own tension ebb, pleased that her partner had also sensed the potential for danger. "I think we're pretty much finished, sir," Louis said. "Uli has been very helpful. We apologize for the intrusion."

Herr Steingarten cocked his head as if something in Louis's choice of words had caught his attention. "You're not Germans?"

"Americans, Herr Steingarten," Uli said, pointing at Bethany. "She was on the train with Hans."

"I hear his accent, yes, ever so slight. But he speaks excellent German. And the one who was with Hans?"

"She speaks no German," Uli said.

"Ah, that would have been too much to ask, I suppose. Americans have little reason to learn our language. Tell her, please, that I'm sorry for what has happened. I trust she will clear her name through these efforts."

Louis translated.

"Thank you," said Bethany sincerely.

"Is there anything that I might offer?" Herr Steingarten asked. "Something that will aid in your work? I trust, of course, that your individual efforts do not come in conflict with the police. That is to say, your goal is to assist the investigation along. Am I correct?"

"Absolutely," said Louis. "And the only thing you might offer to us is some information. Uli told us you rotate workers through the brewery and that the three men who have died happened to be assigned to the malthouse at that time."

"Yes, that's correct. We've suffered through a series of sad coincidences—that's all."

"You agree with Uli then?"

"Do I? I don't know what he said, of course, but I can tell you we're lucky not to have had other deaths in this brewery over the years. There are many dangerous places, many dangerous chemicals. Hans, of course, was a tragic murder. We cannot control what happens on the streets, now can we?"

"Ask him, Louis, if we can get a tour of the facility," said Bethany suddenly.

"No, not now," said Herr Steingarten, smiling, surprising Bethany that he was able to understand her question. "As of the last few weeks, the malthouse has resumed full production. Again, this is a dangerous place. Please remember that. My superiors would frown on my taking you through the building."

Bethany pondered Louis's translation. "What's this about the facility just resuming full production? Was there a mechanical breakdown or something? Maybe a downturn in business?"

"No, absolutely not!" Herr Steingarten laughed. "Neither of those! This is a very old facility, you understand. It was built, in part, before the turn of the century. The basement is quite deep and quite wet because of the malting process. Mold grows as a result of all the moisture, of course, and the old machinery needs its annual maintenance. So as a matter of course, we stop production in the summer. We use the time to clean and repair. Franz—he was going to spray the walls with mold killer. Shadeesh was doing work on the grain transporter. I believe Hans was working on the ventilation system."

"So it seems there is nothing," said Louis dryly.

"Don't be pessimistic," said Herr Steingarten. "What there is, I believe, is pure chance. Bad luck. Why do I think this? Because aside from these recent deaths, we live a very boring existence in this brewery. There can be no reason, because we have no reason for being here. Except maybe to be the worker bees for the company, I suppose."

"And to put food on the table," said Uli.

"Yes, obviously. We don't come here because we love it. Unlike the typical American, we are not married to our careers. We simply exchange our time and labor for money. Sometimes, as you can see, the trade-off is not worth it."

"People have died at their jobs for hundreds of years," said Louis. "Look at Bethany here! She was a police officer back in America. And I'm military. Danger comes with the territory. Hell, it adds something to the job."

"Until you make a mistake. Something that causes injury or death." Herr Steingarten considered the two Americans once more. "You both impress me. This little investigation cannot be an easy undertaking."

"We're only getting started," said Louis, "but that's about as optimistic as I can be right now. We have no other leads. Nothing of any value."

"You maybe should consider leaving it to the police," said Uli.

"Yes," said Herr Steingarten, "He may be correct. You do not want to get into trouble for your efforts."

"It's either try or wait, and waiting isn't something we're willing to do. Especially not Bethany. If she could speak German, we'd have already turned something up."

"See! Confidence! That's what impresses me the most." Herr Steingarten opened his office door. "Come back anytime if you need more information, but now I really must complete some paperwork. And Uli, I'd like you to get back to work. Break time is over."

Bethany and Louis stood outside the office door, waiting for Jake to arrive. Bethany felt exasperated, her mind turning in circles. She hated this feeling, this reliance on Louis to decipher the language and the words their interviewees provided and then recite them back to her. In all her years as a cop, she had never felt so helpless.

"What an irony," she said suddenly.

Louis put his head against the wall. "I never understood the definition of that word."

"Just that I'm a beer expert and I'm inside one of Munich's most famous breweries. And I'm not drinking a beer and probably won't drink a beer."

"That's ironic?" Louis asked.

"That's Jake," Bethany said, coming to attention. She pointed.

It was one hour after the interview with Uli had begun. Bethany could see Jake crossing the courtyard and then mounting the stairs outside the malthouse. He entered the building. Bethany noted the surprise in Jake's eyes when he saw them waiting, but that surprise quickly vanished behind a veneer of stolidity. Louis explained what had happened, recounting the interrogation of Uli and the discussion with Herr Steingarten. Bethany listened closely, trying to catch any inconsistencies from what Louis had translated earlier. She trusted him, but under the circumstances, she needed to verify every step along the way.

Outside, a gorgeous fall day was unfolding. Brilliant sunlight filled an empty cobblestone courtyard. Puffy white clouds dappled the indigo sky. Jake led them out of the musty dark building. He stretched stiff limbs and breathed deeply, allowing the morning warmth to soak into his pale skin.

"Let's take a walk," he said.

They exited the brewery via a side gate. He led them up a narrow street lined with seedy apartments and closed shops. They turned down an alley, walking through cool shadows. The aroma of brewing beer swept over them, a sudden southern gust pushing between the buildings. They hurried ahead to the next street and approached a small café. Its entire façade was a series of windows, providing Bethany with a clear view inside. Nearly a dozen tables filled the tight space, each covered with a starched white tablecloth. Several guests sipped coffee from fine china. Others nibbled on delicate cakes, dabbing the corners of their mouths with cloth napkins. Bethany glanced back, amazed at how quickly Munich neighborhoods transitioned from downtrodden to upscale. In Buffalo, the city's decay stretched for miles in every direction.

They entered and sat. Without asking, Jake ordered three cups of coffee. Bethany cringed. Her mind was still on beer, and if Jake suggested they head back to the brewery for some samples, she wanted her taste buds in perfect working order.

"So Uli was helpful then?" Jake asked after the waiter served their coffee.

"I'm frustrated," said Bethany, subconsciously pushing her coffee an inch or two away. "The language barrier is tough to deal with. I feel like I'm out of the picture, useless. Louis translates, and all that does is slow the whole process down. I can't make quick decisions the way I usually do."

"Uh-huh, and Louis probably lacks your instincts."

"True," said Louis, "but shuttling information to Bethany makes it worse. I can't focus and think."

"I'm sorry to hear this, really, but I don't know what to say. Keep trying, I guess. There are other guys at the brewery to talk with."

Bethany glanced at Louis, her lips tight. "It doesn't seem like it would do much good," she said.

Louis nodded.

"Then what now?" said Jake.

"I don't have a clue. Wait to see what the police dig up, I suppose," she said.

Jake stood, speaking quickly, with sudden cheerfulness: "Well, then that's it, I suppose! You'll know where to reach me if something comes up. Here, let me pay for these coffees. Would you like to walk back to the brewery and catch the streetcar there?"

Bethany shrugged, standing lethargically, wishing now that she had drunk the coffee. Louis rose beside her. Any optimism they may have felt before speaking with Uli was gone now. Sapped of energy and hope, they shuffled behind Jake. They were several feet behind him when he opened the door onto the street.

Thwick!

Wood splinters exploded from the door, peppering Bethany's face. Instinctively, she drew back and threw herself flat against the wall. Louis dropped to the floor, sliding beneath a table. Jake stood frozen, suddenly stepping back as another bullet rammed into the door, this time an inch above his left shoulder.

"Get back!" yelled Bethany. "Get down!"

Jake stumbled backward, tripping over his own feet. He hit the floor with a thud. Bethany grabbed his shirt and yanked him to her side. Quickly, she ran a hand over Jake's chest, feeling for blood.

"I-I'm all right," said Jake.

"Stay down. You too, Louis! Nobody move."

They stared at the half-open door. Two gaping exit holes told Bethany that the shooter had used a big gun. This hadn't been some accidental shooting or some random act of violence. The attacker had sniped the front door, looking to kill one of them, maybe all three. Only bad shooting and a little bit of luck had spared Jake's life. Now the question was whether the killer would come in after them. In the distance, sirens howled. Bethany looked to the back of the café. A man stood, shrouded by a wall, a telephone in his hand.

"They called the police," said Bethany. "We need to get out of here."

"We can't," whispered Jake.

"Out the back," said Louis. Rolling from beneath the table, he sprang to his feet and hurried into the kitchen.

Bethany grabbed Jake by his shirt collar and dragged him along.

Louis pushed open a rear door and leapt into the sunshine. Bethany cringed, half expecting a hail of bullets, and then followed. She scanned the alley and the rooftops but saw nothing. The sirens were getting close. A quick wave of the hand and Jake ran out behind her. Jake pointed to the right. They hurried forward. At the street, they slowed to a walk, easing past the curious onlookers that had collected on the sidewalks. Police cars screamed past, screeching to a halt in front of the café. Jake found another side street that led away from the scene. After several minutes, the din had faded and the only sound remaining was that of their footfalls.

Louis spoke first. "What the hell happened back there?"

"I'm thinking the obvious," said Bethany. "Someone targeted Jake. A pretty gutsy hit too, I might say."

"H-how they'd miss? They had two clean shots." Jake was pale. His limbs trembled.

"Stop for a second, Jake. Relax. Catch your breath." Bethany paused, attempting to bring her own emotions under control. She closed her eyes, visualizing the scene at the café, taking her time before she spoke again. "They missed because they weren't professionals. Simple as that. Whoever tried to kill you probably had as much adrenaline pumping through him as you have now. When the time came to shoot, he yanked the trigger. Same with the second shot, except that time he was too pissed to take good aim."

"You got lucky, buddy," said Louis. He slapped Jake on the shoulder, grinning. "That's living life, eh? Nothing like being hunted!"

"What are you talking about? I nearly got shot!"

"My point exactly. Maybe now you'll have a better idea of what's going on in that brewery of yours! The other three who died—they were all working in the malting cellars at the time! Just like you."

"I, uh—it makes no sense."

"There's something, Jake," Bethany said. "There has to be something. Come on! We can't help you if you don't tell us. Something bad is going on, and we're all caught in the middle of it."

"It's only a stupid brewery," said Jake, resting his sweaty forehead in his palms, his voice quivering. "Nothing but a stupid brewery. There's no reason for people to get killed. No reason at all. None."

The young German pulled a tight hood over his round face. His skin was stained with soot, and his blue eyes carried the weight of fatigue. The long day had slid away toward evening, and after more than eight hours tucked inside the tiny crawl space, his muscles felt cramped and stiff. He moved uncomfortably, and the backpack he wore swayed heavily as he walked. He tried to work out the kinks in his body as his mind ran over the events he had already recounted several hundred times—taking the two missed shots, hearing the sirens, and then breaking down his rifle and retreating into his hiding spot. Everything, except for the fact that he missed the target, had gone as planned. Of course, the target had been the most important objective.

He passed by Casanova's, a Canadian-owned Munich nightclub. Laughter spilled from the open doors. It was comedy night, the sign outside said. On any other evening, he might have gone in for a drink and a laugh.

Up ahead on the corner, a black BMW flashed its headlights. He hurried his pace, adrenaline once more filling his blood. The door popped open from the inside, and a voice from behind the tinted glass invited him in. The soft black leather seats molded snugly to his body.

He placed the backpack on the floor and leaned back, relieved and exhausted.

"You're safe," said Christian Scheubel. "I was beginning to wonder."

"I had to stay in my hole. The police were all over the place."

"Yes, of course." Christian paused to chew a breath mint. "There is a small problem, though. It seems they found no casualties at the café."

"I-I misplaced the shot, yes. I'm sorry."

Christian laughed. "Sorry? Listen. Do you want to know something? We're small, that's true, but I like to think of us as a sophisticated organization. This means, as you know, doing quality control. On missions of this magnitude, we have an operative—in this instance, you—who we trust to get the job done. We have that trust because you have proven yourself in the past. We made success as guaranteed as possible, yet you failed us."

"I missed my shots, yeah."

"But more importantly, you also picked the wrong target. You fired on the wrong person! I find this hard to believe because we gave you the order. You knew the target! I simply do not see how that egregious error was possible."

The young man shrugged. "Nerves. The sun reflected funny off my scope. Hell, what do you want me to say?"

"There's no use saying anything. Perhaps, yes, we mobilized too quickly, but when we learned they had gone to the brewery, we had to act fast. These are the moments, my dear boy, that bring victory or defeat to our movement. We cannot accept the latter. I'm sure you understand. Only the former will suffice, both for our leader and for me." Christian tapped the backpack. "The rifle is in there, I assume."

"Packed and stacked. Yes, sir." The young man tried to smile.

Christian started the engine. "I'll take you to the train station." He sighed. "You are to buy a ticket to Garmisch. Do you recall the apartment?"

"It's in Grainau, right?"

"Exactly. On Alpspitzstrasse. The key is inside the base of the bird feeder, the one just beside the door. You'll see there's a little trapdoor built into the bottom."

Christian pulled into traffic. They were silent during the drive, reaching the Hauptbahnhof in less than ten minutes. The young German opened his door and climbed out.

Christian, speaking softly, stopped him. "You failed us today. You know that. In most instances, you would be dead now. But there are reasons you still live. Your youth. Your loyalty. Your past success. These gifts are invaluable to our movement. You will discover that your rewards will exceed any fear you may feel now."

"I will, sir. And thank you."

Christian motioned to leave the backpack. "Check the timetables to Garmisch," he said, "so you can be prepared to leave quickly. Buy a ticket you can use at any time. But before you leave Munich, I have more work for you first."

CHAPTER 6

BITTER GROUNDS

As Polizeihauptkommissar Fritz Weyermann entered the small Munich café tucked back from the street at the corner of Türkenstrasse and Theresienstrasse, his smug smile and cherry-red lips reminded Bethany of corrupt Buffalo cops. She knew the kind that believed their shit didn't smell, that strode with impunity through the most dangerous situations, that had official palms greased and local crooks in their back pockets. She hated cops like that, and right now, she hated this damn German.

Fritz Weyermann had the youth and stature to lend credence to his attitude. His olive-shaded skin held tight to his round, lean face. He had large blue eyes that glinted with pleasure at the pleasant smells of the café. Bethany watched him move confidently in their direction, bending to excuse himself at each table filled with ladies. She knew right then that the man was part cop, part actor and should be treated as such.

"Thanks for staying in touch, and thanks especially for meeting with me," Fritz said. "I thought a trip to Munich might be easier for everyone involved, if only because I hardly get away from Garmisch. But I'm sure you understand that, eh, Ms. Judge? Anyway, let's see now. You know, we've been doing some quite significant investigating since you came back to Munich."

Louis sipped his coffee, and Bethany simply nodded. She had ordered a Hefeweizen and now swirled the glass gently, taking a moment to enjoy the signature aromas of banana and clove. She loved this style of beer. In fact, she ranked it near the top of her list when it was brewed right. And nobody could make it better than the breweries of southern Germany. The beer consisted of a blend of malted barley and wheat, plus the all-important yeast that made German "hefe" so different from the American wheat beers that dominated the landscape back home. Even the natural cloudiness in the beer made it special. Rather than filter it away, German brewers allowed for remnant yeast to lend a touch of flavor, character, and nutrition to the final product.

Fritz grinned when the waitress approached the table. She blushed, his charisma washing over her. "We've had some luck, of course," Fritz said. "It's always interesting when your chief suspect is a police officer."

"Am I the chief suspect?" Bethany asked, feigning ignorance. "I never realized that. Perhaps an unfortunate fool, sure."

"That bit of information about you yielded additional facts. At least to me, that is. I always liked your personality, never saw you as a killer. And I happen to believe a cop—no matter how drunk and no matter how long retired—would never murder so foolishly. Unless she's a psychopath." Fritz smiled at Bethany. "Are you a psychopath?"

"Absolutely not."

"I'm glad to hear that. Of course, psychopaths make quite skilled liars, don't they? Anyway, I believe you, even if your superiors describe you as a troublemaker. I'm not one for misjudging personalities."

Bethany shot a glance at Louis. "What does this mean?"

"We're considering other alternatives," said Detective Weyermann, "though I should warn you that this doesn't mean you're entirely off the hook. Quite simply, I believe we're wasting valuable time focusing the investigation on you. After we run some other leads, we can always put you under the microscope again."

"She's left dangling until you close the case?" said Louis.

"I'm afraid so, yes. She was a police officer. I'm certain she understands."

"Sadly, I do," said Bethany.

Her eyes roved over the room, resting on the front door. A bell jingled, the door opened, and suddenly, there she was. The woman from the airport. Dressed with casual elegance in a black sweater and tight black pants, she flicked a friendly wave at the man behind the counter and ordered coffee. Her hair fell straight to her shoulders, a touch darker than Bethany remembered. Possibly she had colored it since arriving in Munich. A round silver pendant lay suspended by a chain just above her breasts, and two silver rings decorated fingers on both her hands. When her gaze drifted across Bethany's face, she frowned slightly. Then recognition dawned.

"What a surprise," Herta Stocker said, approaching the table. "I had expected to hear from you already, but my phone has been only silent. You're enjoying your stay in Munich?"

Herta sat without asking, and Detective Weyermann stood quickly to push her chair to the table. The four of them stared awkwardly at each other, searching for something to say. Herta sat directly across from Bethany, her eyes encouraging a response.

"Yes!" Bethany blurted finally. "Eventful. The trip has been unexpectedly exciting."

Herta's coffee arrived. Bethany shifted uncomfortably in her seat. This wasn't the type of congregation that made her comfortable. The old friend and drinking buddy Louis Frey. The attractive but academically astute Herta Stocker. The powerful, charismatic Detective Weyermann. At various times in her career, Bethany had been required to sit through meetings with odd combinations of people, from Buffalo's mayor confronting the city's most notorious drug dealer to the mother of a murdered child speaking with the murderer. It was always stressful. Trying to find an emotional middle ground had never been her talent, and awkward groups like these always seemed to charge up strong opinions.

Detective Weyermann had scooted his chair a bit closer to the professor and was now lavishing attention upon her, their conversation little more than background chatter to Bethany's thoughts. There was something unsettling about this coincidental meeting. An instinctive feeling weighed heavily in the pit of her stomach. Her gaze floated over the other three at the table, not fearing that they would read her thoughts, so enraptured were they in their conversation. Why? The question had to do with the professor. Certainly she had the right to drop into any café she preferred, and certainly she seemed to be known here. But to arrive so conveniently in the middle of their meeting? Alarms jangled quietly in Bethany's mind.

"It was one of those moments," said Herta with a laugh, again directing her gaze at Bethany. "A boring flight. It seemed far longer than usual, I can tell you. We were waiting for the luggage and simply begin speaking. We hit it off fabulously right away."

Bethany agreed with her sentiment; they had hit it off well. Herta had eased up beside her, brushed against her, shared stories about her career as a German professor, and even shared a quote from that famous German author. What was his name again? Damn, she knew it was in her search history from the time she discussed it with Louis.

But despite those pleasantries, she thought back to that brief interaction and couldn't help but ponder why the professor had ever given her a second thought. Here she was back home in Germany, with people to see and work to do. Bethany, meanwhile, was the simple lonely traveler. It struck Bethany that the professor remembered things about their first meeting too closely, too detailed, while all she had were the fuzzy edges of their conversation. What had Herta Stocker found so memorable?

Detective Weyermann and Louis behaved like bucks in the rut. Not like Bethany could blame them. The professor carried an air of sensuality and self-assurance. Pheromones were probably wafting off her in thick waves. Bethany supposed that, hidden in her guttural German, the professor was directing the conversation away from anything troublesome, and that was good. She enjoyed discussing herself, her profession. The professor giggled like a teenager, rolling her eyes and twisting her hair. Every now and again she made eye contact with Bethany. With little doubt, she held the rapt attention of both men. Somehow, through very few words, she created the feeling that passionate lovemaking was in the not-too-distant future. Perhaps Louis or Detective Weyermann would be the lucky one. But her gaze at Bethany said something otherwise: It was pure folly, play. The good stuff she was reserving for Bethany, whenever she wanted it. Now? Why not now?

The foursome stretched their visit into three long hours, the conversation lagging only when Bethany finished her fourth half liter of Hefeweizen and excused herself to visit the bathroom. Bethany found herself guessing that the professor wanted it this way, this trio transfixed by her every word and movement. Bethany determined that the professor was a lonely sort, the professional recluse who once in a long while fed her soul through human interaction. She possessed a distinct coldness, didn't she?

When she returned to the table, Bethany realized the professor was staring at her and holding her gaze, her lips turned up into a curious smile, her eyes creased with pleasure, her mouth speaking words that simply blended together. Warmth washed over Bethany's body. Her cheeks flushed. Herta's face suggested they leave. Bethany widened her eyes in a way that asked the obvious question: together? The nod was subtle but real, at least to Bethany. She wanted to find out where this might lead. Following the professor was her only way.

Herta stood suddenly. Louis and Detective Weyermann did the same.

"No, no," the professor said in English, pointing at their chairs. "The two of you stay here. My dear Beer Judge and I are going for a walk."

Bethany stood, almost entranced. She felt pulled into Herta's orbit, helpless to the expectation that she should follow the command. She glanced at Louis, who was again sitting. His mouth moved silently, forming the words "be careful." Bethany fluttered her eyes, signaling her response. Of course she would be careful.

Detective Weyermann sat as well, his body language screaming irritation, his voice tinged with jealousy. "Then I suppose we will just continue the discussion," he said. "Perhaps we'll discover something without any new information."

Outdoors, the cool fall air swept over Bethany. She wished for a moment that she had ordered coffee, not beer, if only to have kept her warm. In the low light of the street, the professor's face lost its sultry, desirous appearance. They stood across from a bakery, a butcher shop, and a small bank. The sweet aroma of fresh-baked bread mingled with the acrid stench of fresh meat. Cars sped past, adding gray exhaust to the air. The professor observed herself in the long windows that ran the length of the street, preening her hair before turning hard eyes on Bethany. Which, now, was the real Herta Stocker? She bounced between them seamlessly, it was true, almost as if she were playing two parts. If so, she was a fabulous actress. If not, perhaps a split personality. Bethany's curiosity led her to follow the professor up the street.

They had covered two hundred yards when a sudden noise erupted behind them. A breaking window. Yells. Screaming. Louis shouting for calm. A pistol shot. More screams. Bethany turned to run back, but the firm warmth of the professor's hand on her shoulder stopped her. The professor's smile had returned, deeper now. She tipped her head toward an archway that led into the English garden.

"It's getting worse," Herta said as the sounds dimmed behind them. "Germans are emulating the Americans now. It started when the soldiers left, did you know? German youth began wearing jeans and baseball caps, watching MTV and acting urban. Now they find illegal weapons and shoot indiscriminately, mostly for effect. It was bad for a while in East Germany—the result of decades of Communist rule and little economic hope. But now it has found its way to the big cities. Munich, Berlin, Frankfurt, Hamburg. A disgusting breed, don't you agree?"

Approaching sirens reminded Bethany that Louis might be injured. She was not being a friend right now, following this woman, but something kept her from returning to the café. Perhaps fear that she'd never see the professor again? Perhaps the thought that their meeting wasn't an accident? Perhaps the hope that she might land her in bed? It was one of those unexplainable moments in life where logic and desire conflicted and exploded into chaos. She couldn't think straight, didn't even want to.

"The children, they're forgetting what it means to be German," Herta said. "They shaped their identity since the war, of course, and the Americans were always part of that. Your army was everywhere, your troops a staple of our daily existence. And then one day that ended. The Berlin Wall falls, East Germany joins with the west, Germany becomes one nation devoted to being a peaceful partner in Europe, and the Americans go home. But what do they leave behind? A vacuum. Our children fill it, of course. First with American clothing. Then the cultural things, like from American television. Now the behavior. Did you know I coined the phrase, 'the MTV effect?' I have built my career on the theories embedded in those simple words."

Bethany listened but felt her mind drawn back to the scene at the café, her imagination flooding with horrible pictures. Was Louis dead? Or the detective? Was it now a hostage situation? She had seen all these things before on the job. They weren't something she wanted to see on vacation.

"Now they come to shooting teachers and students at schools," the professor continued. "And it looks like they robbed our little café. I suppose your friends are fine, don't you think? They are grown adults, smart, trained to handle situations like this."

"It would be nice for us to go check," said Bethany.

"There's no use, don't you think? If we had gone back before, we might have been shot. And now the police will not let us close. The situation will resolve itself, hopefully without any harm having come to your friends."

Presently, the two of them were strolling along a concrete path through the English garden, having agreed to a more roundabout route back to the café. Bethany, her spirits lifting despite her newest worries, strode with leisurely pleasure, drawn ahead by the magnetic beauty of this irresistible woman. Herta talked ceaselessly, inflicting a bit of history about this piece of architecture or that particular side of the creek that flowed through the middle of the park. Bethany caught glimpses of words—"beer garden" and "nude sunbathing" being the two that stood out in her mind. Sadly, though, it was late autumn, and neither could be experienced or enjoyed right now. The professor suggested that Bethany return sometime in the summer to see the English garden in all its glory. Her wan smile started the professor on a tangent.

"Of course you can come back!" Herta said. "Why, I'd even suggest to you that you might stay for good, at least while I'm here. This, of course, requires a bit of commitment on your part, like the beer expert thing, for instance. Perhaps you can do some research, write some articles or even a book? You strike me as the type who might one day be famous. But that might be too grandiose to stomach while abroad for the first time. Of course, the point is that you'd have a place to stay, if you'd want it. And you'd have a friend who speaks both languages, English and German. Who knows? Maybe you'd end up learning a thing or two."

"As it turns out, I'm extending my stay indefinitely," Bethany said.

"Oh?" Herta said. "You've been bitten by the Euro bug? We'll turn you into an expatriate before we're through."

Their stroll brought them out the south exit of the English garden, within earshot of the Isar River. Bethany knew less about the professor than she might have hoped, having enjoyed merely listening to her voice. Interrupting with questions or stupid comments— she hadn't been able to bring herself to that. Probably a feeling of inadequacy. Fear that if she opened her mouth, some stupid comment would roll out, bathed in her horrible Buffalo accent, and the professor would shrivel her nose in disdain. The professor was, after all, highly educated. Bethany was little more than a gutter dweller by comparison, a commoner compared to a queen. Just being near Herta Stocker was glorious.

"We return this way," the professor said, pointing up Von-der-Tann-Strasse. "There is a beautiful path along the Isar, though. That is, if you'd like to explore the city some more."

"The city? It's a nature walk more like it! Wonderful, if I might say so myself."

"The Isar isn't as clean as it once was, you understand. We still have some residents who sunbathe nude along the shores or skinny-dip in the water. Myself, I'd hate to touch the river even in a dry suit. It's the type of thing we need to have cleansed, to revitalize the spirit of our people, to reclaim a river that is all German. If I had it my way—" The professor stopped.

"What?"

"No, you find it boring, I'm sure. We should return to your friends."

Bethany felt a sudden rush of anxiety. Had she really forgotten so quickly, truly been pulled out of reality and into this strange conversation? For all she knew, her friend Louis was injured, maimed, or dead. She should get back there. And yet, here she was, listening to the next words roll out of her mouth.

"Really," Bethany said. "I'd like to hear. It's nice to listen to passion in someone's voice. People in Buffalo—they're a defeated bunch. They see the city as hopeless, the politics as corrupt, and the future as bleak. Obviously, I'm learning that not all people share that view of the world."

"I imagine you'd find it quite boring. German politics is quite regional and is very burdened by history."

"I'm sorry—what do you mean?"

"See? Already I have done it. Regional in the sense that we think of Bavaria before we think of Germany and think of Munich before we think of Bavaria. By *history*, I mean our collective memories aren't as weakened as the Americans', if you'll excuse my choice of words. We recall the Second World War, even those who didn't live it. We know our culture dating back to Germany's unification in 1871 and even back to when we drove off the Roman invaders. Americans, by contrast, are lucky to remember last century, let alone last week. Perhaps it gives you more flexibility in your politics. I'm not certain. We Germans must always bare the old wounds first."

Bethany laughed. "Buffalo has its culture. We remember our blizzard of '77. And how our Buffalo Bills couldn't win a Super Bowl in the '90s. And maybe even the World's Fair in 1901!"

"My point exactly. Those are important moments in the life of your city, but I certainly would not consider them culturally transcendent. The weather? Professional sports? Fairs? Don't you find it amazing that American history is plain forgotten? Like it never happened?"

"We live our lives, I suppose. It's the American way."

"The American curse, more like it. You stay here in Germany for some time and I promise you'll get a different perspective on your world. How history and the present aren't separable. Even if you don't know the past, the world is filled with people who do."

Bethany allowed those words to drift past unanswered. Merely shrugging, she turned right with the professor, up Ludwigstrasse. For a moment she thought the professor could be leading her astray; she hadn't paid much attention to exactly where they had walked. But suddenly they were there, back at the café, its front window shattered, the police gathered around. Louis stood aside from the crowd, giving a statement. He waved to Bethany as she approached. Interestingly, Detective Weyermann was nowhere to be seen. A sinking feeling hit Bethany's stomach. She felt nauseous. The closed ambulance doors—could the detective be behind them, lying on a cot with a white sheet over his head?

The professor rested a warm hand on the back of Bethany's neck, whispering in her ear and pointing inside the café. Ah, there he was, hard at work, as if he had lived in Munich all his life. It was hard not to admire the detective, even if the guy still might decide to throw Bethany in jail.

Marienplatz was total silence. The square was a model of cleanliness, though the lack of cigarette butts, broken glass, or other garbage among the cobblestones was hardly noticeable in the dim evening light. The pedestrian zone was peaceful, as if everyone had decided to stay home after the incident at the café the day before. One person killed, a woman.

"It was targeted," Louis said to Bethany as they crossed beneath the shadow of the Glockenspiel, "even if the authorities claim it was a random act of violence. The dead woman looked a lot like that Stocker lady. And there's no sign of a perpetrator."

Two shootings in hardly more than a week. Three since Bethany had arrived in Germany. But they had agreed, hadn't they? No one must know about the shots fired at Jake. Especially not Detective Weyermann. They hadn't been there, hadn't even heard about *that* shooting incident.

But the professor—there was something odd about her, wasn't there? To leave a café with a near stranger, to hear commotion coming from the café moments later, to react so coolly. All that flew in the face of Bethany's training, of her experience. Something didn't smell right, she knew. But her usually acute senses were jaded with curiosity. Maybe even lust. She had to admit that too. Under those circumstances, it might be difficult to reach the right conclusions.

Bethany exhaled thin white wisps that quickly dissipated in the light evening breeze. She covered her face with her hands, saying nothing, thinking only through the evidence that, so far, made no obvious sense. The malthouse workers—were they targeted? If so, why? And now this dead lady in the café. The professor hadn't seen the resemblance to her, yet there it was. Things were getting tight, confused, not as simple anymore as one dead man on a train. Poor Louis hadn't expected a full-fledged intrigue when he came to Munich. Now, like it or not, he was stuck in the middle.

"I'm tired, Bee," Louis said as they approached Sendlingor Tor. "Let me catch some rest. Maybe it will clear my mind, help me come up with some new ideas."

Bethany watched him descend the stairs to the U-Bahn. He would catch the subway, zip underground, and be to his hotel within fifteen minutes. She envied him. Sleep was nowhere on her radar. Even if she dropped her head onto a pillow, Bethany knew the drill: she would toss and turn, and her brain would keep buzzing with scenarios that could not come together.

A beer sounded good now. Maybe a Dunkelweizen to soak up some of the evening chill. Or at least just a Dunkel to soothe her parched throat. She cast away her thoughts of the last week, feeling the tension melt as she pulled the pub's door open. Laughter and smoke spilled into the street. The aroma of spilled beer beckoned, and soon Bethany found herself leaning against the bar, a glass to her lips. The first sip was deliciously cool and then warm as the alcohol pumped through her veins. She closed her eyes, relaxing a little more, and by her fourth beer was again enjoying the signature banana and clove characteristics of a Bavarian Hefeweizen. She would try a few more beers to compare styles and maybe then find a shower. Maybe then, finally, she could put today, and the last few days, in the rearview mirror.

A hand touched her arm. "Are you okay?" a woman asked in English.

Bethany smiled, her eyes still closed. "Fine. Just trying to relax."

"A difficult day?" the woman said.

"A difficult vacation. Nothing but trouble since I got here." Bethany looked at the woman. "You're an American?"

"Same as you, sure. On a drinking tour of Europe. How about you?"

"It started as a visit to the Oktoberfest. It's become a bit more."

"Germany is a crazy place, don't you think?"

"I don't know. My experience has been a bit jaded. I haven't had much time to slow down and experience things."

"But you have! You're enveloped by it every minute. Here. At the Oktoberfest. Just walking down the street. You need to be open, let it flow naturally. If you try to see it like back home, you'll get nothing out of your stay."

Bethany nodded thoughtfully. "What's your name?"

"Amanda. Amanda Lang. From Salt Lake."

"Utah? Never been there. Mormon country, right?"

"Big-time. And I'm one of them."

"You? But—"

"But Mormons don't drink. I know. And we don't smoke either. Listen, I came over on a mission trip three years ago. Did nothing but preach my faith. Last month, I decided exactly what I was just trying to say: to see the world through a filter that isn't my own. I put my Mormon faith back here." She tapped the back of her head. "And I'm putting German faith in this beer glass, pouring it in my mouth, and swallowing it. You'd be surprised at the clarity."

"Yeah, I got that my first night."

"A little too much? You got to be careful. This German brew kicks!"

"You talk like you've been drinking all your life."

"Close enough. You ever heard that joke 'Why don't you ever go fishing with only one Mormon?'"

"Why?"

"Because he'll drink all your beer!" She laughed. "Damn Mormons watch over each other. It's worse than the Stasi."

"Stasi?"

"The old East German secret police. Kind of like the Gestapo. You heard of them?"

"From the Nazis, right?"

"Brutal bastards, I'll tell you. And I'd bet there's something like it now, even in modern Germany, even after East and West reunified. There's an undertone in the society, something unspoken, just a murmur at the most. Can't you hear it? It's like the fact that from here, we're maybe, what, ten or fifteen miles from Dachau? That was a big concentration camp, you know. Political dissidents, the works. A nice wall for the firing squad. They had showers, ovens. And today it's what? A curiosity for visitors like you and me? A way for Bavaria to generate tourism dollars? It's so entrenched in their psyche, the Germans don't even see it anymore. Just like me being a Mormon. I don't *see* my religion, or at least I didn't. To see the present, it's necessary to break with the past."

"I see."

"I wonder about that."

"Look. I only came in for a drink. To unwind a little."

"I never got your name."

"Bethany Judge. From Buffalo."

"Wyoming?"

"New York. Snow capital, you know? Home of the Bills? Where President McKinley got shot?"

Amanda shrugged.

"You've never heard of Buffalo. Really?"

"Buffalo, Wyoming. I was there for a rodeo championship in high school. But I don't know much of America east of the Black Hills."

"But you know so much about Germany?"

She laughed. "It's beautiful, isn't it? I love the irony."

"Rather makes it hard to put much faith in what you've said. It all sounded good, granted, but it's sort of like window dressing."

"You doubt me? That's understandable, of course. Meeting a stranger in some Munich bar, engaging in a conversation about something more than the weather—it's enough to give anyone pause. But I'm happy to show you."

"Show me what?"

"Proof, if proof is what you desire. It's easy to come by, you know. It requires asking the right questions. And being curious."

"It seems like that's all I do—ask questions. Would you like another beer?"

"Absolutely!"

Bethany held her glass to the dim light, observing the beer's hazy appearance, the result of yeast suspended in solution, the classic look of a Hefeweizen. After a satisfied nod, she tapped her glass against Amanda's, toasting the moment before touching the glass to her lips. Seconds later, half the brew had disappeared down her throat, not a drop spilling on her shirt. Amanda watched admiringly.

"Great stuff!" Amanda said.

Bethany shared her enthusiasm with that beer and the next and the one that followed. Sometime after midnight, Amanda tendered an arm to help Bethany out the door, leading her to a black BMW parked just outside.

"A cab?" Bethany said, her words a drunken jumble. "Very thoughtful of you."

Amanda opened the back door. "Get in."

Amanda slid in beside Bethany. The driver punched the gas before she had closed the door entirely. They turned down an alley and then circled the Altstadtring. Minutes later, they entered Stiglmaierplatz and then sped out Dachauer Strasse. Blond haired, tight-lipped, and with hands tensed on the steering wheel, the driver weaved through the quiet nighttime traffic, never saying a word.

"I'm afraid I have no idea where we are," said Bethany, her eyes drooping with inebriation.

Amanda wiped the sweat from Bethany's forehead. "We're heading in the right direction," she said, a light German accent invading her English. "A little diversion tonight, but we'll have you home safely before long. You're wanted, did you know? Quite popular for an American just arrived in our fair city."

CHAPTER 7

AXIS AND ALLIES

Amanda opened the door and exited quickly, her heels striking the ground before the car tires had come to a rest on the jet-black driveway. Bethany came out behind her, feeling sobriety creeping back into her brain, but her legs were still fighting for balance. She gripped Amanda's left hand. Amanda led the way up the narrow staircase, entering the house without the slightest knock on the front door.

A pleasant place, thought Bethany, her mind still fighting the fog of one too many beers. Clean white walls and waxed hardwood floors. Colorful photographs adorning the rooms, mostly of idyllic outdoor scenes. A lingering aroma of mulled wine in the air. Bethany could make out the clove and cinnamon. She grinned despite herself.

The first floor was sparsely furnished. Two wooden chairs filled the middle of what should have been the dining room. The kitchen had little evident cookware. No toaster, no mixer, nothing. Just pristinely clean. Even the sink sparkled. Bethany had the impression nobody lived here regularly; the current occupants were temporary at best, perhaps only for a brief meeting with her. The thought chilled her.

Two people sat in the back room, which had large curtainless windows and a view of some distant mountains dimly visible in the thinning darkness. Sitting on the floor beside the windows, with dozens of papers and documents spread around him, was a skinny, tall man with shifty eyes and a pasty face. He stood and arranged himself in such a way that, to Bethany Judge's newly internationalized mind, seemed thoroughly American. There was nothing familiar about the face, nothing except the look behind the eyes. Maybe this guy was a cop. But if so, what the hell was he doing here, somewhere in the middle of Europe?

With nervous agility, the man strode forward, kissing Amanda on the cheek. He grabbed Bethany's hand and squeezed, giving it a fast pump.

"This went off better than I might have hoped," he said. "Wonderful work, Amanda."

"Thank you. Ms. Judge was quite cooperative. She should be commended for keeping her head under the most trying of circumstances."

"My beautiful consort deserves the credit," said Bethany, trying to play a part she couldn't quite understand, trying even harder not to jumble her words. "I have seldom felt more at ease."

"That's good, that's good. Yes, you should feel quite comfortable. We are here to help. My name is Albert Treanor. You already know Amanda. And perhaps Francis Eberhardt as well?"

Recognition flashed through Bethany's mind. She remembered hearing all the stories about Francis Eberhardt, a sort of legend among America's law enforcement circles. Always prowling the nastiest edges of society, always ready to drive his claws in for the kill, always bringing infallible cases that ended in high-profile prosecutions. Rumor had it that he had moved overseas after unprecedented professional success in New York City. Now, solving international crime was his forte. The years had made him a very wealthy man. Yes, the brushed-back, thick brown hair, the pensive black eyes, the broad nose set too close to his full mustache. Bethany had heard the man never smiled, and so far during this first meeting, that reputation held true. Francis Eberhardt nodded but did not offer a handshake.

There was little doubt where things stood. Bethany had stumbled into something of unbelievable magnitude, something beyond the petty indiscretions of her work experience in Buffalo, something she could only hope to grasp but probably never would. Just the sight of Francis Eberhardt took the wind out of her lungs, made her feel weak, exhausted, and scared. Whom could she trust? What mistakes had she made? Bethany replayed all her experiences since arriving at the Munich airport, thought through all her efforts since leaving Garmisch. Too many connections, she was certain now, and nothing but an array of errors. It had been an unbelievable miscalculation on her part to have even tried to solve this mystery. But Francis Eberhardt would set things straight. The man lived in the shadows, knew the enemy, always stayed one step ahead. A master chessman if one had ever lived in the real world. There was something comforting about Eberhardt's presence, if not also unsettling. What the hell had she gotten into?

"Now that we're all friendly, perhaps we should take a seat," said Albert Treanor. "I'm sorry the accommodations aren't more comfortable, but this was the best we could do under the circumstances."

Amanda left to retrieve the chairs from the dining room. She returned, dragging them clumsily through the hallways, twice bumping the walls with the chair legs. Bethany took a seat immediately, her body sinking heavily, enjoying the reprieve. Amanda huffed back to examine the dark scuff marks her clumsiness had left behind. She went to the kitchen cupboard and returned with a bucket of white paint and a brush. After several even strokes of paint on the wall, she appeared satisfied.

Dawn had struck, and with it, Bethany knew at least one thing: the room they sat in faced east. Brilliant sunshine streamed through the windows, killing the evening chill that had hung in the air. Albert

Treanor squatted and shuffled through papers at his feet, squinting and sighing with exasperation at the sudden glare that hampered his work. Bethany had a sudden desire for coffee or juice—something to get the morning started. Even better, a beer. That would pack some calories with it. She hadn't eaten since—since when? Certainly too long, and that sudden realization sent a wave of weakness through her limbs. She guessed she was in bad company for sympathy. Albert Treanor had the skinny limbs of a high school cross-country runner, and Amanda had a muscular, athletic physique. Francis Eberhardt showed few signs of physical existence. Had he not blinked every thirty seconds, Bethany might have thought the man was dead.

"Why should we care about you?" said Francis Erdhardt suddenly. His voice was deep and booming, a powerful, resonant force. "You may have plenty to share with us, but you only recently arrived from the States, isn't that true?"

"Buffalo. That's right."

"And we should believe that your sudden arrival will illuminate our years of hard work? That somehow your limited experience gives you the expertise to consult with us? I suppose you might. That's the nature of the workplace today. All the young people today think a minute's worth of expertise is worth two hundred dollars per hour in the marketplace. Well, thankfully, we're offering you no money, Ms. Judge. I'd be quite skeptical of your motives, indeed, were that the case."

Bethany looked at the others in disbelief. "My motives? I was … Amanda brought me here. I knew nothing of this meeting."

"Of course! That is true!" said Albert. "Francis, why must you torment the young lady? I suppose you find it humorous in your sick kind of way."

Relief swept through Bethany together with a sense of foreboding. She knew this little game of good cop, bad cop. But why they were turning it on her? It made no sense, not if they had brought her here to be of help and to be helped. Perhaps this Francis Eberhardt just had an ax to grind. That was his type of personality, wasn't it?

The professional that sneers down his nose at everyone who tries to emulate his success. The snoop who trusts only his own fine-tuned judgment. Or perhaps Bethany did not yet know the real meaning behind this meeting. She let her guard rise and took a deep breath.

"Humorous? Yes, quite humorous, in fact," said Francis Eberhardt. "Can you imagine the improbability of traveling halfway across the world and accidentally landing in the middle of this? I'd suppose the chances are worse than winning the lottery. Her little hornet's nest is a bit too neatly arranged—that's all—and I'd prefer to knock it to the ground before I climb the ladder."

"What the hell is that supposed to mean?"

"I want verification! Proof she's not acting on their behalf."

"What—you think I'm involved with the murderer somehow?" asked Bethany.

Amanda smiled, patting her knee. "No."

"Speak for yourself, miss! If you let your gender drive your alliances, I promise you death will not be far behind. I demand more, Ms. Judge, regardless of what—or who—brought you to us this morning."

Bethany's eyes jerked nervously between Amanda and Albert. She had feigned anger on suspects hundreds of times, but she still felt unsettled despite her own experiences. The strange faces. The unknown environment. The rapidly changing situation. There was nothing here for Bethany to grasp. No home, no friends, no comfort foods. Everything was foreign, even these Americans. And for that matter, was Amanda even that? Her sudden change of accent hadn't escaped Bethany. It had surprised her, yes, but it had not slipped by unnoticed. She had to wonder. Except for Francis Eberhardt, how did these other two fit in?

"You're always suggesting I'm naive, Francis," said Amanda, her voice cool. "Could you have brought her here tonight, I wonder? It seems to me that you lack some of my assets."

Albert said, "That's right! We're a team, ha! Each possesses particular skills, yes. We've discussed this before. But as you can see, Ms. Judge, our little triumvirate must contend with pride. It's a terrible force, isn't it? Quite destructive, even during moments of success."

Recollections of her own lifetime flickered dimly through Bethany's mind. Her successes as a police officer. Her successes as a wife. Her successes as a daughter. Pride had shattered them all, destroyed them, reduced them to rubble. Pride was her greatest enemy, the invisible force that pushed everything to arm's length. Or further, preferably. Nothing could prove her wrong, nothing could reveal her faults. When something threatened her protective bubble, she stomped it out mercilessly. And to insulate that bubble, to ensure extra distance from the world around it, she had pushed away everything, pushed herself all the way to Munich to ensure nothing could ever come close to touching her. She only wanted to practice her new talents, put her Master Cicerone skills to the test, drink the beers of Germany and Europe, and wipe away the past. But then, she could never get far enough away. She was still a cop from Buffalo. An ex-cop at that and, in the back of her mind, a complete failure.

Bethany forced her thoughts back to the immediate situation. "I'll admit I'm confused. I have no sense of why I'm here. You haven't told me anything about yourselves. Only—"

"Only what you need to know," said Francis Eberhardt.

Bethany tried again. "I know about you, Mr. Eberhardt. Your reputation precedes you."

"Understandably."

"Yes, sir. And Amanda told me about herself when we met. Assuming that was true, of course." She looked to Amanda, who blushed and lowered her head. "From her reaction, I might assume there were some falsehoods in the things she said. And you," she said, looking to Albert Treanor, "are a complete mystery."

"Absolutely. I don't doubt that," said Albert. "A drink perhaps?"

"A good German beer?"

Amanda rose. Moments later, she set a foaming glass of Bavarian Helles on the floor beside Bethany's chair. Bethany was not going to drink it right away. She would wait to make sure she trusted these people. Albert's crystal-green eyes sparkled mischievously, as if he expected something interesting to happen. He shuffled some papers and flashed a pleasant smile.

"Your stay in Munich has been exciting," he said.

"It hasn't been quite the vacation I expected," said Bethany.

"Yes, and we do have some questions regarding that."

"Wouldn't it be fair to give me some information about yourselves first?" Bethany asked. "Something to level the playing field a bit?"

"The playing field," said Francis Eberhardt, his voice tinged with irritation, "has not been level for decades. An uphill battle! That's what we face."

Albert cleared his throat. "That's right, and unfortunately you've rather, er, dropped into the battle three-quarters of the way up that hill."

"Which is exactly what I don't understand! What battle? A guy was killed on the train, and the cops considered me a suspect. I worked to clear my name. That's all." Bethany's tone was one of exasperation.

"Calm down, please. We don't expect that you'd know." Albert paused, casting a sideways glance at Francis Eberhardt. "Well, perhaps not all of us. But the fact remains that we can use your assistance. That is one of the reasons you are here."

"I was a victim," Bethany said. "That might sound odd coming from me. I heard that all the time on the job. You'd think I wouldn't buy into victim-speak."

"Not strange at all," said Amanda.

"Tragic story," Albert said. "But things have been far too public lately. Too much to be a coincidence. That's Mr. Eberhardt's theory, anyway."

Francis Eberhardt cleared his throat at the mention of his name. He shifted perceptibly, attempting to conceal his thin smile. After a dramatic pause, he spoke: "Criminals have always filled the world, and some places seem more prone to crime than others. New York City, for example. Places with large congregations of people. That's quite reasonable when you think about it. If you're alone in the jungle, there aren't many others to steal from. And when people surround you, human nature simply is to covet what they have. But there are, shall we say, 'other kinds of criminals.' They covet not the tangible things—money, jewels, cars. They want the intangible. It's power, if I may use the most basic term. By the simplest definition, they seek little more than that. But questions arise for persons like me: Who is it that is seeking this power? Who are those criminals? And the answer is simple. One word. Politicians. The twentieth century saw the ascendancy of politicians who used the mind as the ultimate source of power. Adolf Hitler was the first genius of this. And with that, Germany has a special legacy that must be watched, lest we discover its reemergence too late. The ideology that scares everyone, Ms. Judge. Fascism. Most now call it the Far Right."

He gestured toward Amanda Lang.

"Amanda is our bloodhound. She knows as much about fascism in Germany as in America."

Amanda fixed a strong gaze on Bethany as if willing her to understand. "It's a strong political force in both countries," she said, her voice calm and quiet.

"But nothing compares in strength to the German movement," said Francis Eberhardt. "Nothing! It's the blood of this society, not so easily purged by trails, hangings, and decades of prosperity. Call it what you will today, but the longing for that kind of power remains an immense lure."

Bethany shook her head. "Just a second. You're telling me ... I'm supposed ... What? I've fallen in with Nazis?"

"Or the like," Albert said, moving forward. "We can't be certain, you understand. Only suspicious."

"As I said," Francis Eberhardt continued, "Amanda tracks our suspects. Her investigations suggest something is percolating here in the fatherland. Something big enough to cause some very public deaths."

"And assassination attempts," added Amanda.

A palpable pause gripped the room. All eyes fixed on Bethany as if the three expected her to share something relevant. For her part, Bethany wondered how they might know her little secrets. The shooting when she was with Jake and Louis. The murder at the café. Just a guess perhaps?

"How did you know?" she whispered.

Albert laughed. "She's the bloodhound!"

"Three Americans talking loudly in a German café don't escape notice, Ms. Judge. I only had to ask some questions, gather some descriptions, run a couple of physical tests for confirmation. You can't deny you were there, though perhaps you don't realize your good fortune."

"My good fortune? They were shooting at Jake. He is the lucky one."

Albert's eyebrows rose. He threw a glance at Francis Eberhardt.

"This was the third person in the party? The other American besides your military friend?"

"Yes."

"And you came to know him how?"

Bethany offered a brief but thorough explanation.

"Fair enough," said Amanda. "We'll need to gather more information on this Jake Stoddard person. In the meantime, you need to realize that he likely was not the target. They want you, Ms. Judge, because they realize their error. On the train, by leaving you alive, somehow you have drawn near to exposing their ambitions."

Francis Eberhardt spoke. "It's either something on her person, something she possesses among her belongings, or the actions she is taking."

"Probably the latter," said Albert. "Sniffing around gets you in trouble. Right, Amanda?"

She laughed. "Every time."

"Indeed. And we're back to asking what the motivations of our adversaries might be," said Francis Eberhardt. "Nearly eight decades of relative quiet—barring, of course, the recent far right political victories in Austria, France, Germany, and now, even America—and they choose to crawl out like cockroaches now when nothing overt is apparent. We see nothing, not even movement among the rank and file. There are no indications of increased money flowing into their coffers, either from internal or from foreign sources. Only this sudden and unmotivated extremism."

"I expect they are taking a page from the book of other extremist influences," said Albert.

"But this is too tame, too targeted. Don't the murders seem more like purposeful assassinations to you?" Francis Eberhardt shook his head, the bewilderment evident across his taut face. "I see the other extremists blowing people up indiscriminately. Pure terror, that is. What we have here is something completely different. If it weren't, wouldn't you expect our Ms. Judge here would have perished on that train?"

Bethany whitened, quickly reaching to gulp some of her beer. Clumsily, she knocked the glass to the floor. "I'm sorry," she said. "A little flustered—that's all."

"Understandable," said Amanda. She flashed Francis Eberhardt an angry glance before disappearing to find a towel. When she returned, Albert had already continued the conversation.

"The shot came from the top of the neighboring building. We traced that through ballistic evidence. I suspect the police have managed to do the same by now. No evidence of the shooter, though. It's quite surprising, in fact, that he escaped detection. Either he had help or an outstanding place to hide. And the death in this other café? The place you went for your meeting with the inspector from Garmisch? Any idea who that woman, the victim, might have been?"

"None," said Bethany. "What? You were following me?"

"Don't be surprised, please. That's almost offensive. You know the murder on the train caught our interest. And the shooting at you and the other two Americans. You know the circumstances of your survival were quite curious. We had to look, and to our pleasant surprise, we discovered that your investigations were stirring up some concern. But two murders and at least one attempt on your life—we felt it appropriate to step in. To inform you of our presence. You can be an outstanding ally to us, Ms. Judge."

"How? I'm sorry, but I just don't see—"

Amanda Lang turned suddenly to Albert. "I don't think she understands entirely," she said. "She's rather out of her scope, don't you think?"

"It doesn't matter," said Francis Eberhardt. "I'm still interested in learning about what was going on at that café. And about her little walk with that woman."

"Yes, I was coming to that," said Albert.

"The professor? Yes, we happened to meet when I arrived in Munich. At the airport. She gave me some helpful advice. Well, I say helpful, but in a way, she got the idea in my head that I should find a place to sleep and suggested an overnight train ticket to Garmisch. Figured I'd just sleep it off on the train, you know?"

"The fateful ticket," muttered Francis Eberhardt.

"That was all. She had given me her phone number. You know, as a contact. A person to know while I was in the city. I thought of calling her maybe once or twice, but by the time we went to that café for our meeting, I had quite mostly forgotten about her. Then she just walks in. We sort of recognized each other right away, and she joined us at the table. She's quite the dominant woman, really took control of the conversation. Finally, we left for a walk."

Francis Eberhardt interrupted. "Just the two of you!" he barked.

"Just the two of us—that's right. We hadn't gone far before we heard something happen back at the café."

"But you didn't go back? Not even knowing your friends were there?"

"Only one friend. The other guy was that cop from Garmisch. He came to update us about their investigation."

"That's quite kind!"

"I was relieved to hear they were focusing the investigation elsewhere, yes. But he wasn't specific about where they were going to look, and besides, I had the opportunity to go for a stroll with a friendly and beautiful woman. She was a nice diversion."

Francis Eberhardt sighed audibly. He waved a finger at Amanda. She stooped, shuffled among the papers on the floor, and rose with a page-sized black-and-white photograph in her hands.

"This is the woman?" said Francis Eberhardt.

Amanda placed the photograph on Bethany's lap.

"Yes."

"And her name?"

"Herta Stocker."

Albert Treanor shifted nervously. "So that cuts it then. In case there was ever any doubt."

"Doubt? About what?" said Bethany.

"Herta Stocker's reputation precedes her as well," said Albert. "I'm surprised that you hadn't heard of her, being that you're from New York. Her adversaries claim she harbors certain sentiments of the far right form. Some of her lectures have erupted in very unsightly displays. Reactions to her inflammatory comments, the students say."

He sighed. "So we suspected there might be a connection. Herta Stocker begins a sabbatical in Munich just as certain odd things begin to occur."

Amanda interrupted. "But she's so ordinary! Nothing abnormal. Spends the day writing, it seems. Or doing research. She's quite devoted to her profession."

"And to her twisted ideas! Look, Ms. Judge, let's cut to the quick. You might not give a damn either way, but the simple fact is that a woman of great interest to us has approached you. This presents us with a unique opportunity to uncover some very useful information. The moment is crucial, particularly given the strange events of recent weeks. Our hope is that you will contribute to our cause."

"But I still don't understand your cause! You never made that clear. I have listened to this confusing exchange and even the occasional accusation, but the reasons behind bringing me here are no clearer than when I first arrived."

"Ms. Judge, rest assured that we are acting in your best interest," said Francis Eberhardt. "Not only that, but in the interest of the entire world. I share your mistrust, but mine is directed at you. Still, it appears we are forced to trust each other, doesn't it? Two complete strangers must surrender their pride and work together for a greater good. You know about pride. Yes, that I can see. So you'll bristle when I tell you our work is strictly classified. We can't share anything more about our operation. Ultimately, it protects you. But should we succeed, you can expect the highest possible rewards from our agency."

"So this is like the CIA or something?"

Francis Eberhardt only shrugged. Amanda and Albert studied their feet.

"Okay. So say I agree to do something. Then what? Do I throw on a swastika and learn the goose step? I doubt it will be so easy as to simply walk in among them, these Nazis, without gaining their confidence somehow. And for that matter, what would a person do about them anyway?"

"There's nothing to do," said Amanda. "Only gather information. Get as close as you can, learn faces and plans, but never reveal your intentions, never reveal anything that might endanger the operation or your life. We're bloodhounds, remember?"

The words hung between them, Bethany uncomfortable with the supposition that she was already onboard. Whatever suspicions she might have harbored before now were completely tossed out the window. This odd scenario here in this—where was she exactly, anyhow?—confirmed the complexity of the original murder but dashed hopes that she and Louis might somehow solve it through their own sleuthing skills. Cooperation perhaps was the only way to gain access to the truth.

Uncomfortable as it made her feel, Bethany nodded slowly, agreeing to a partnership. "Understand, though," she said, "that I need some more information. Let's start with where the hell we are right now."

Albert turned to face the mountains. A morning haze painted the trees in a thin white sheen. "You've no doubt noticed we're close to the Alps. Quite close, in fact, to where misfortune struck on the train."

"We're back in Garmisch?"

"Not quite, no. A neighboring town. The location is most favorable. Good access to American technology. Easy transportation to Munich. Beneath the enemy's radar. But mostly it keeps us in a neutral location, away from the fray. There are always things going on in the city, things that might be subtly attractive, even to our trained minds. Enthusiasm for the movement, for example, is growing in the streets. We can't afford distractions that might derail our efforts, so we keep an arm's length away unless there's work to do."

Bethany shifted in her chair, her tongue feeling thick and dry.

"I don't understand. There's no sign of fascists in Munich. Not that I saw, anyway. Perhaps among an isolated few, but not the whole city."

"You'd be surprised. It isn't a matter of Munich breaking out the Nazi flags and dangling them from their windows. We aren't waiting for brown shirts to march through the streets. It's better to listen to the murmurs. They tell you everything, like the trickling of a stream. Subtle comments told in confidence. Amanda had an older German whisper something in her ear recently at an event at the city's history museum. 'It's a shame all of Munich had to be destroyed because a few Jews died,' he said. And that's just the beginning. What we've discovered is a nation cloaked in subterfuge, all sharing the dirty secret of their truest beliefs, all living with one foot in civilization, the other in barbarism.

"They say there's no longer anti-Semitism in Germany. That's partially true, but only because the Jews are dead or gone! Now the Germans despise other foreigners. Turks. Poles. Whatever. It doesn't really matter. Their historical fear of isolation, of being surrounded by enemies. It is stronger than ever now, whether they recognize it or not. The whole vicious circle bites them in the ass when some charismatic person foments a movement. The Germans want someone with power to lead them. Why? Because the burden of history forever forces the world to see Germany with a jaded eye! But the Germans, well, they want to come out of the proverbial closet and do great deeds for the fatherland."

"This is …" Bethany shook her head. "It's just too much. I'm sorry. Impossible to believe. I can't even understand what you're saying, mostly. I was a Buffalo cop for fuck's sake. We didn't deal with this kind of shit. And what we dealt with was bad enough. That's why I retired. That's why I became a beer expert. I'm just here for good beer." She pointed to the empty beer glass. "Can I get that beer now? Shit, some international conspiracy? I'm lucky if I understand local politics. And I'm gullible too. Look how easily Amanda tricked me. That is your name, right?"

"Amanda Lang, born and bred. And I did grow up in Salt Lake, a Mormon, but I'm first generation out of Germany. My parents converted and moved to America when I was still in the womb. But we came back often on missions. You notice the accent, no doubt, because I still spent most of my life speaking German. Germany, Salt Lake, parts of the West—that's my territory. And when some Nazis murdered my parents, that sealed my future for good."

Bethany blinked. "They what?"

"They murdered my parents," Amanda said slowly, exaggerating the words. "Point-blank, bullets in the back of the head. Executed for being Mormons. And guess what? Nothing happened to the killers. The police said it was a misunderstanding. A misunderstanding! That the murderers believed their home was threatened when my parents came knocking on the door, doing their Mormon missionary work. Two elderly folks in nice suits, a threat? No, more like a bunch of fascists covering each other's back."

"And that's why you're here?"

"Absolutely. For revenge. To destroy what I can before they finally kill me. I find that inevitable, you see, but that's okay. Not fearing my own death gives me greater courage. I do things I often find surprising, but never would I shirk from my duty. Not until my last breath."

Bethany turned to Francis Eberhardt. "I know about you," she said, her voice steady. She looked at Albert. "What about you?"

"Just a job. A stupid way to live, I suppose. Some might call it a relic of the Cold War. But events have shown there's nothing like having good intelligence on the ground, right? We're the scouts, the frontline grunts. If we succeed, the sparks are doused before the fire gets started."

"You've been at it long?"

Albert shrugged. "Long enough to not like what I'm seeing. Things have changed since I started this career, Ms. Judge. I can tell you that. The world is becoming a more dangerous place, and Germany is part of that current. What we do is stem the flow and then move on to the next breach in the dam."

"So what do you do? Or should I ask instead, what should I do? Are there things you have in mind?"

"There are lots of things you could do. Many others you shouldn't even attempt. You aren't skilled in espionage, Ms. Judge. Please don't pretend that you are. And please don't allow your former profession to give you a false sense of security. The people we deal with—they are absolutely the most dangerous people you have ever known. Be cautious. Be smart. Those are the simplest answers I can give."

"Then do nothing?"

Amanda looked at Albert again. Francis Eberhardt answered the unspoken question that passed between them.

"We'd be foolish to request more from this woman. Security is the last thing that protects us. We know very little of her and may already have shared too much. How are we to know that our entire operation isn't compromised now?"

"Trust," said Amanda, smiling kindly at Bethany. "I trust her. And besides, she provides a conduit into their organization. It's something we never had before. It's the reason we brought her here!"

"Amanda is right, Francis," said Albert. "At some time we have to play a card or two. This is a good opportunity for us. We shouldn't squander it."

Francis Eberhardt sighed. "But the question remains: What can she do for us?"

"That's easy. Just three words. Fall in love. You can do that, can't you, Ms. Judge? Fall in love? She's a beautiful woman, perhaps the kind a woman like you wants hanging on her arm. And she seems to feel a certain affinity toward you. Otherwise, I suspect she would have shot you in the English garden. Or had one of her men do it. Yes, she went from wanting you murdered to wanting you alive. Now she only needs to start wanting you."

Amanda leaned close to Bethany's ear. "Can you do it?" she whispered. "Don't be afraid to say no."

Bethany knew how she had felt about Herta Stocker that day at the café, the day she followed her into the English garden, tangled in the professor's web despite the chaos that had erupted. The pull was unmistakable. Bethany was drawn to the professor, even sensing that the outcome could be bad. Worst of all, Bethany knew this excuse, knew it never held water. She had heard the story time and again as a cop and had never believed it, always hearing it as a cover-up, probably because she had never experienced it. Everything was different now.

"I can. I'd be lying if I said there wasn't something between us already," Bethany said. "And this intrigue? It kind of adds something." She smiled. "Something kinky. But you know what?" The others looked at her, their eyes questioning. "It isn't so much whether I can fall in love with the professor. I'm wondering if I'll actually mean it once I do."

Francis Eberhardt muttered that it wouldn't be a problem, not after Bethany got a whiff of the professor's murderous tendencies and the sort of scum she called friends. At that he declared their meeting finished, saying any further discussion was redundant and that action was the only next logical step. Amanda left to pour Bethany another beer. After that, she would put together a lunch. Already it seemed too late to eat breakfast. By the time Amanda returned, however, a fresh Bavarian Helles filling the glass, Bethany was sleeping in the hard chair, her chin resting on her chest, a light snore rolling from her throat.

CHAPTER 8

A SUDDEN STORM

They exited the Hackerstubl to a surprise snowstorm dropping light, lazy flakes that melted on Munich's roads. Along the darkened street, only two people stood, gazing into a well-lit shop window. Behind them, the door swung shut and the sounds from the crowded bar fell silent. Louis Frey wiped sweat from his red face. He wore handsome black slacks and a fine Loden coat. Bethany Judge had on the same wrinkled clothing from the day before.

"You can't simply disappear!" barked Louis at Bethany. "Imagine how I felt, waking up in the morning and finding you were gone."

Bethany looked hard at her friend. She had known him for years. Decades, really. Secretly, perhaps she had wished he had been her first kiss, her high school lover. Maybe even the man who took her virginity. But those days were long past, and Louis had lived a life in Germany that Bethany could not imagine. All these people she had met—Herta Stocker, Jake, Amanda, Francis Eberhardt, Albert Treanor—were they any different from Louis? Any less of an enigma? In truth, they were all strangers. At least to her, anyway. And maybe there was some connection, some thread between them that she just could not yet see. Even Louis. Looking back, it was strange that he had materialized at the Garmisch police station to rescue her. Was that orchestrated? Was the professor involved? Was there anyone Bethany could trust?

"You kept your head," Bethany said finally. "Coming to our meeting place."

"Kept my head? I'm quite upset! My face is burning up. Blood pressure's probably through the roof. You can't do that, Bee. Just run off! If we're to be successful, we have to work together."

"You heard what he said. They aren't looking at me as a suspect anymore."

"Oh, come on! Bee, you were a cop. They haven't tossed your name out, and you know it. Maybe he said that to see if you screw up. Maybe he's telling the truth. Either way, you aren't safe until you or the police find the real murderer."

They started walking through the swirling snowflakes and skin-biting wind.

"I just had to get away, Louis. Clear my head."

"You could have told me where you were going."

"Too many people getting killed or shot at. I wasn't thinking clearly, I guess. Things are better now."

"I'd have expected more. Feeling ill is the stuff of rookies and tourists, not a seasoned veteran like you. Can't handle this, being on the other side of the fence? Come on, Bee! You're innocent, so do what you need to prove that! And don't rely on me because you can't speak the language. Don't entrust anything to me."

"Can I ask you something?"

"Sure."

"And you'll give an honest answer?"

"All the time. You know I'm a man of honor."

"Do you think there's something more here? Something we aren't seeing?"

"Of course. Otherwise, we'd have solved this by now."

"Not that, no. More than just what happened on that train. If it were that simple, don't you think we'd feel like we could solve this thing? As it stands, I'm totally confused. People are shooting at us.

105

Strangers act like our friends. All I want is some beer to even out my thinking."

"You're being impatient. We can't rush the investigation."

"I'm not talking about rushing. Right now, I'm not so interested in proving anything. All I want is a sense of what we are dealing with here. Like the guy on the train was killed for his money. Or Jake got shot at because he's sleeping with someone's wife. Or the lady at the café was killed for stealing chocolate. Anything but this sense of nothing."

"Nothing?"

"This place. The country. I'm not understanding what any of it means. I don't know anything, not even the language. Everything I know is filtered through you."

"I'm giving you the best I can."

"But everything?"

"Everything, yes."

They came to a corner café and went inside. The room was dim and empty. The coffee warmed them, and the pastries were rich and creamy, satisfying a certain emptiness that they both felt at that very moment. Only once did the waitress come past and ask them if they wanted something more. Another coffee perhaps? They both shook their heads, trying to smile with gratitude. The waitress cleared the table and returned with a bill. The price caught Bethany by surprise, but Louis seemed not to mind. He fished euros from his wallet and laid them on the table. The tip, Bethany noticed, was more than modest.

A cool draft touched Bethany's neck. Louis lifted his gaze, which lit with recognition of the person entering the room. Half turning, Bethany caught the shadow of the approaching form. Cold fingers touched the back of her neck. Then Herta Stocker stood beside their table. She wore a fashionable winter overcoat, black boots, and a fur-trimmed hat. Wet snow dripped away to water. Her teeth flashed brilliantly against her red lips. Bethany couldn't understand how she had come here. She found herself looking at Louis. Had he arranged this and her other surprise visit the day before? Would the two of them have met even if Bethany hadn't shown up? Was there an arrangement here she wasn't aware of?

She took a deep breath and forced a smile, saying, "A lovely coincidence! It is a coincidence, isn't it?"

The professor laughed. "I live right near here. You should know that by now, Ms. Judge. You are a talented woman in that respect, I understand."

"She certainly is," Louis said. "I have the feeling I hold her back."

"Each person comes with their own talents. Yours, I am certain, are talents that would boggle the mind. Particularly the mind of a woman."

Louis stared silently and then shifted his gaze back to Bethany.

"It's always a pleasure to see you, Professor," said Bethany, struggling for a polite tone.

"And always a surprise, isn't it?" the professor replied. A hint of sarcasm tainted her words.

"Becoming less so perhaps. I trust your work isn't suffering from the time away from your desk."

"Hardly! It is time to collect my thoughts, to focus more clearly. Sit in front of a computer all day, Ms. Judge, and I'd challenge you to think coherently."

"That's a reason I picked my former profession. Desk jobs—I just couldn't imagine."

"And you, Mr. Frey?"

"A combination of the two. The military offers flexibility that way. The mind and body need to stay fit, you know?"

Herta nodded thoughtfully. "Americans are very practical that way. Germany has always misunderstood its greatest asset. The mind is forgotten. Only the body matters. To fight war, invade, and conquer. Or make babies."

Bethany coughed. "Aren't things different now? Since the war—what'd they call it?"

"What did they call what?" asked Herta. "How do you label brainwashing? Call it the Nuremberg Trials? Denazification? What do you think? Would you be so easily swayed from your core beliefs? This is what the Allies believed. They bragged of their successes, as if they actually succeeded."

"You sound unconvinced," said Louis.

"Unconvinced? I built my career on the truest feelings in the German heart." She lowered her voice. "I speak the party line, do you understand? I proclaim what Germany's Führer might say to his countrymen today. That," she said, tapping her temple, "is what the academic mind can do."

"What does that matter? I still haven't met a goose-stepping German, not during all my years over here," Louis said.

"Why should you? What fool would dress in a swastika and march around? He'd be arrested in a second. That is the law, and the hope is that that law will change Germany's heart. It hasn't worked, of course. Little has changed since 1945. That is my point. I'm criticized for uncovering it, but the results of my work are clear. Research does not lie."

"This is"—Bethany looked at the ceiling, searching for the right words—"an unexpected confession. If that's what it is. I get the feeling that nobody else knows of your, uh—"

"Charade?"

"That's it, yeah."

"Do you really believe that's all it is?"

"Seems like it to me. What do you think, Louis?"

"I think you're demeaning her work," Louis said.

So that's that, thought Bethany. Why was he defending the professor? Perhaps they were already allied. Perhaps this little bit of chaos had been orchestrated from the start. Louis and the professor knew each other in ways beyond their brief meetings. Her instincts told Bethany that was true, even if she couldn't put a finger on it. She chuckled.

"Nothing demeaning meant by it. It's what she said."

"I doubt she believes it's a charade." Louis glanced at the professor. "Do you?"

She shrugged. "You're Americans. You understand the power of controversy. By different means, certainly, but you enjoy controversy just the same. Look at the internet or television. Look at your president. You'd be challenged to find one entertainment that doesn't play on emotions, that doesn't yank or pull on its viewers to elicit some sort of response. And then there are the more overt shows. The polarizing cable news talk shows with the screaming, yelling, and finger-pointing—those are the first that come to my mind."

"People like that are everywhere in America now," said Bethany. "They're real."

"But the internet and television legitimize this behavior, don't you see? This becomes America's culture. The nation's lowest common denominator is the national aspiration. Think, by comparison, of Germany's great minds. Goethe, Brahms, Mann, Wagner. They inspired a nation to greatness."

"You consider the Holocaust greatness? The Second World War?"

She flicked her hand at Bethany's words. "A blip in history. You need to look at the longer trend. That's exactly what I do, and that is what excites my critics."

Bethany was silent for a moment and then said in a reflective tone, "This is all very confusing to me. Back home we have our buffalo wings to keep us fat and happy, and we talk about the Buffalo Bills, and I'm learning about good beer. You're saying stuff I can hardly understand. It sounds like you're telling me that America has no culture. Or that what passes as culture comes through internet or TV."

"And all the consumables, yes. Like your Buffalo Bills. Like your chicken wings."

"Meanwhile, Germany's cultural history is higher-minded or something? And that this should mean it is of more value?"

"Yes, my dear friend. It possesses legs, doesn't it? The ability to withstand the brutal test of time and yet still knit our society

109

together. We Germans can look back on some painting by Käthe Kollwitz and understand how the turmoil she portrays weds itself to our people. We can smell the German countryside as described by Theodor Storm in his poems and novellas. It's all there, hundreds upon thousands of years of German history."

"But I don't care about paintings. It is ancient history, for crying out loud! And boring! What I want is the taste of your beer!"

Louis cleared his throat. "Didn't Henry Ford say, 'History is bunk'? I think it was him. I always took that to mean Americans are future-minded. That we don't dwell on the burdens of history like old feuds or lost battles. We consider the endless possibilities of our lifetime instead. Nothing is beyond us."

"The optimistic American. Yes, I really must write that book someday. Something that portrays the American psyche exactly as you just described it. An amazing thing. I'd hardly believe it could be possible for humankind, yet an entire nation proves me wrong. It'd be one thing if only the European Americans felt that way. And perhaps that is the case. But it seems that even the Asian and the African Americans share the view in one way or another. Don't ask me why. A true cultural phenomenon."

"So why do you do this then? You never made it clear." Bethany tried to smile. "How is it that your work is a charade?"

"I never said that, my lovely Beer Judge. You did."

Bethany grinned, enjoying the sound of her nickname. "But you said—"

"I told you I do my research. I uncover truths. I espouse them. My work stands on its own." She glanced at both of them. "Have either of you read my work?"

Bethany shook her head. "Hadn't even heard of you before we met."

"Me neither," said Louis.

"Then perhaps it is time we took a stroll. You're both welcome to visit my humble little apartment. Beer Judge, I'll admit to having expected you long before now. Now's the chance to view my 'etchings,' as the old saying goes. Interested?"

A curious glance passed between Louis and Bethany. Then Louis shook his head and stood, seemingly filling the room with his muscular body. "It wouldn't be a good idea," he said. "Bethany was ... It's been a long day for the poor lady. A long bunch of days, really. We should get home. Enjoy a nice night's rest."

"That's fine. Disappointing but understandable. The invitation is always open, you understand, not just a one-time thing. There are things to be gleaned from my work, things better understood in a"—she looked around—"more favorable environment. And now, I mustn't forget the reason I came in the first place. The strudel is superb! Did either of you try it? No? That's a shame. Well, you must stop by again." She paid the waitress and took a small plastic bag. "Thank you, my dear. Now, my friends, until next time."

Louis nodded. Bethany stood, blushing when the professor placed her lips lightly on her cheek. The professor whispered something Louis couldn't quite understand, something that escaped Bethany too, for the words were in German. With a flurry of her coattails, the professor swung toward the door and into the night. The room filled with silence once she was gone.

CHAPTER 9

A CASE FOR BEER

They exited onto the damp street. Snow fell heavier now, brightening the night and silencing their footsteps. Bethany looked but could see little through the blanket of thick flakes. Squinting, she stayed beside her friend, trusting where he was leading them. Occasionally, someone walked past, eyes to the ground, hurrying through what most certainly was a strong storm. *Wimps*, Bethany thought. They knew nothing about the true fury of snow, the way Lake Erie could wind up a winter low pressure system, sucking up moisture as the cold air passed over the warmer waters of the Great Lakes, dropping it inland by the foot. There was the blizzard of '77, of course, or the November storm of 2001 and the big dump of Christmas 2002. Almost eight feet fell during those insane two days in 2002. Enough to paralyze the city, if only briefly.

"Can you believe that bi—"

Bethany cut Louis off. "Is there something going on with you two? I mean, how else could she have found us here tonight? Coincidence? She certainly didn't follow me! Hell, I had just gotten back to the city when I found you at the bar."

"You think ... Damn, Bee, the way she's eyeing you, I might have thought you spent the night giving her some Buffalo lovin'."

"Not the case. I was indisposed. Taking in some local culture. I was hoping for some clarity but ended up more confused."

Louis touched his friend on the shoulder. "Well, don't take it out on me, okay? I'm here to help. You need to trust me or I can't do anything for you."

"Yeah, of course. It's just—"

"It's nothing, Bee! Listen, we haven't seen Jake since the other day, you know? We'd be smart to see how he's faring. What do you say we head over in his direction? The walk will do us some good."

"No subway?"

"First snow of the year? Bee, there's nothing like early winter in Germany. They really capture the holiday mood. Street vendors selling Christmas wares. The smell of roasted nuts wafting through the air."

"You sound like her!"

"Do I? Hmm, yes, well there is a certain magic to the old country. It's part of what brought me, part of why I stay. Take your mind off your troubles and perhaps you'll see it too."

"Yeah, but from what Detective Weyermann said, I don't have any more troubles. They were looking elsewhere."

"Is that how you heard him? Funny. I heard it different," Louis said. He stopped, suddenly distracted. Bethany followed his gaze.

They had come to a short building that, architecturally, appeared identical to the others that lined the street. Most of the windows were dark. In one they saw the colorful flashes from somebody's television. In another they watched a nude couple dance amorously past, unconcerned that their shades weren't drawn. The rest of the residents were readying for the day ahead, Bethany thought, suddenly feeling an urge to be back at her job. The routine, the predictability. These things had been stripped from her life.

They resumed walking and soon turned down a narrow street. "Jake lives right around here," Louis said.

"Close to the brewery, right? Weren't we near here the other day?"

"That's right. He prefers to be near his work, I guess. Doesn't like dealing with the subway or the commute. I don't know. If you don't need to drive—"

"That's about the only good thing about Buffalo. Twenty minutes to almost anywhere. The traffic is never bad."

"But pathetic public transportation, don't forget. Europe has us there. You hardly need a car in this country. And everything runs on time."

"I've noticed that."

"Pity the disorganized German!" Louis said. "Imagine living in a country where precision is part of your merit. All my years abroad and I still admire the American way—ingenuity, creativity, the ability and willingness to adapt to challenging situations. It's what made our country great, you know. Ah, here we are!"

They continued several buildings farther and were climbing the steps, looking to find the button that would buzz Jake's apartment, when a young man turned the corner on the last set of steps inside. He was moving fast, running, and a quick glance over his shoulder told Bethany someone was following. *Nothing in his hands*, Bethany registered quickly. But just as that thought passed into oblivion, the door slammed open. It crashed into Bethany's chest, knocking her off-balance and backward down the stairs. Louis stretched a hand that grasped only air and then chased half-heartedly down the street, stopping when the fleeing man disappeared into a dark alley. Louis returned to the stairs to find Bethany rubbing the back of her head.

Jake knelt over her, looking worried. "You took a nasty hit. I'm surprised there's no blood," he said.

"It's all right. A bump—that's all. Never lost consciousness."

"Are you sure?" Louis asked. He felt the swollen lump and frowned. "Should we find a hospital?"

"I said I'm fine! No doctors. I don't want to meet my version of a Dr. Mengele."

"No problem, Bee." Louis ran a nervous hand through his disheveled hair, apparently not liking Bethany's reference to the infamous Nazi doctor. Josef Mengele had been a member of the German Schutzstaffel—the SS—and had earned the nickname Angel of Death.

"No luck catching him?" Bethany asked, bringing Louis's attention back to the moment.

"Too much of a jump on me. And faster."

Bethany turned her head to Jake, wincing at the stabbing pain behind her eyes. "You were chasing him down the stairs. Why would he be running? It didn't look like he had stolen anything. An attempted break-in?"

Jake shrugged. "I was getting ready for bed. Work again tomorrow, you know? I had just turned off the lights and was settling into sleep when I heard a noise. I kind of jolted awake. It sounded weird, like something rattling. At first I thought something was knocking on the window. Like when I was a kid, branches from a tree used to knock on my bedroom window. But then I realized where I live, right? Middle of the city, not a tree in sight. So I listened a little more closely, and I heard it again. Definitely a rattling. It reminded me of a doorknob, quite honestly, and two seconds later I heard the hinges squeaking. On the door, that is. I yelled something like, 'Who's there!' The guy bolted down the stairs. I hurried down. That's when I found Bethany."

This was nothing new. Bethany had heard it before. Felt it. Something passing through the air, the unmistakable hint of a lie. This time it felt like relief. As if they had come closer to something and Jake had escaped unscathed. Maybe it was Jake's long, relaxed breath. The indication that he felt safe despite what had just occurred. It didn't make sense, of course. Why should she suspect Jake? Why would anything connect to him?

Jake squatted on the stoop between Louis and Bethany, saying very little. Bethany recognized an unmistakable twinkle to his eyes, as if Jake were struggling to decide what story was best to tell. It was easy, after all, for him to fabricate something. If Bethany had learned anything in her career as a cop, it was that lies came easily to people.

They just rolled off the tongue, this magical cloak that protects humans from the harsh realities of their bad decisions. Easier to lie than to face the truth. Perhaps that was what had drawn her to beer. When it came to malt, hops, water, and yeast, there wasn't too much left to deny. Your beer was either great, good, or garbage. And there was no denying when it was garbage.

Bethany guessed how Jake saw her: a simple oaf. And why not? Just mention the city of Buffalo, admit you were from the region, and you immediately earned the badge of stupidity. She blamed it on the local accent, on the fact that recession had hit Buffalo and Upstate New York long before the country had felt the pinch during and after the financial crisis of 2008. But few people really understood what had dragged down Buffalo. Not the weather. Not the people. No, these two things existed in a form of symbiosis, each strengthening the other, forming a tighter bond.

The real culprit was simple economics. High taxes had sucked the life out of Buffalo. Encouraged businesses to flee to the southern states where low costs allowed their companies to thrive. The stupid New York politicians had been too greedy, too slow in their response. And the city, as a result, had died a slow but steady death.

"You're okay to stand?" Jake asked finally. "Why don't you come in, get out of the weather. This sucks, doesn't it? Snow this early in the season isn't normal in Munich."

Bethany heard an internal voice ask what exactly was normal in Munich. Certainly, she had stepped into a shitstorm, and things had only progressed from bad to worse. She eased behind Jake into the foyer, enjoying the rush of warmth. There would be no climbing the stairs. At least not now. *Sit, relax, and get your strength back*, she thought. The marble step was a remarkably comfortable seat.

Jake smiled, his lips brittle from the cold. "What brought you out this way?" he asked.

"Checking in with you," Louis replied. "Hadn't heard from you since, well, you know. Wanted to make sure everything was okay. And if you'd heard anything new."

"Nothing," Jake said, shaking his head. "I'd rather forget about the whole thing, to be completely honest. Concentrate on my work."

Bethany tried to smile at his words, her pain forcing her mouth into more of a grimace. She liked what he said but knew a lie when she heard one. "You like your work too much. Hell, sounds pretty dangerous to me."

"At least people don't usually shoot at me."

"This intruder," Louis asked. "What could he have wanted? Do you have anything valuable in your apartment?"

"Valuable? On a brewer's salary? Ha! Probably drug money or things to sell for drug money. That's my guess. Crime has gotten worse lately. That's what all the Germans say."

"You are on friendly terms with your neighbors?"

"Somewhat. By Germans, I mean the ones from work."

"Obviously crime is up for them. All these deaths. But your neighbors here—nobody has come out. Why?"

"It's too late. Germans go to bed early. They get up early. A very regimented bunch. It took me a while to get into that groove."

Louis nodded. "Way different than back home."

Bethany shook her head gingerly, wincing. "This guy tonight, Jake. You're sure he was a thief?"

How many times had Bethany seen that look? Shock, surprise, the "How dare you doubt me?" stare. It was all Bethany needed to confirm that something wasn't right. The realization slowly and steadily took her breath away, as if a weight were pressing on her chest. Their partner—this American—had been tied to Bethany from day one, hadn't he? He had approached Bethany at the Oktoberfest. Maybe he'd picked her as a patsy. Perhaps Jake had slipped onto the train and murdered Hans himself, leaving Bethany alive to divert the investigation. The possibility was legitimate. And like unseasoned neophytes, they had trusted him. Probably a mistake, Bethany now admitted.

"It's the only thing that makes sense," Jake said. "Unless your theory is correct."

"Theory?"

"That someone is killing everyone in the malthouse," Jake said. "Maybe I was next on the list."

Bethany had forgotten about that possibility. Damn, she must have knocked her head hard. A malthouse serial murderer remained a distinct concern. But what would be the motive? Sex? Doubtful. An old grudge? Neither Uli nor Herr Steingarten had mentioned something like that at the brewery. Revenge? Against three different people? Also unlikely.

Louis waggled his finger. "I think it's different here. You think your murderer would have run so easily? He still had the element of surprise, even if you were already awake. The apartment was dark, right? You were presumably half-asleep. He would have come ready to finish the job, regardless of the circumstances."

Bethany forced a nod. "He's probably right, Jake."

"I guess you're right," Jake said. "I don't know. Just throwing out ideas."

Bethany lightly tapped her right temple. "I'm constantly sorting things. Sooner or later we'll find the truth." She leveled her gaze on Jake. "So far, it's been lacking."

Jake returned the stare. He swallowed hard. "At least you've had my complete cooperation."

"I suppose. It's difficult to tell when people are concealing things. Sometimes there is only a hunch."

"There's nothing for me to gain. You've seen it yourself. I was threatened at the café. And possibly tonight."

Not according to some people, Bethany thought. And if her hunch was correct, she figured Jake knew he wasn't a target. A convenient cover. Yes, quite convenient indeed. The pain in her head vanished suddenly, so quick it was almost alarming. Bethany felt a rush of clarity, not like she was on the brink of solving this mystery but as if she finally had stepped in from the outside. The web was intricate, not just a simple murder on the train. Knowing that would be a powerful tool.

She said nothing, of course. A thoughtful look, a hand on the chin. Those were enough to break beads of sweat across Jake's forehead, even if otherwise he looked impervious to the pressure. A little battle of wills was going on here. Who would crumble first? Bethany hardly imagined Jake would snap. Maybe the guy knew very little and was trying to protect something simple, something he deemed valuable. But there was the chance of more. That made this game of chicken worthwhile.

Louis cleared his throat to speak. Bethany stopped him with a wave of her hand. A frown lit across Jake's lips. He forced a smile, accented by a twitch below his left eye.

"I didn't ask you to come here," Jake rasped, the words dry and desperate. His tongue darted over his lips, seeking moisture. "You both should leave now."

Bethany checked the door. "Are we safe out there?" she asked.

"What a ridiculous question!"

"Is it? I'm willing to bet that person is still nearby. Perhaps just outside that door."

"Bethany!"

"Let me finish, Louis. If Jake has things to conceal, this is the only way to hear the truth. I'm sorry if my conjecture is wrong, of course. I have little recourse."

"You're absolutely wrong," Jake snapped. "Get out!"

Jake threw open the door. A brisk wind swept over them. Snow swirled into the foyer.

"Cast out into the night, Louis! You'd think our ally would do the opposite, eh? Maybe a cup of tea to warm two weary travelers. Or preferably a beer. Instead, we're kicked to the curb."

"Get your drinks down the road," Jake said, pointing. "About three blocks on your left. Now, get on your way."

The bar was already in sight when Louis finally spoke.

"What the hell was that about, Bethany? He was supposed to be our friend. I'd say you can forget getting any more help from him."

"It was about time," Bethany said, the words rolling dreamily from her mouth. She couldn't expect her friend to understand. Louis was, after all, a military man. He had never experienced old-fashioned investigative intuition. But Bethany knew it when it came. An old friend, it calmed her nerves like the beer she was about to drink. And the one that followed. And those that would come after. Tea? Some other day perhaps.

CHAPTER 10

DARKNESS

I did it again, dammit, Bethany thought, the words floating across her mind, shrouded in the haze of one beer too many. Stress relief, that was what she had called it. How could someone be stressed when drinking a true Bavarian Helles? Light gold, an underlying maltiness and a very subtle hint of hops. The Helles boasted superior drinkability. A true session beer. She had enjoyed the first beer and then the second. Just a couple more liters to ease her worries. And then things had blurred.

Now where was she? Inside, yes. She wasn't cold. Her damp clothes were nearly dry. But the room was so dark. No windows? Bethany couldn't make out a streetlight or anything of its kind. She rubbed her eyes just to make certain they were open.

Sounds emanated from nearby, probably from the neighboring room. Bethany focused her hearing, crawling over the floor toward the noise, eventually bumping her head against the wall. She ran her hands over what felt like painted concrete. Standing, she pressed an ear to listen. The smooth, cool walls deadened sound. Still, that was a German speaking, wasn't it? The coarse tone and the guttural sounds. Yes, there was no denying the nationality of the person doing the talking.

But that other voice. It came like a whisper through the concrete, the singsong of the language familiar enough to remind Bethany of English. But she couldn't be sure. And sometimes it sounded like German, didn't it? Yes, there it was again. So soft but definitely German now. Two people having a conversation? Maybe a third?

A sudden shout drew Bethany closer to the wall. The voice rose into a screaming tirade, still muted but clearly German. A voice responded, at first muffled beneath the other's yells and then rising to match its opposition. Bethany heard the terror, the implacable fear, the fact that whatever was happening, or was about to happen, pressed the limits of torture. But that was all secondary. Something else was registering with Bethany, something that slowly chewed the toxic edge off her hangover.

That screaming voice belonged to Louis.

Her mind raced back to the bar. The man who had stood beside them, slowly sipping on a beer, occasionally throwing a glance in their direction. The woman with the smile. Her lipstick had been too red, her glass of pilsner always half-full. Nothing there had seemed out of the ordinary. Bethany had sensed no danger. But come to think of it, was her hangover earned? Had she really drunk that many beers?

Bethany remembered her eyes roving over the woman's Germanic face. She had smiled at her, hadn't she, accepting the compliment? And then she had come to her? And Bethany had set down her beer? And they had faced each other for a moment? And Bethany noticed something curious. What was it? A passivity of the cheeks? A brief flicker of the eyes? Nothing too alarming at the time. But now her stomach twisted, the dread working its way through her limbs. A couple of liquid drops in her beer? Probably. Not long after that, the lights had gone out.

The thick darkness pressed into Bethany's skin, carrying with it the rising tenor of the German's screaming voice. She heard Louis respond, also in German, still under control. An interrogation perhaps? Or maybe they expected Bethany would still be unconscious. This might be a business conversation.

Bethany drew close against the cool wall. Tuning out the mental clutter—that was the challenge right now. She needed to listen. Perhaps she'd catch a word she understood. Perhaps they'd switch to English. But fears that Louis had betrayed her swept through Bethany's mind, followed by guilt, followed by rationalization. She had suffered over the last few weeks. It was only natural to trust no one.

What was that? Bethany pricked her ears. The silence. Why so sudden? It seemed to last a lifetime, so quiet it was deafening, but that first gurgle, the sound of air rushing over blood, came only a second later.

"Why?" Louis asked, the question posed in English, the clarity of the word masked in viscous fluid.

The response came in German, the tone nonchalant. "Einfach so," said the voice. He punctuated the sentence with a single gunshot.

The dark dungeon swallowed the echo, bringing silence once more.

Watching through the tinted glass, Herta Stocker saw Louis's head snap back, a splatter of blood exploding against the wall behind him. A stream of dark red followed, flowing from the base of his skull. It formed a dark puddle beneath his chair.

Christian Scheubel holstered his pistol and then pulled open a heavy door and stepped into the room where Herta waited.

"That's it then," she said.

She looked through the glass at Louis's lifeless body, noting her reflection, wondering if her face looked paler than usual. Was it shock at Christian's brutality? No. Likely just the overhead lights. They did have the tendency to wash out even the blandest of colors. She sighed audibly.

"We have eliminated a threat, yes." Christian stepped closer, brushing the back of his hand across her hair.

"But created other problems perhaps. He was military, after all. American military. We can't expect that people will not come looking for him."

"Nobody will know where to look. Not after we take care of that problem in the other room."

The professor turned away. "I think differently," she said. "Perhaps it's time we start letting the cat out of the bag."

"It's still too early. Not until—"

"That is exactly why! By the time the puzzle is pieced together, we'll have already secured our prize. Our destiny will be secure."

"Too risky," Christian said. He looked through the window, his eyes coming to rest on the opposite wall. The last remaining threat was just beyond those bricks.

"Politics is risky, Christian. It isn't like she knows who we are. She can only suspect. Proof is a distant mirage."

"You've become too fond of her."

"Perhaps. These things aren't always controllable, you know. She's a simple woman with few redeeming qualities. Her mental power is underdeveloped. I imagine I shall bore of her easily. But for the time being, I shall enjoy our little game."

Christian smirked. "Cat and mouse. It is your favorite game."

"We've done it to an entire nation, haven't we? Our lonely American is nothing more than a simple test. To be used in the future."

Herta's mind went to all the great things their movement had accomplished. Why should Christian doubt his leader? Especially after she had spent so many years in America. She knew the mind of this adversary and certainly had plans that reached years into the future. What she did today was advanced planning, nothing less than that. She smiled at her own brilliance.

"You want me to release her now?" asked Christian.

"Not right away. Take the body from the room. Kill one of your assistants and place him in the chair. Make certain the American gets a glance when we lead her out. Tonight, before dark. Blindfold her and dump her in the country somewhere. We'll see how long it takes before she arrives at my door."

"At your apartment?"

The professor smiled. "Of course, Christian. Don't you understand? Right now, I'm all the poor American has left. She has lost everything now, including her freedom."

"But not if we release her—"

"No, exactly when we release her. Trapped in a foreign country like this, surrounded by adversaries. The woman is vulnerable. She doesn't know what to believe anymore. Her profession may have granted her some analytical powers, but they are useless to her now. She operates on instinct alone, and even that can't be trusted. In that room over there, she knows nothing less than horror. Complete darkness and absolute dread. Wonderful tools that shall serve us well."

"But why not just run? She can fly back home."

"She's under investigation. As a former police officer, she can't bring herself to leave. Not until she receives permission. And so, she'll seek something solid." Herta looked through the window again. "First, her dead friend. That will yield nothing, of course. That's when she comes to me. Remember, I met with them both. Twice now. It established the connection of a triumvirate in her mind."

"The three of you?"

"All three of us, yes. Now she must tell me that one was lost. It's not unlike losing a family member. Or a limb, I suppose. Sharing grief is part of the healing process."

"You are a woman of genius."

"Don't be silly. Any of my ideas may backfire. Failure is one of my greatest concerns. But as it has happened, I haven't suffered this in my lifetime. My work has a way of seeing its way to fruition. For what reason I may never know."

"Look no further than yourself."

"Is that all? The woman in the mirror? I wonder. After all, the movement is far greater than me. I am nothing more than a mouthpiece."

Of course, she knew it was more than that. She looked again at her reflection, seeing the sculpted features of a true leader. She was the present and the past, the continuance of what was and what should have been. Perhaps she had been endowed with the führer's spirit. A certain possibility, she thought. Surely, she felt his power coursing through her veins. Surely, she knew the future with clarity.

"I should call an assistant to move the body," he said. "It will be easier before the limbs start to stiffen."

"Have you decided which shall take his place?" she asked when he finished the call.

"It's immaterial. They are all disposable. The only challenge is not alarming the others. Then we may lose their loyalty."

"Or instill such fear that they never dare betray us. That, of course, was the way of the past."

"And those days may come again."

"I believe they will. There is sometimes a necessity to purge the ranks, displeasing as that may be. But why, I ask, should we hold back our youth? Catapult our future leaders forward, I say! Our duty is to prepare them to replace us. We'd hate to see another lull of nearly eighty years, don't you think?"

"Those years have been horrific. I would hate to see them repeated."

"Exactly. Like good managers, we train our staff to replace us. It is, Christian, how I always saw our relationship."

"You see that in me? The ability to lead the movement?"

"Of course. Are my expectations misguided?"

"Certainly not!"

"As I suspected. You are youthful and strong—the kind of thing that attracts the disaffected in our country. But those more mindful of our political history, those who might resist swaying to a face too similar to our former leader—they will view me as unthreatening. I am, after all, only a woman."

"Not only!"

"That is how some will see me. I do not oppose it. In fact, I embrace it. We live to understand the feelings of our followers. But more so, we must understand the thoughts of those who oppose us. Our preference is to win their support. If that proves impossible, we'll have to crush them."

A door opened inside the room. Three assistants entered. Each man wore blue coveralls and black shoes. Their hair was slicked back neatly, and their beards were cleanly trimmed. They gathered around Louis's body, silent in their work, hoisting the body onto their shoulders and disappearing out the door. Moments later, one man returned with a bucket and mop.

"He lost the lottery," said Christian.

The professor nodded. "Complete silence," she said.

With one quick motion, Christian withdrew his sidearm and attached a silencer to the muzzle. He was through the door, the pistol extended, and a round through the skull of the assistant before the mop touched blood. Christian caught the body as it crumpled. He guided it to the chair, careful to keep him from toppling to the floor. Satisfied, he carried the mop from the room.

"You'd have been a wonderful cowboy," said the professor. "A superb performance."

"You left little choice but perfection."

"Am I really so difficult?" She chuckled. "I only ask for the best possible work, especially from you. Even a queen bee has her favorites."

"And sometimes the drones are sacrificed."

"For the greater good—exactly! I expect our friend in the other room will come to that conclusion. She has escaped the miserable Buffalo existence, kicking and screaming, no doubt. Too bad we don't have a camera in that room. I'd love to see how she's reacting."

"How she reacts to her release should sate our curiosity."

"Absolutely. If she fails my expectations, you are to schedule her termination. Without hesitation."

"That's understood."

"You have someone capable of the job?"

"He seeks redemption, yes. I doubt very much he would fail me twice."

The professor arched an eyebrow. Twice? So Christian did have a soft spot. Or was it perhaps an agenda of his own? She could only expect that he'd branch out from her teachings. It was her objective. That was true. But this story had a strange sound to it. Almost as if he had acted out of character. Softhearted. Kind. Forgiving.

"You've not punished him?"

"In a sense, yes."

"What does that mean? I thought we were clear on how to deal with failure."

"We are. It's just that, well, this one is special. I see in him the same thing you see in me, I suppose. I could discount his error because of that, and besides, I was close enough to managing the project. We have his target in custody. We could finish his task today. In a sense, I suppose, that job is half-done. Her friend was there that day, the one we just eliminated."

"You mean her? In the other room? The woman from Buffalo? I'm wooing her to our party while you try to kill her?"

"The reasons are obvious."

"To you, yes! My God, we need to improve communication between us, Christian! Working in opposing directions like this? Inexcusable." She giggled slightly. "I suppose this means we must eliminate each other."

Christian bristled. "Is the movement really that unforgiving? Without you, there is nothing."

"Without *us*!" Herta said, emphasizing the word. "I'm sorry for not telling you my intentions. I knew of them since the airport. Too many years in America, too many years keeping secrets. Some habits are hard to break."

"I'm sorry, Herta. I just can't forgive you."

"You can't? What's that supposed to mean?"

"Inexcusable," he said. The corners of his mouth turned upward.

She slapped him on the arm. "Asshole! Now, get on with it. Darkness is coming up quick."

CHAPTER 11

BRILLIANCE

They pulled Bethany from her darkened dungeon shortly before midnight, conveniently forgetting the blindfold until they had halfway crossed through the room. Bethany had ample time to study the dead man in the chair. It wasn't Louis, and for that she breathed easier. The last several hours had been pure hell, imagining the death of her friend. At that instant a hand slapped the side of her head and someone screeched something in German. Then a burlap sack was pulled over her head and cinched tightly around her neck. Oh yes, Bethany remembered. There was still her own health to worry about.

A car drove Bethany and her captors from their location. Though she was blinded, the winding road suggested they were somewhere in the country. The lack of stops supported her hypothesis. They cruised on, many miles and many minutes passing in slow silence. At times, Bethany felt like dozing, such was the warmth from the bodies that sat beside her. And then the car began to climb. The engine strained a little louder, and the air felt a touch thinner. Bethany's ears popped. Suddenly they stopped. The door beside her opened, and a hand shoved her shoulder. Bethany fell from the car, hitting the ground hard.

"Consider yourself lucky this time," a German voice said in heavily accented English. "Others were not so fortunate tonight."

There's no doubt about that, thought Bethany, remembering the figure slumped in that chair. But it made no sense that they released her, especially not after viewing the dead man. *I'd have killed me that very instant*, she reasoned, suddenly thankful for her strange meeting the other morning with Francis Eberhardt, Amanda, and Albert. They remained odd figures in her mind—illusions almost—but there was little doubt now that their warnings had served her well. Without them, she might feel panicked by now.

Fortunate that they hadn't bound her hands, Bethany had the rope untied and the sack off her head in a matter of moments. The darkness, however, was so thick that she hardly noticed the difference. Slowly her eyes came to discern shapes and dim lights nearby. She rose and began walking, the uphill climb quickly turning into a tedious chore.

Within twenty minutes, she reached a small mountain village, which would have been bathed in total darkness were it not for a lighted sign from the local bar. There was irony in this, Bethany realized, but dwelling on it was an unaffordable luxury now. She continued, searching for an indication of her exact location and quickly reaching the other end of town and a veil of blackness that stretched upward toward the stars and a distinctly close mountain peak.

Something white beckoned ahead. Bethany approached it and discovered a cross and shrine set neatly back from the road. A wooden bench offered worshipers a place to sit. She accepted the invitation, lowering herself with an exhausted sigh. Her limbs felt suddenly stiff and heavy, so she reclined and soon was resting flat against the bench. Several flutters of the eyelids later, she rested heavily, only waking when a finger poked the flesh of her ribs.

"Get up!"

Bethany swam back to consciousness. She stared unknowingly at the person who had roused her, her mind racing to connect the place and the language and the familiar face. None of it gelled until the person smiled and spoke again.

"This isn't the best place for us to meet again, is it?"

"Albert?"

He laughed and grabbed Bethany's arm. "I suspected with your training you wouldn't forget a face. But it does appear you have stepped beyond the line we warned you about. You're lucky to be alive today, you know."

"I was, um, thinking that last night."

"Certainly you were." He glanced over his shoulder. "Come now. It isn't safe here."

"Safe for what?"

"They're watching, of course. Do you think they'd just drop you here and vanish? Of course not. It's all a test of some kind. God knows what."

"They killed somebody last night."

"Did they?"

"I thought it was Louis. My friend. But I saw the body when I left."

"It wasn't him?"

"Nope. Somebody else."

Albert nodded knowingly. Words perched on his lips, but he refrained, appearing to decide his comments could wait for later. With a firm hand, he gripped Bethany's neck and pulled her down the road.

"I parked down this way. The mountains—they were tough on my poor engine."

"Where are we?"

"Near Berchtesgaden. Do you recognize that name? It was the so-called Eagle's Nest of Adolf Hitler. A country retreat for him, I suppose, though plenty of evil was organized there, I'm certain."

"We're still in southern Germany?"

"Not that far from Munich. It's a couple of hours to the north by car."

"We drove about that long last night, I'd guess. But why here?" Bethany stopped, glancing suspiciously at Albert. "And how'd you know where to find me?"

"Don't think we'd leave you unobserved, Ms. Judge. The same is true for the other side. You are in the middle of a very delicate struggle, the exact end of which we don't understand. All we can do is play this game of chess. Hopefully the result will be in our favor. Now, as for why they left you here, I can only guess. Probably it is a clue to the broader drama."

"So that's all this is to you? A drama?"

"A man loses his life last night, sure. I'd call that dramatic. And what our adversaries are arranging could be quite dramatic as well. Right now, trapped in the middle, we are clueless. Relying on wits to survive is never any fun. I should know. I've done this job for long enough. Now get in the car."

Albert slammed the car into gear and sped down the mountain.

"I don't understand," Bethany said.

"What's to understand? We're dealing in layers of secret. Some of it may be decades old. Our goal is to outwit the enemy, even if how we will succeed remains unclear."

"Groping in the darkness."

"An appropriate phrase, yes. You must remember not to panic. Let them lead you down the path they choose."

"But you say they are watching me. That must mean they know about you."

"Quite likely, but that's part of the game. We can't be invisible, Bethany. Only smart. In a sense, you're a lure, though I admit to not knowing exactly why. For some reason they find you irresistibly attractive."

"You might believe that, but not me."

Albert jerked the steering wheel, forcing the car fast around a sharp left turn. "Sorry," he said sheepishly, shifting down and tapping the brake. "These little cars can get away from you. Listen, we talked about that professor woman the other day. Herta Stocker."

"Right."

"And you've seen her since. That's something we find excellent, by the way."

"You do follow me closely!"

Albert smiled. "She's a very smart lady. It's been quite impossible to touch her over the years. And then you come along. They've gotten sloppy since then. Almost like they are crawling out of the dark holes they live in."

"Maybe they're tired of hiding."

"Exactly my sentiment!" Albert yelled. "A brilliant deduction on your part. Yes, they must be preparing for something. Lurking about in the darkness is no longer a viable option."

"I still fail to see how I fit in."

"That doesn't matter. I'd guess the professor feels a sort of infatuation with you, perhaps a form of separation anxiety from leaving America. It would make sense. Lust often causes mistakes. You must remember this, Bethany. Our success may hinge upon how well you play your role. Don't you think there might have been thousands of moments like this in the course of history? Maybe when America tried to oust Castro or certainly during the Cold War. Little efforts by apparently little people make all the difference. They have stomped out some of the nastiest ideologies on earth, I'd dare say."

"I'm beginning to forget I came to Munich on a vacation."

"Consider that a lost opportunity. Fate has beckoned you to a higher cause. You'll see it that way, I'm sure, once we declare checkmate."

"You're quite confident."

"Failure, my friend, is not an option. In this era, when countries like America or Britain or Germany have such precise military power, do you believe radical movements would risk complete destruction unless they had some unknown wildcard in their favor? Under normal circumstances, we raid their compound and kill the entire leadership! But now we're left to wonder if they will unleash smallpox or a wave of suicide bombers. It forces us to be restrained. But in this instance, Bethany, I don't think they have reached that point yet. My guess is they don't have that leverage yet. If they did, we'd be hearing the threats by now."

Bethany interrupted him. "I have to know something," she said.

"What's that?"

"What is going to happen next?"

Albert laughed. "If I knew that, Bethany, our job would be much easier. I can guess they want something from you. Dropping you near Berchtesgaden—it is supposed to tell you something. Probably that your captors were fascist sympathizers."

"A veiled threat?"

"Of sorts. It's also information for you."

"Information?"

"To use later, probably. You'll know it when it happens."

They said nothing more for many long miles. Bethany stared out the window, admiring the German landscape. Morning was coming, casting a soft glow over the trees and fields.

Finally, Bethany turned to Albert. "And where are the others?" she asked.

"Amanda and Francis? Doing their jobs. They have people to look after, as you might imagine."

"The professor?"

"Or similar such people. We're not far from Munich now. Any place you'd like to go?"

"Not back to my room, though I'd like to find Louis. He'll be expecting me there."

"Perhaps."

"Downtown, I suppose. A beer might be the best thing right now. I need something to break the tension. And besides that, I'm parched."

"Ah, the old standby! Coffee is my morning drink of choice."

"After that, I don't know," Bethany said. "I should probably visit that Jake Stoddard fellow."

"The one from the brewery?"

"Yes. He acted quite strange the other night. Someone had tried to burglarize his apartment. We saw the man just as he was fleeing. Louis gave chase but had no luck."

"You think there's a connection?"

"Why should there be? But then again, someone shot at us when he was around, right? I have to believe Jake knows something. Or has a connection to someone that might play into this."

"It'd be quite a coincidence, though. Didn't you meet Jake Stoddard by accident?"

"He introduced himself to me. Is that an accident, or was it planned? Maybe the professor orchestrated the whole thing after I met her at the airport."

"She'd have done an amazing job of pulling the whole thing together."

"I agree. It would seem they planned for all contingencies, even the most random of events. I doubt that would be possible."

"They are an amazing group," said Albert. "I wouldn't put anything by them. Start with Jake. That sounds like a good choice. You'll hear from one of us soon."

"I guess that's the best I can ask for," said Bethany. "Now, his apartment isn't so far from the Augustiner Bräu brewery. There is a bar nearby. Do you know where that is?"

CHAPTER 12

ACTION

In a corner of Augustiner Bräu's malt cellar, Jake Stoddard quietly went on with his work. He had arrived earlier than usual this morning. His blue overalls and matching jacket gave some protection from the basement's chill, but a few minutes of labor had brought beads of sweat to his brow. Not to mention the nervousness that made his tools feel slick in his hands. This might be the big day.

Months of careful planning all came down to mornings like this. First, there had been the letter. He would admit doubts of its veracity, but to deny the possibility? Impossible! Hadn't he read over that text hundreds of times by now, touched the decades-old yellow paper, pondered what it might mean? Yes! And finally, he decided to find the treasure it proclaimed was buried in the brewery's basement.

That it was to have been there since 1923—that was the clincher. Jake had only been doing his job that day, cleaning an old storage room per Herr Steingarten's instructions. Old things up there, Steingarten had said. Take good care not to break anything. Some of it might be valuable. Brewery history. Try to keep it organized.

And so he had come to those stacks of ledgers. Nothing exciting, Jake had thought as he leafed through the aged pages. Lots of numbers that showed the ebb and flow of the brewing business. Maybe the only interesting fact was how much more malt the brewery had produced back then. But, of course, that was before they had converted large portions of the malt cellars to fermentation space. These days, malting was a specialty—economies of scale and all. Huge volumes of grain were malted as easily as small lots but for far less money. Yes, the modern practice had made beer brewing that much more profitable.

He had started slowly, not really trusting his command of the German language, believing it possible he was reading the letter wrong. Finally, he had purchased a translation dictionary and slowly, secretly, in the privacy of his apartment, turned the German words to English. They read:

Darling Gustav,

You are too young to know why I write this tonight, though someday you will understand. In that truth I take much consolation.

After all, what am I but a common brewery manager? Our life has always been simple and predictable. Even during these years when inflation made our money worthless, I have always put bread and beer on the table. Indeed, perhaps we will never be more prosperous than now!

There are temptations in life, though, aren't there? These make the status quo insufficient, the predictable boring, the adequate inadequate. Avoid the material things in life, my son. They are poison to the soul. Trust your father on this.

For I could not heed that myself, and my pursuit of fortune and fame led me into circles better left avoided. Names are not important, since I hardly know many myself. But yes, Gustav, you read this next sentence correctly: your father has some power in the Nazi Party.

Perhaps I should write "had some power." That's more accurate. I accepted a charge from your Uncle Adolf to gather weapons and gold. The former would ease our movement's transition into leadership. The latter would fund it. Never, Gustav, have I been more successful! I surprised even myself, quite honestly. Call it a natural ability. I simply was able to convince anyone of our cause. We are rich and well armed thanks to me.

But just the other day, Adolf was the fool. Trying to overthrow the German government with a political declaration? And in a beer hall, of all places! Shooting a pistol into the ceiling? Now he has been arrested. What could he have been thinking? I suppose that doesn't matter, for that was when I failed him. The weapons and money should have been made available, but where was I? Drunk, reveling in my successes, oblivious to what our leader was conducting. Only too late did I learn. And by then, he was in jail. My life became dispensable.

They are after me, Gustav. For my failure, I shall likely pay with my life. What happens to your uncle, who knows, but for their betrayal of me, the Party shall never learn where I hid the treasure that I collected for them. It is now my gift to you.

Look no further than the malt cellars, Gustav. It is all there, in that place where you once napped. Do you remember where that was? I certainly hope.

You are a dear child, Gustav. Please do not be angered by my mistakes. In the end, they were meant to do you good. Perhaps they still will.

Your loving father,
Otto

How such a personal letter would end up stashed in a brewery ledger, Jake didn't know, and after a while, he didn't care. Maybe they came for Otto that day, and Otto hid it and ran. Or maybe he never needed it after all. The worst possibility was that the treasure had already been found. Whatever. Jake wanted the treasure for himself, if it was to be had.

The process was so damned slow! Find the likely hiding spots. Where would a child sleep when his father brought him to work? Where were hollow spaces that a treasure could reside? He worked and spent free time easing away grout and tile and searching by hand. He had to be close. He simply knew the end was coming near. In his mind, Jake was already spending the money.

There had been close calls, of course. Moments when people had nearly discovered his operation. Shadeesh—that ridiculous foreigner who really thought he might learn how to make beer—had appeared around the corner one morning. It hadn't looked good for Jake, having a piece of the floor raised like that. Shadeesh said something in his stupid Indian accent about talking with Herr Steingarten. That was when Jake had simply, well, reacted. A casual approach, just strolling up like he had done nothing wrong. A flick of the switch to turn on the grain transporter. A strong shove to push Shadeesh into the machine. Sure, listening to his legs snap and tear away had been horrible, probably worse than Shadeesh's screams. But Jake's problem had been solved.

Then there was Franz. The poor guy showed up early one morning, probably to get a jump start on cleaning the walls. He hadn't been bothered by what Jake was doing. Interested was more the word. "Looking for something?" Franz had asked, and Jake could already hear what would come next. "We'll share the treasure—unless you want me to tell somebody." Franz's lye bath had been the only reasonable choice.

As for Hans, what a pity but what a stroke of fortune! Jake couldn't have planned it better. Ever since Hans had been murdered on the train, nobody but Jake wanted to work in the malt cellar. Not alone, at least. That left Jake the whole day to search and explore. Things were speeding up. To just touch the treasure ...

Upstairs, a horn buzzed. Jake checked his watch. Time for the morning break. He wasn't surprised to find his stomach rumbling. Sometimes he felt like a conditioned dog reacting to his master's commands. But that was the result of the working life, wasn't it? He covered his tools and headed for the stairs, checking once back over his shoulder. Yes, the shadows concealed everything.

He was musing over his coming wealth as he climbed the steep, narrow staircase. The walls were damp. The musty air had bothered him at first, but it had become more tolerable with the passing months. Upstairs was the worst. Grain dust floated thickly, casting a light blanket over the machinery and the concrete floor. There were days when all they did was vacuum and clean—a necessary precaution, really. If not, there was always the off chance of a spontaneous fire. Maybe even a dust explosion.

Several of his colleagues filed past the top of the stairs. They always rushed to the morning break, especially on Thursdays when Hefeweizen and Weisswurst was the meal of the day. It was a tradition Jake had never quite fathomed—sausage and beer at 9:00 a.m. He had to admit, however, that he enjoyed it. Maybe it was the sweet mustard. Perhaps it was the distinct banana and clove taste of the Bavarian Hefeweizen. Whichever, just the thought was making him hungry.

It made the appearance of Bethany Judge all the less desirable. There she stood beside the door to the break room, looking a bit disheveled and the worse for wear since the last time they had met. Bethany still managed a smile and an outstretched hand. Jake reciprocated.

"You haven't taken to sleeping on trains again, I hope," Jake said.

"Not so far from that, I'm afraid. But it wasn't intentional, I'll assure you of that."

Jake threw her a curious glance, uncertain whether to take the comment as a joke. He decided a half-hearted laugh was noncommittal enough to not offend. "I doubt you'd make a habit of it," he said. "You don't seem the type."

"More strange things have happened," said Bethany.

Jake raised an eyebrow. "Not another shooting, I hope! The German police will be at a loss if people start shooting firearms everywhere."

A long sigh slid from Bethany's lips. She shook her head. "Someone was killed," she said. "I saw the body. The bullet hole. The blood."

"Where was this?"

"I don't know. I was being held hostage."

"Hostage!"

"Dark room. No food. The whole works. And I heard them interrogating someone. I thought it was Louis. I heard this gunshot. They bring me out later, but the body is someone else. And then they stick a bag over my head and drive me to the country."

"Savages!"

Bethany shrugged. "I'm starting to enjoy the uniqueness of my German experience. I doubt such things are written about in the tour books and blogs."

Jake took Bethany's elbow and led her outside. The early morning light revealed the deep circles under Bethany's eyes. She stooped, her body looking drained and exhausted. And yet, Jake noticed something sprightly in her step.

"It was a mistake," Bethany said.

Jake stopped, a worried wrinkle creasing his forehead. "It's possible, I suppose, but improbable," he said.

"Not in that way, no. They misjudge me—that's all. I'm feeling they may regret their error."

"Ah, confidence! And how do you propose you'll accomplish that?"

Bethany was slow to answer. She simply stared at Jake as if reading his face. Finally, she nodded as though she had reached a decision. Then she spoke: "I'll need you. Don't ask me how just yet, but somehow, you are part of the equation. The train. The shooting. You've been involved from the start."

Jake swallowed hard. Hadn't he known this from the start, felt it deep in his bones? His intuition had warned him. That treasure, still locked in the dark confines of the malt cellar, was more in danger than ever before. So maybe Hans's murder hadn't been so fortunate after all.

He could tell Bethany, enlist an ally, and double the pace at extracting whatever was down there. No, that wouldn't work. There was no way to know how large the treasure was. Split between two people, he might be left with next to nothing. Besides, how would Bethany get into the cellar to work? And who could guarantee she'd go along with the idea anyway?

And there was the off chance that Bethany was a con artist. Had he really considered that possibility? No, Jake hadn't. But henceforth, he'd watch this American with a jaded eye. Perhaps a little "accident" might be the best solution to the problem.

CHAPTER 13

TOKEN

In the kitchen at 20 Alpspitzstrasse, located in the southern Bavarian town of Grainau, Francis Eberhardt poured himself a cup of thick black coffee, took a seat at the table, and floated his gaze over his three partners. His smile tried to hide feelings of general disdain, but his eyes revealed the deepest feelings in his soul. He despised the exercise of seeming to care, but he was, after all, a professional. Lying, cheating, and deceit simply came with the career. He had risen through the ranks because of carefully constructed relationships, strategic alliances, and plenty of feigned caring. He was perhaps least adept at the latter. Still, it had served him well. And now that he had reached the pinnacle of his career, tending to unimportant relationships caused him pain, not for the fakeness but for the effort.

He looked closely at Albert Treanor, who seemed lost in thought. Old, reliable Albert had been that way since Bethany Judge's kidnapping and subsequent release the week before—quiet, distant, contemplative. There was also Michael Persaud, a grizzly compact man and head of German operations. He clicked gum between his teeth and drummed his fingers, nervous ticks for a man who had recently given up chewing tobacco. Amanda Lang was her regular bouncy self. She preened her hair and checked her lipstick, typical of a girl who thought more of herself than her job.

Three men and a token woman. Francis hated that. He couldn't stand the made-for-television team, as if someone in the agency had decided diversity was necessary when hunting the new generation of Nazis. Plenty of other talent existed within the walls of their organization. Why did they have to settle with Amanda? The next threat to global peace should be the focus of the operation, not playing babysitter to placate the executives in human resources.

"There's little reason to feel optimistic," Persaud said between the snaps of small bubbles. "I think the three of you would agree. So many deaths—murders. It's undeniable that we are seeing a convergence of events here. Yet we're totally in the dark as far as where this is heading."

"Stocker is the key," said Eberhardt.

"We've known that for years now," said Albert Treanor thoughtfully. "It does us little good to know this, though, if we can't tie activities directly to her. There's nothing to build any action upon. We're left to be simple speculators, guessing the next move without being able to see the chessboard. Blindness, you know, is rarely an asset."

"The power of subterfuge," said Persaud. "Whatever else we might say about our adversaries, they are cunning and patient. I can't believe they haven't shown their hand somehow. And yet ..."

"And yet they have," said Amanda.

Francis laughed, saying, "The expert speaks!"

"Shut up, Francis," Amanda said. "You all know the murders are related. You all know that has tipped their hand. But what you don't know is how. And Bethany Judge, the only connection we have between us and them, is unconditionally mistrusted by Mr. Eberhardt here."

"Because she may work for them!"

"Amanda has a point, Francis," said Persaud. "Given the nature of this investigation, it's best not to be too cautious. Hell, I'm willing to throw our cover to the wolves if that's necessary to reveal what's going on here. It stinks, I'm telling you, and the boys at the top are getting nervous. Small potatoes or not, southern Germany bears a history that has the power to drag Europe back one hundred years. Does anyone want that again? A repeat of Europe on the eve of World War I?"

Albert Treanor cleared his throat and ran his palms over the table. "I'll give you the facts. These people are using symbols and aspects of the Third Reich. They are using them against Bethany Judge and against the German population. But they are so subtle in their application that nobody notices. We hardly notice! Yet here I am rescuing our charge when they dump her near Berchtesgaden. And we chase a leader—female this time—that possesses artistic inclinations, charisma, and real devotion to the movement she adopted. If you ask me, we're far beyond the eve of the First World War. I'd guess we are looking at something more like what Germany would have looked like in 1950 had it won the war."

"You mean nuclear?"

"At least down the road to being nuclear, yes. My guess is that Stocker and her people are quiet because they know this is big. If they were going conventional routes, boisterous positioning would attract sympathetic parties and swell their ranks, which would normally be good. But in this case, whatever they're trying to get must be equal to hundreds, maybe thousands of supporters."

Francis shook his head. "They know the German government would shut down their operation in a second. German law motivates them to stay quiet."

"Quite so."

"Yet they're not afraid to go around and shoot people."

"The world makes that quite convenient, actually," said Albert Treanor. "Extremists of all nationalities and religions make it easy to forget those closest to home."

Persaud nodded. "Another smoke screen?"

"Call it that if you will. It's just what is, and groups that follow the likes of Stocker remind me of water. They flow to the weakest spot and exploit it. In a social and cultural sense, this is no different. America and Europe look to the Middle East for terror. Resources are engaged to fight the threat. Bad guys fill the void where the defenses have fallen."

"And you think they'd have nuclear weapons?" asked Amanda in a horrified voice. "That they'd be crazy enough to blow up London or Paris or New York City?"

"Logical targets," said Francis.

"We'd need a report out to put nuclear specialists at all the ports and transport hubs," said Persaud, jotting himself a note. "I'm not sure we can get funds appropriated for this type of security action."

Albert smiled, his unfocused eyes rising toward the ceiling. "It's premature and tactically wrong," he said. "They will not challenge those places with the highest security. They are like water, remember. And they want an impact."

"Munich? Berlin?"

Albert shook his head at each suggestion. He smiled. "I'd hazard to guess Israel."

Amanda's eyes widened. "It would be quite the coup."

"A notable strategy too," added Francis.

"So much attention is lavished on the Jewish-Palestinian conflict, it's easy to minimize the disdain for Jews that still simmers below the refined German countenance. Beyond that, a revived Nazi movement should want to finish the work left undone by Hitler and his boys. In a way, Israel becomes a blessing. Millions of Jews are collected in a relatively small area."

"An easy target."

"Easy when you have the right kinds of weapons, yes."

That comment hung in the air, everyone pondering the depth of its meaning. Francis pursed his lips, concentrating. "And the collateral impact would be enormous, wouldn't it? I mean, let's say they nuke Israel. That draws the US into battle. They would assume

147

the attack came from Iran, Syria, Egypt, or some terrorist group getting funding from state sponsorship. I wouldn't doubt they'd throw some tactical nukes at some of the big cities."

Michael cleared his throat. "I agree. The region would already be saturated with fallout. Our military ethicists wouldn't have to worry about being first to the party. I suspect they would take out any potential supporters of the attack. And I stress *potential*."

"But that would mean strikes against almost every country in the Middle East," said Amanda.

"Quite astute, my dear."

"But that's terrible," Amanda said, her cheeks blanching. "America would never be so random in its use of force."

Francis laughed, the sound coming out like a bark. "Don't be so naive. Who could stop us?"

"It isn't a question of someone stopping us," said Albert, turning to Amanda, "but I'm afraid to say I agree with Francis on this one. With Israel decimated, we'd have plenty of reasons to destroy our enemies completely."

"What could justify murdering millions of people?"

"National security. Unlimited control of oil. Regional control. This means the wholesale destruction of anti-Israeli nations."

"And there isn't one in the neighborhood that isn't."

"So America is forced to conquer, subdue, and resurrect a huge block of real estate? And one they've contaminated nonetheless?"

Albert shrugged. "America wants a reason to destroy the rising threat of terrorism. Give them a good excuse and anything is possible. Stocker might be relying on that possibility."

"Another reason for them to stay under the radar," said Francis.

"Like if they say nothing now, nobody can pin the blame on them later?"

"Sure, Amanda. Even global politics is no different than the schoolyard."

Francis tossed a wad of paper at the garbage can. "I can imagine Stocker's spin masters now," he said. "Take the events they want, shape them to suit their needs, create the image that justifies their actions—"

"And behind that smoke screen, Stocker sweeps in and grabs power in Germany?"

"Yes, and likely with America's blessing!"

Amanda looked horrified.

"Why not, my dear? Don't look surprised. As reprehensible as an attack on Israel might be, the subsequent destruction of our enemies would give us wholesale control of the entire region."

"You're saying … Do you mean our government employs us to stop Stocker and her kind, but in truth they want them to succeed?"

Francis shrugged. "Pure speculation, of course. Except perhaps for the attack on Israel. Stocker is planning something big. And she's keeping an excellent secret. Have we any trustworthy information about their capabilities?"

Albert tapped some papers. "Nothing concrete, you understand, but intelligence suggests they possess very little. Stocker isn't known for her riches, and there's been no unusual banking activity. Book sales and lectures provide some income, but nothing like what she'd need to fund a coup."

"Anything been done with her computers?"

"The systems at the university revealed nothing unusual. Book stuff, lecture notes, emails to students. Nothing suspicious."

"Any chance she uses code?"

"Some excellent people are working on that right now. So far nothing."

Amanda leaned back in her chair. "Clean as a whistle. A sharp lady."

"Too clean," said Albert. "That's what I've been thinking about. Where's the speck of dirt? What can we exploit?"

"The same old story." Amanda sighed. "Nothing. If I had friends to complain to about this job, they'd tell me we're crazy. Barking up the wrong tree. Paranoid over nothing."

"Not quite," Michael said. "We know they are extremists. They are just quiet about it. We believe they have weapons or are seeking them. And we are confident their motivations run counter to civilized government."

"Unless America chooses to back them."

Albert waved his hand. "Ignore that possibility. Trust your government. Believe in your job. If you doubt either, this work will become impossible."

"Fine, but it still seems we're chasing ghosts."

"Except we're not."

"Except you believe we're not. There's nothing except this same damn discussion. Nothing has changed since we got here. Nothing!"

Albert reached into a pile of papers. He removed a single photo of Herta Stocker. "This has changed," he said. "She came home."

"There are no weapons. There's no money. So far. But we will find something. They will give it to us. They always do." Francis moved to the sink and poured a glass of water. "This Bethany Judge gives us a chance. I hope she's making a mistake."

"I thought you didn't trust her."

Francis grinned. "Who said anything about trust?"

"Always going for the kill, aren't you, Francis?"

"The job's nothing without the hunt, Albert. You should know that after all these years."

Albert dropped his eyes, saying nothing. Francis let a smile crease his lips. He lifted the glass and drank the water.

"But you should know, a lack of alternatives makes me nervous. Only having the Bethany Judge lady doesn't make me comfortable."

"Should we bring her back?"

"Too risky. We broke protocol twice already with her. I'm starting to think we're desperate."

"It was necessary to move things along."

"But dangerous. They might know we're here."

Albert shook his head. "Couldn't be helped. She does us no good wandering through Munich drunk and even less good lost in the mountains."

"You both presume the worst of her," said Amanda. "Perhaps the Buffalo gal will surprise us in the end."

"Spare me the talk of someone from Buffalo making good," snapped Francis.

Amanda's cheeks reddened. "She might prove to be your equal."

"Yes, certainly! My thirty years of international experience are worth nothing. Imagine that! Perhaps we should just follow the lead of our Buffalonian beer expert!"

Michael Persaud, known as the Thundering Bull of US Special Ops, had mostly listened up to this point, but now he lit up like a red-hot candy. For every inch he lacked in height, Persaud made it up in sheer stature—broad shoulders, a thick chest, bulging arms and thighs. He was the rare man who could boast a perfect center of gravity and perfect control of his emotions. But not this time. A crimson glow spread up his neck and face, his fists clenched, and his breaths came quick and shallow.

"Don't allow your fame to give you the mistaken impression that you can act like an asshole," Michael snapped. "Especially when you know little about your company."

Francis raised an eyebrow. The muscle under his left eye twitched.

"That's right," said Persaud. "Grew up in Orchard Park, just south of Buffalo. Home of the Bills stadium. And I'll tell you this: Buffalo is a mess these days, but the quality of life is great. We have Lake Erie in the summer, decent skiing in the winter, easy access to the outdoors for biking, fishing, hunting, whatever. DC has nothing over Buffalo, if you ask me."

"Unless you like concrete and powerful people."

Michael shrugged. "There's no denying Buffalo is the armpit of America. The city has no pull. Hell, it's going into the crapper each day. But we've contributed our share of American presidents and famous folk to the history of our country."

"I've heard," said Francis as he rubbed his chin, "that people from Buffalo live their lives mostly in the past."

Amanda struck her hands sharply against the table. "Gentlemen! That's enough. I have little interest in the merits of Buffalo or the lack thereof. And I've had enough of everyone jockeying for position. We're supposed to be a team! Our objective—"

"Which is the point of this entire conversation," Francis said, interrupting. "We are lacking a clear objective and have very little information."

"And demeaning each other will do any good?"

"My record speaks for itself," said Francis. "Independent, reliable, hard-hitting. As for the sloth of your stunted, bureaucratic cube-drone existence—"

Michael raised his hands in mock surrender. "The lady is right, buddy. My fighting's over."

"I don't intend to surrender so easily, Mr. Persaud." Francis glanced at his audience. "At least not thanks to the talents of my excellent partners."

The sarcasm floated heavily across the room. Albert stood, audibly sighing as he stepped to the large picture windows. Gray mist painted the distant mountains. "Francis isn't all wrong. He just communicates poorly. And his distrust of others is a liability to maintaining operational efficiency. Personally, I believe we have run the course of this one. Bethany is our answer, and if she isn't, then we are back to square one. We try for some kernel of information. We get it or we don't, but at least then we can move forward."

"And if she betrays us?"

"Then we fail. Perhaps we die. Who knows, but I'm certain after so many years in this business that risk rules the equation. Nothing comes from nothing, Francis. I doubt you learned otherwise in your career, so it's unclear why you relish that strategy now."

Albert turned back from the window, facing his partners. "This hasn't been a total waste, but we're certainly doing nothing to advance our interests. Our enemies are quite keen. Excellent planners, if we can say nothing else. Smart. Being cautious will be a wise move for us."

"But it shouldn't paralyze us either."

"Casting everything else aside," said Albert, abruptly steering the conversation, "there are no swastikas or brown shirts, no 'Sieg Heils' and goose-stepping. If I might use some modern parlance, I'd describe it as a gigantic sleeper cell."

"A brilliant assessment," said Michael.

Francis nodded. "The support is there. East Germany has experienced only a fraction of the western promise of affluence since the collapse of the Berlin Wall. The whole region is a hotbed of radicalism. Communism, fascism, it doesn't matter. They want some sense of control over their destiny. But I don't know how they can keep their support of Stocker quiet."

"Because she hasn't stepped out as leader."

"Flying under the radar? Waiting for the right moment?"

"She has all the potential backers she could ever hope for. But something's missing from her plans."

Francis smiled. "It can only be one thing."

Albert nodded, turning back to the window. "Enough of this conversation. Time to take a walk."

CHAPTER 14

STALK

Mist never bothered him. Gray sky—now, that was a different story. Down in the Alpine foothills, sometimes the warm air blew up from the Mediterranean, through Italy, over the mountains. The Germans called it *föhn*. With it came cloudless blue days. He loved that weather—he lived for it.

Not this kind of crap.

He shivered from the chill and from the feeling of being wet to the bone. Something waterproof, breathable, and a bit on the warmer side would have been nice to wear right then. Something besides the standard-issue wool sweater and old fatigues. Those damn things did nothing once dampness invaded their fibers. They just felt heavy and worthless. Like this job.

But Christian had told him what to do, and he had to listen. Was there a choice? He had flubbed that other mission, missing both his shots, and now he had to prove himself again and again. Like earning his place in the weeds. Admittedly, he was lucky to be alive. Nobody ever failed Christian and lived to tell about it. Why had he? How could he be the first? There was only one explanation.

He was special.

For what reason, he couldn't guess, but his innate wisdom led him to a simple conclusion: Christian intended great things for him. The movement was on the rise, wasn't it? Loyalty would be rewarded. Authority would be allocated. The future held great things.

Which was the only reason he crawled among the weeds. Just obeying orders, as good Germans always said. "I give the order, you go!" had been his father's favorite words, and he had learned at a young age that refusal meant punishment, pain, and wounds, both physical and mental. Nobody could ever call him a bad student; as an adult, he never paused to doubt anything he was told. He just acted.

Were it not for the damn weather, he'd be done by now. Christian had called and given the command: "Use the ticket to Garmisch today. Get to the house in Grainau. Get the job done."

Inwardly, he had feared a reprimand. Something like "And don't screw it up this time." But instead, Christian had been the voice of confidence. *He believes in me,* he had thought as he hung up the phone. And that was a strong enough thought to quell any consternation.

A look over his shoulder forced a grimace. The mountains were totally obscured. A good thing, but bad also. They couldn't see him, but how would he see them? *Just a little closer.* He inched forward several feet before pausing to peek through the weeds and grass. Lights glowed in the modest southern German home. The kitchen and living area were occupied with some bodies sitting at a table, others moving about. Obviously, they were discussing something.

Under normal conditions, this was close enough. Remove the weapon from the bag, drop the tripod, deep breaths, aim, take the shot, get gone. But these conditions weren't normal. And his past failure had sowed the seeds of doubt about his capabilities.

Trust yourself! The thought arced electric, snapping his veins with adrenaline. Success was the only option. No variables would stand in his way. A bit closer was best. The 7mm slug was powerful but not unstoppable. Wind, rain, the window. It must be given the best chances against these additional hurdles. With a silent grunt, he eased ahead once more.

On the upside, struggling against nature offered an opportunity for personal reflection. Like how he might be living among the homeless, how his father had threatened that to his "worthless child." He tried to imagine that life, fighting the elements every moment, every day, and shook his head. Those men and women who lived on the streets—they were the ones with true fortitude.

And how slithering among the weeds could be viewed as a metaphor for his previous failure. Sure, for those with no vision, no destiny. It signified much more to him. Like control. Success. He moved among the bugs and the worms, yet he was so much greater.

He was close enough to feel the house's heat. The light through the windows was brilliant now, almost blinding him to the surrounding landscape. *Close enough.* Beyond here and the going would get dangerous. *Can't watch my back, my sides. Always leave an out.*

The weapon slipped nicely from the bag. The synthetic stock ignored the veil of water on its surface. The action moved smoothly. He smiled. Taking care of his weapons was the first guarantee of success.

The bullet wed with the chamber, silent and effortless as it entered its temporary home. A rising anticipation sent a ripple across his muscles. He exhaled, searching for his calm center. The moment was near.

He balanced the weapon on its tripod, the scope catching the briefest reflection of his round, cherry lips. They pulled tight, involuntarily recalling the pain from his youth. It didn't bother him, not anymore, what Father had done with his hunting knife that day now fifteen years ago. He had deserved it, earned the punishment. Hadn't he? And his father had been swift and merciful. Just a quick flick of the wrist, a twelve-inch gash from elbow to shoulder, now a thick red line on his dominant arm. The scar had hurt for years, the tissue healing and then yielding to his constant movement. But then the pain stopped. Or he just forgot to notice it. Yes, that was it. To be a good leader, you must not dwell on the past or the present, or on misfortune and pain. Only the future mattered.

He positioned himself behind the rifle, settling his hips into the mud, his stomach over stiff grass, his feet against a rock. The scope's large eye relief made this his most comfortable weapon to shoot. And it was the most accurate too. Unlike that other one, now disposed of. But that situation had dictated a special rifle, one that broke down into pieces, easy to pack and carry. Convenience brought issues of muddled sighting. Maybe that explained the miss.

His thoughts shifted abruptly to the picture. That man had pulled it from a stack of files, flashed it around, jawboned some more. And the photo was of her. The most beautiful leader. The woman he adored. Not sexually. Never. But for the control and power she wielded. They were like silk in her hands, fine and smooth. Yes, those same things would be jagged and rough were he in control.

I'm so young, he thought. *So much to learn.*

And he wanted to learn. That was his strength. It would make him her right-hand man. Possibly someday, Germany's great leader.

The man inside put away the picture and now faced the window. The crosshairs rested on his chest, a bullet only milliseconds away.

What do his eyes see in the reflection? Outside or only themselves? He imagined the older man as narcissistic, that he turned to observe himself at every opportunity. A handsome man, surely, but weak inside. Only the infirm wasted physical and mental energy on the uncontrollable. Surely that was a sacred truth.

This man, the one who would die tonight, was going to be the first of many. Christian had told him to eliminate just one. That order was clear. He was to send a message. *Let them know we are here, we are watching, we are coming.*

It seemed to him a shame, though, taking only one. His field of fire swept the entire room. All four were exposed and confined. He imagined their reaction to the first shot, the bullet exploding the glass, ripping the man's chest open, blood splattering and spurting.

They would panic, disbelieving, not moving while he reloaded, aimed, and squeezed. The second one, a head shot, to make sure of the kill. The third probably a bullet through the back of the girl fleeing to the door. The fourth was a possible escape. It all depended on their reaction times.

He saw words form in the man's mouth, the lips moving slow, slower, slowly, until he read with complete clarity some dangerous words: "time to take a walk." *They're coming*, his brain warned, and his finger responded in kind. A steady pull of the trigger released a deadly load that sliced the glass open, shattered a sternum, shredded a heart, and glanced off a backbone. The body slumped and collapsed in a heap, the white room now stained in red. He ejected the shell and took aim, dry firing once, twice, thrice. They would all be dead.

He rose, sopping wet. *Good thing I loaded only one shell.* Time was short now, his window of escape narrowing. The empty shell glinted at his feet. He paused to retrieve it before hurrying toward the mountains, disappearing among the gray. He heard the wails and cries behind him from those three that should be dead.

Spared today, he thought, *by minds greater than my own.* Someday he might share Christian's vision. Or better, hers. Then he'd understand. Then he'd share the foresight. Then he'd be twice the man he was today.

Wouldn't that show his father?

CHAPTER 15

DECISIONS

"This is completely unacceptable," said Herta Stocker, flipping strands of hair back from her eyes. Her apartment felt smaller than usual this morning, the air thick. She was in no mood for lovemaking. "I was absolutely not wrong about her. She wanted to come to me first! If ever there was a predictable person, Bethany Judge is that woman. This is very disappointing. I don't know what to think anymore. We're going to need to reassess our situation, I hate to say. This is a grim situation."

She touched her pockets as if searching for a cigarette, coughed lightly, and reached up to pinch her earlobe.

"Of course, I'm always willing to admit the potential of making a misjudgment," she continued, "but consider who she went to instead. That boy Jake from the brewery. From the brewery! Under ordinary circumstances, I might think her action worked to my advantage. Something smells funny, though. They've been tied together too long. From the beginning of this whole mess. I don't like it. Not that I suspect Bethany. She's simple, naive. I couldn't expect much more from a child of Buffalo. And that's what makes her so perfect! Yet somehow this Jake Stoddard fellow—he simply smells like a rat. How he's tied up in the things of interest to us—the brewery and Bethany in particular. All far too coincidental for me to feel comfortable. It's almost as if he's trying to hold us at bay."

She stopped and squared her gaze on the man sitting across from her.

"I admit to losing sleep myself," said Christian Scheubel. "We're on the brink of major changes, and it's in moments like these when history is made or lost. Good decisions, and our successes will resonate through history. Bad decisions, and history shall easily forget us."

"Must you be so morose?" she asked plaintively. "I'm not feeling my peak at this very moment. *Flustered* is the correct word perhaps. I'm a hard person to satisfy, even when I act on behalf of myself. Little errors, plans gone awry, and my whole compass is thrown off."

"You should expect more rocky roads to come, more expectations dashed, more disappointment. You must steel yourself to their eventuality and forget them as they occur."

"Easier said than done, I'm afraid. High aspirations are not easily quelled. Neither are they neatly tucked into a corner and controlled. They are a furnace waiting to be stoked. When it happens, the fire often burns uncontrollably."

Christian shrugged. "Be aware then of its potential as a liability. If you can recognize your faults, you can shield yourself from them."

"Oh? How?"

"Seek counsel. Search for quiet to clear your mind. Anything but confrontation. For it is during battle that you awaken your internal demons. They will rush out and attack, and by then, it's too late."

"You watch out for me, don't you?"

"Every great leader needs great followers."

Herta smiled. Christian, his cheeks blushing, rose from his chair.

"You should know I have taken some liberties."

"Liberties?" said the professor, her eyebrows rising.

"To protect you. To protect the movement. Understand, the threat is real."

160

"What liberties?

"You remember my little protégé? The boy—"

"The boy who failed in his previous mission. The one you kept alive for personal reasons of some sort. Yes, I remember the story and have wondered what you had planned."

"There was no plan. Just intuition. I have learned this from you, I suppose. And he has performed as expected. Superbly."

"Shall you keep me in suspense any longer?"

"I have kept it from you. Precisely, I suppose, for the reasons you just described. I needed you keen witted, not distracted by the inevitable attempts by outside governments to influence the flow of politics in our country. In any case, a small team, I believe sponsored by the Americans, has had its nose to the ground for you, getting what I deemed to be too close over the last several weeks. They are afraid of you and what you might become. They recognize your power and ability and could very well intervene in our efforts at any moment. I waited for the right moment and took action. Last night, their lead man was eliminated."

"Your protégé did this?"

"Precisely. A wonderful assassination, really. They will be so caught up in the legal mumbo jumbo of German law that we shall have completed our task before they reach peak operating capacity again."

"What about replacements?"

Christian shook his head. "Not a concern. They are men of ego. And there is a woman among them as well. Now that a friend and partner has gone to his grave, they will insist on finishing this job themselves."

"A reasonable assumption. And this woman?"

"Not a threat. We've seen her among the people in Munich, trolling for information, using sex as a tool. She speaks wonderful German. American born. It seems some friends in the party assumed the task of eliminating her parents."

"They were Communists?"

"Mormons."

"What a disgrace! They are a plague of locusts on Europe! Riding about on their bicycles, the neat suits and dresses, preaching heresy. Germans would be smart to cast them away from their homes. Deny them access to their minds. It is a poison, you know that, Christian? Let that bit of information into the brain and it takes over."

"Like a virus."

"Yes, a virus! A perfect description. I'll remember that. It shall be part of our campaign to rid Germany of the Mormons and the Scientologists. Oh, just speaking of them makes me shudder."

"It's my fault. I'm sorry."

"Not at all, Christian," she said, reaching to stroke his cheek. "You're reporting progress to me. And that pestilence is part of that report."

"She was not the target of the action," said Christian. "Perhaps that should have been the case, but we sought to massively disrupt their operations. Leadership, as you understand, had to be eliminated."

Herta suppressed a smile. "I take it your efforts were successful?"

"An absolute coup. With a single bullet, their operations were sliced apart. This"—Christian paused, recalling the name—"Albert Treanor died moments after holding a picture of you. A fitting tribute, don't you think?"

"Indeed. And you've shielded me from all this? That they are conducting clandestine meetings to discuss our party? That these men have pictures of me?"

"Yes. I'm sorry if I've offended you."

"Offended? Hardly! You have done your job. Quite well, it seems. As has your protégé. It shall be interesting to see how long they stay away. And how far. I'm not surprised, you know, for I've developed enough of a reputation back in the States. To be watched is nothing new. But to be suspected of pulling my ideas into an actionable form? Never."

"We can't be certain how knowledgeable they were." Christian sniffed. "They certainly weren't discussing their intelligence outside their squad. But we witnessed one connection, one that caused great concern."

"What was that?"

"Bethany Judge."

"Her again! The loser American seems to be everywhere!"

"That's true. And we can't determine the connection. Perhaps they wanted to use her."

The professor nodded. "Absolutely. They saw I had connected with her. Perhaps they assume I'm loose and easy, looking for some easy sex away from the microscope of America's media."

"Doubtful. I think they believed she was leading somewhere."

"And indeed, she was. But we must be careful not to impose what we know to be true as the thoughts of our adversaries. Quite likely, they knew little beyond the connection of Bethany and me. They would have been trolling for more."

"And so they shall troll no more."

The professor laughed. Then her face hardened. "Until they are ready. That could be in two years. It could be tomorrow. If nothing else, they know we're for real. A threat to them *and* others. That we'll take extraordinary steps to reach our goal, regardless of the dangers to us. And they will realize I'm shielded, that such an overt act by a member of our party means layers of organization exist between Bethany and me. To some extent, I'm afraid to say, we have played our hand. Whether it was too soon, I can't say. But your action does necessitate that we accelerate our plans. Methodical steps and patience are, as of now, discarded policy. We must be people of action."

"I, well … It seems like an abrupt shift."

She laughed again. "Does it? And what about assassinations? They, and the party, are not mutually exclusive. Together, they sink or float. You chose a course of action. It was, by all accounts, successful. Now we must adjust, and my argument is that the adjustment must be quick and radical. We need what we've been waiting for. Now we must go and get it."

"You're panicking, Herta," said Christian, reaching for her hands. "Be calm. There's no need to overreact."

She jerked away, sneering. "Overreact? Am I the one ordering murders? And never call me Herta! I am your leader, not a schoolyard chum! We go for my birthright now! We rally the party within the month."

Christian squeezed his temples. "It's too soon."

"It's never too soon to take control, Christian! Have courage and faith. It has served you well thus far."

"The brewery?"

"My birthright is there, Christian. My father, Gustav, promised it waited for me, for when the time was right. It is the only gift ever passed down in my family, and it connects us directly to the glory of Germany's greatest leader, Adolf Hitler!"

CHAPTER 16

DIVISIONS

Bethany Judge was afraid. She had tried to achieve emotional detachment from the whole chain of events since her arrival in Germany. To some extent, indeed, she had been successful. Despite a few dead bodies, getting kidnapped, and now Louis missing, she had managed to laugh the whole thing off as bad luck. Very bad luck. But as an ex-cop, she knew things came in streaks like this. And once your feet got dirty, it was hard to stay out of the mud. Putting the whole thing into perspective required just flipping on the professional goggles. After that, she could step back and see things for what they were.

Not that she wanted to admit she was in the middle of some complex international intrigue. Espionage? Covert operations? Those concepts surpassed her qualifications. She preferred to think in terms of street thugs and the law. But who was the law here? Could she really trust Albert, Francis, and Amanda? It seemed she could, but experience beckoned caution. And the professor? She had faded to dark gray in her mind's eye, a distant memory. But it had only been weeks since she had last seen her, right?

And then there was Jake. She still didn't trust him, still felt the tug of intuition telling her that he had played a key role in recent events. But on that day when she visited him at the brewery, Bethany had asked that he stand ready to help. She hated her own duplicity. Perhaps, like the words in a book, things would get clearer if she edited him out of the story. Perhaps her real focus should be somewhere else. Just the thought of that made Bethany shiver.

Though maybe it was her desire for beer that was giving her the chills. Had she really been drinking every day for the last two weeks? Time had seemed nonexistent since she left the brewery with Jake, gone to his apartment, and stayed ever since, drinking liters upon liters of freshly bottled Oktoberfest beer.

"Fresh?" Bethany had asked. "The Oktoberfest ended long ago."

"This stuff stays in the lager cellar," explained Jake, "at temperatures near freezing. They bottle it only when inventories are low. It's as fresh as at the Oktoberfest itself."

Bethany had savored the thick malt sweetness, balanced with a generous portion of noble German hops. The alcohol was warm on her tongue but not off-putting. She remembered that, with the first drink, the beer had been the cleanest flavored that ever met her tongue. And she had discovered that her share of ten liters went down very easily and left little damage the next morning.

Perhaps that was why Bethany had fallen into the habit of starting each day with a half liter of Oktoberfest. And another. And another. The total count hardly mattered anymore; it was impressive by any standards. It didn't hurt that Jake was always there to offer another. Hell, the guy was a veritable beer warehouse, always bringing more cases home from work. Always giving her another sample to add to her growing beer knowledge.

"It's part of the benefits package," Jake had explained. "Seventy-five liters of free beer each month. And that doesn't include free beer at the brewery's beer garden and twenty free liters of beer at the Oktoberfest."

They had both fallen silent, filling the room with an awkward quiet as if each expected the other to speak first. Jake had taken the honor. "Have another beer," he'd said.

Bethany had taken that as sage advice. Perhaps the best of her entire trip to Munich.

But not today. Not fourteen days into her drinking binge. Equilibrium was still at bay. There was no doubt about that. But her conscience tugged at the edges of her blurry mind, reminding her, urging her, that greater things were at hand. How to define them, she didn't know, but it did offer a warning siren that things were slipping past.

She uttered a long, incomprehensible sentence that might have sounded German to the unrefined ear.

"What'd you say?" asked Jake.

Bethany forced spit onto her tongue, relishing the moisture. She had always drifted toward dehydration when she drank, and today was no exception. A cold glass of ice water would be the perfect elixir.

"Ice water?"

"No dice, sorry. Germany isn't a fan of ice. Straight from the tap is frowned upon too. You'll have to run to the store to buy some carbonated water."

The thought made Bethany's head hurt. Now she needed aspirin. She walked to the kitchen and stuck her mouth beneath the faucet. The metallic-tasting water washed the barbs from her mouth.

Jake smirked. "Germans drink so much beer because the water is bad, you know. At least that's the tradition, probably dating back to before municipal water. They think Americans are crazy the way we drink H_2O."

"I'd rather be crazy than parched," said Bethany. Water trailed from the corner of her mouth, dripping from her chin. She wiped her face with her forearm, pausing to eye the yellow crust that came from her lips. She frowned.

"Yeah, you puked last night. In the bathroom, thank God."

"When the hell—"

"Middle of the night. I heard you retching and thought you might pull a rock star move. You know, choke on your own vomit. So I dragged you to the bathroom and got your head into the toilet."

Bethany dropped her head into her hands. "I am so sorry."

"No worries. You're my guest. It's been fun."

"I've taken advantage of your hospitality. Gone over the edge. This isn't reasonable. My drinking—"

"Your drinking is perfectly normal. At least that's true among the people I work with. Now, maybe if you had a job it'd be too much."

"My point exactly! I'm wallowing. I haven't been outside in two weeks! Since we walked here from the brewery!"

"There was no reason—"

"There's always a reason! Christ, I'm sure there are people looking for me. They probably think I'm dead."

"Tell them you escaped. You deserved it."

Bethany forced a sarcastic laugh. "I'm not an escapist," she said. "A beer expert, but not an escapist."

"However you want to define it."

Bethany sighed loudly and sat, dropping her head back into her hands. "I have to get out of here. This has to end."

"Giving up on the good times, eh?" Jake asked.

He disappeared into the kitchen and returned a moment later with a jar of pickles. The lid snapped open as Jake gave it a twist. He pulled a plump green pickle from the jar, sucked the juice, and took a bite. The pickle issued a loud crack.

"Pretty fresh for Germany," said Jake, nodding with approval.

"You don't like it here either. Why do you stay?"

"There's work. And I have things on the side."

"You can find work back home. And hell, it's not like you have any friends. I don't remember any visitors during the last two weeks."

"I have more important things to worry about. Not meaningless friendships."

Bethany paused. "I'm not meaningless? Or am I? If you care for nothing but yourself, there must be some motivation to stay."

"Finally!"

Bethany glanced around, confused. "Finally what?"

"The rubber meets the road! Two weeks I've waited for this. I was starting to doubt my suspicions."

"Suspicions? Now I'm confused."

Jake stabbed a finger. "Don't backtrack! Don't you dare!"

The makings of a severe headache flared behind Bethany's eyes. She squeezed her temples. Maybe she was dreaming all this. After all, experience had taught her that drunken stupors and hallucinations usually existed in tandem. She groaned.

"You're up to something, after what's mine!" Jake continued. "I don't know how you know or who put you up to it, but I'll stop you! Mark my words!"

"Please let it end," Bethany whispered. "I'll stop."

"Damn right you will!"

Resignation swept through Bethany. "What's yours is yours," she said, eyes closed, head drooping toward the floor. "I won't touch anything."

She felt sudden pressure against the back of her head, her mind struggling to realize its origins were hard, cold, metallic, and attached to Jake's hand. *Hallucinations can't get worse than this,* she thought, controlling the inner urge to panic.

"I should kill you, you know that? You come into my world unannounced. Screw everything up at the Oktoberfest. Get the cops chasing around. Link up with God knows who and run around the city like you own the place. Now you're after my stuff. What I've worked years to get!"

You will sober up. You will sober up. You will sober up. Bethany silently chanted the thought, blocking the threats, bowing under the weight of the gun.

"I've eliminated lesser threats than you," continued Jake, his ire rising. "With no hesitation! You want my shit, you gotta come through me! Maybe thousands, maybe millions. But it's all going to be mine. Mine!"

"Yours. Copy that."

"Stand up," Jake said.

Bethany rose, keeping her eyes shut and her head low. Jake dug the muzzle into her chin, raising Bethany's head.

"Look at me," he snapped.

Bethany fluttered open her eyes, finding focus. Things in Jake's apartment were remarkably clear. In the past, her drunken romps had ended with blurred vision and crazy distortions. Not today. Jake looked, well, like Jake, excluding the snarl on his lips and his hand wrapped tightly around a pistol.

"This is too real," Bethany said.

Jake smacked the pistol against Bethany's cheek. Pain seared through her head, shattering the fog. It dawned on Bethany that she was again in a dire situation.

"Damn right it's real," barked Jake. "Buffalo drunk, stupid piece of garbage. Idiot! Don't play me for a fool. I've been at this for too long."

"Whatever it is, Jake, it's all yours."

"Whatever it is? Whatever it is?" Jake smacked Bethany with the pistol again. "What's that? Playtime? A bug bite?"

"What happened to you, Jake?"

Jake shoved the barrel into Bethany's nose and twisted it. The front sight tore skin, causing Bethany's nose to bleed. Tears threatened to well in Bethany's eyes. It was a natural reaction, like sneezing from sniffing pepper. She fought the tears back, struggling for equilibrium.

"Nothing, Bethany. I haven't changed since the day you set foot in Munich. My goal has been set for years now. I've been methodical and patient. And I've never taken kindly to people disrupting my plans."

"You act like I'm supposed to understand."

Jake drew close. "I don't know who you're with," he whispered. "Maybe a renegade like me. But you stay away."

"I am. I will."

Jake stepped back, sweeping his eyes over her. "I enjoyed having you stay, Bethany. And you should know that I spared your life the last two weeks. I like you too much, even now, to kill you like I killed the others. So I'm asking you to leave. Just leave." He raised the pistol again, pointing it between Bethany's eyes. "Let me have what I've worked for, or I promise you one of these."

"There's no reason for you to worry," said Bethany, trying to look decisive. "You have my word, Jake. I'm cleaning up and getting myself out of this city. I'm looking forward to some buffalo wings and gray winter skies. I want to bury this entire trip in my past."

Jake searched Bethany's eyes, finally sighing after several long moments. He lowered the gun. "There's a pun in there somewhere. And, Bethany, I'm sorry it had to come to this. In another life, we could have been good friends."

There was silence.

"Don't you think?" asked Jake. "I mean, overall we get along well. There's just this little issue between us. I can't overlook that."

"I would never ask you to do that," said Bethany, taking a tentative step toward the door. "Nor would I ever ask you to believe the opposite, that I am innocent of all charges. I understand the power of perception in matters of the law, be it common law or street justice. I'd only thank you for your mercy and then part ways."

Jake glanced around the apartment.

"Don't worry if I forgot something," said Bethany. "I've been wearing mostly the same clothes for weeks. Everything I brought to Europe is garbage now."

Jake shrugged. "Someday I'll wonder if letting you go was the right thing to do. It's like, what if the Germans had kept Hitler in jail after his failed *putsch* attempt in 1923? I imagine plenty of people spent nights pondering that. Some may have given their lives as a result after he came to power. You will not make me regret this decision, will you?"

"Absolutely not. I'd like to say I have a date with an airplane, if I'm allowed to travel internationally by now."

"There's been nothing in the papers. You're probably considered free to go."

Or dead.

"I'd rather make sure before getting hung up in an airport somewhere. At least here I have a modicum of freedom."

"You are a woman of contradictions, Bethany Judge. Please don't use that as an excuse to outstay your welcome."

"Absolutely not! No excuses. I simply believe the authorities will want to clear me. It's what we would do back in the States. You never let a suspect off the hook without some official fanfare."

Jake nodded. "All the more so in Germany."

"Excess appears to be the rule of thumb—"

"It's not only the rule of thumb," said Jake. "It's simple fact. Drinking, law, and specifically, social justice. Germans made beer into food. They proved enemies could be eliminated. No one else has matched their precision."

"Though imitation is the sincerest form of flattery."

"It is indeed." Jake smiled and reached for the door. "Now I bid you farewell. I hope and pray our paths don't cross again. You've come close enough. Please don't come any closer."

The midmorning sunlight warmed Bethany's skin, welcoming her like a long-lost friend. She stepped down the stairs and soon reached the clean and empty sidewalk. She turned and looked back up at Jake, who stood patiently guarding the door.

"I'm leaving, Jake, but whatever it is you're doing, I know nothing about it. I've had enough of my own messes to worry about yours. Seems to me that every corner I go around, some other shit flies in my face. Yeah, I'd rather get the hell out of here. Hopefully they'll let me go. Even if they keep me, don't worry. Your secret is safe with me."

Bethany turned away and started down the sidewalk. She imagined Jake's hand inside his jacket pocket, fingering the pistol's trigger. She guessed the word *liar* hung on his tongue, begging to be screamed. Just one quick shot and Jake could finish it all, get her out of the picture. But then he'd be doomed just the same. Now she was loose and perhaps doubly the threat. Time would tell, and the results might prove unfavorable. Perhaps to Jake. Perhaps to her.

CHAPTER 17

DYING BREATHS

These had been the longest two weeks of his life. Christian Scheubel had done some dirty work in the past, and sometimes it had led to unsavory situations, but never had he suffered so gravely. And it had all started from a plan that appeared so certain for success. They had dropped Bethany Judge in the mountains, observed her rescue, and eliminated a portion of that threat. But, of greater interest, they had watched Bethany flee to the American who worked inside the brewery. Herta had been quite troubled but intrigued by her actions. And so, for the greater part of two weeks, Christian had kept surveillance over the apartment. He had noted nothing of interest. Neither had his occasional replacements. Bethany Judge had gone inside and never come out. Christian had started to wonder if Jake had killed her.

He was stuffing Bauernbrot into his mouth, staring into a cup of lukewarm Tschibo coffee when, from the corner of his eye, he saw Bethany exit the building. Christian spat out the bread, threw on the headphones, and pulled binoculars to his eyes. Bethany looked gaunt and tired, hardly a surprise for someone holed up the last fourteen days. And she seemed agitated. There was a definite tension between Bethany and Jake. Christian listened with interest to Bethany's declaration of not knowing what Jake was up to, of wanting nothing to do with it. *You're already involved, my friend*, he thought, smiling broadly at Bethany's inadvertent lie about how the secret was safe with her.

There was little at this moment to prevent Christian from killing Jake. *He is a threat, after all*, Christian thought. But also an asset. Jake was after the same thing as them, and he had been on the inside for a long time. That told Christian several things: what they were after was tough to find, or it was too big for one person to haul out, or it didn't exist at all. The latter was an unacceptable option. It would, after all, render their party paralyzed. No money and no arms? That equaled no power.

The romantic side of Christian hoped the load was too big for one person, though that left open the chance that Jake had been hauling items out piecemeal. Even that was doubtful. Jake was acting like a man with something to protect. He seemed scared and uncertain. Why else get so involved with a lightning rod like Bethany? Most assuredly, Jake wanted to keep close tabs on something he perceived as a threat.

Christian turned his binoculars to see Bethany nearly invisible down the street, now little more than a brown speck against gray buildings. Jake remained erect on his front stairs, his hand fiddling inside his coat pocket. Christian had little doubt about Jake's struggle. On the open street, however, it was unwise for him to use a weapon. He shook his head. Ineptitude stretched across all strata of society. Killing, the most banal act of all, was not to be confused with rocket science. Jake was obviously someone who had overthought the process.

But it was the former possibility—that Jake had found nothing yet (but was likely close)—that made it impossible for Jake to think straight. Christian couldn't blame the man. Imagine the allure for one person if, as was promised, the riches in that brewery were enough to fund the entire party. The thought of so much wealth would shatter Jake's logic and reason. Christian vowed to pay him dearly for losing that edge.

Though then there was the question: How did Jake know?

Not worth pondering, he thought, reaching for his cell phone. For the first time, Christian noticed his hands were sweating. Not the typical physical response of a trained killer, but he shrugged it off. Things, after all, were coming to a head.

The phone bleated in his ears. Once, twice, and then her sweet voice abruptly spoke her last name: "Stocker."

"The drunk left the bar."

"Did she? Are you sure?"

"I am absolutely positive. Made the identification myself. She looks a bit beat up, and I'd guess she wore out her welcome. She stormed off in the direction of Marienplatz. I'd guess she winds up on a train."

"Back to where it all began."

"And judging by the conversation I picked up, her brewery contact is the one we want to key on. Sounds like he's after the mother lode. Maybe already found out."

"You have any proof of this?"

"There's no proof. Anecdotal evidence, but the coincidences are too distinct. This other American is after something. Bethany knew it and got turned away."

"You think she spent the last two weeks trying to swing a deal?"

"Why not? Retiring rich would beat the hell out of being a Buffalo cop."

"Sure," said Herta, hesitating. "But how would she know about it? How could anyone? It's my birthright, passed down by word of mouth. It was never discussed. Never!"

"It's too late to revisit that question. We must focus on the risk to us. It must be secured posthaste!"

"Agreed."

"And this other American is the one who will benefit us most. I suspect he'd be most helpful in our custody."

"Then make it so," said Herta.

The phone clicked in his ear. Silence filled the line. Christian held the receiver tightly, finally relishing the shifting of tides. Waiting had been ejected. Action had taken its place. New winds were guiding the party's course. His goal to achieve greatness was perhaps attainable in his lifetime.

He trained his binoculars on Jake once more, pausing to admire the broad shoulders and lithe muscles. A wonderful physical specimen. Certainly, this man wasn't a career brewery worker. He lacked the requisite paunchy cheeks, sallow skin, sunken eyes, and protruding stomach. Here was a carnivorous creature, one who relished the hunt as much as the kill. How Jake had slipped past their reconnaissance, Christian didn't know, but his newfound appreciation did not alter the simple actions that must follow. He set the binoculars on the seat and took a 1940 vintage Krieghoff Luger pistol in their place. Christian checked that it was loaded before stashing it in his shoulder holster. He fumbled in his briefcase, emerging after several moments with a can of mace.

Easy way or the hard way, he thought, glancing out the window again. Jake remained frozen in the doorway like a tiger waiting to pounce, still fingering the pistol inside his jacket. After a moment's thought, Christian grabbed a second loaded clip. Had he to guess, things were about to get ugly.

Bethany had passed out of sight of Jake's apartment, the building just a commingled haze on the city's horizon. She had walked briskly for the last several minutes, putting distance between herself and whatever had changed back there. Her mind sought answers, finding none.

Another confusing day in Germany.

She chuckled at the thought, but it was the truth behind the humor that struck her most. Now she was lost and without a map. She had been in Munich long enough to have a basic compass.

But she had no sense of landmarks. She turned full circle on the sidewalk, trying to decide on her next direction.

"Lost?" a voice asked. A soft hand grabbed Bethany's elbow.

Bethany pulled away, shocked, her quick reaction proof of a woman on the edge.

"Amanda?" asked Bethany, blinking her eyes heavily.

"Yeah, and you look like shit too," Amanda said as she brushed strands of the curly wig from her eyes. "Staying holed up for so long hasn't treated you well."

"You've known where I was the whole time?"

"We always stay close." Amanda paused, reaching out a hand. "Give me some change."

"What?"

"Give me some change, please. This needs to look authentic."

Bethany absently stuck her hands in her pockets. "I'm tapped," she said, bringing out empty hands.

"Good. Listen. Things have gotten crazy. They killed Albert—"

"What?"

"Keep your voice down. Don't overreact. Somebody shot him—assassinated him—through the window of our safe house. Whoever it was, we were left standing. They were probably trying to scare us off. I don't know. I went to the street, deep undercover. Fortunately, Albert told me where he had taken you. So I've been living in the alley near Jake's house the last couple of weeks. It wasn't pleasant. You could have shown yourself earlier."

"I was—"

"No need to explain. We've all been there one time or another."

"Two weeks?"

Amanda turned. "I've spent fourteen days sleeping beside a guy who has been homeless for eight years. If you ask me, it takes time to get out of a funk. And for each person, the time needed is different. Just don't let it become a lifestyle."

Bethany floated her eyes over Amanda's ratty clothes. She found her ripe street aroma oddly attractive. Perhaps it was a memory of home. She smiled.

"So you've been following me?"

"We call it surveillance."

"Surveillance, right."

"Listen, when Albert was killed we had two choices. Back off from our investigation or act on our hunch. And you, my friend, are our hunch."

"Me?"

"You and your connection to the professor, yes."

"Professor Stocker?"

"Don't be surprised. She has a shady past. You know that. And things just aren't right the way she hovered around you. I hope you aren't offended when I say I doubt she found you attractive."

"Come on!"

"It's not about you. It just doesn't fit her profile. She has always been about career, about herself, about driving some agenda forward. Neither women nor men have ever found a place in her life. There's no reason for it to be different here."

"She's on a break, right?"

"Please, Bethany! Set your own opinions aside for now, okay? Things are happening. There's little time to waste."

"What could possibly happen—"

The distant sound of gunfire floated over them, stopping Bethany midsentence. Both turned their heads toward the source of the sound. It was too far to tell, but it had definitely come from the direction of Jake's apartment.

"Shit!" shouted Amanda. "We have to hurry."

Amanda sprinted toward the source of the gunshots, quickly outpacing Bethany, who lumbered slowly in her wake, struggling to pace her breaths. She had ignored her fitness and was paying the price now. This wasn't the first time her in-shape body had eroded into a mass of jiggly flesh. Her muscles felt weak. Every joint below the waist protested each connection of foot to pavement. Her breath seared hot in her chest. The adrenaline surge from the sound of gunfire had done nothing to help.

When Bethany finished the sprint to Jake's front step, her lungs rasping from exercise-induced asthma, her mouth gaping, her hands on her knees, she saw between heaved breaths something akin to the Old West. Jake sat on his front landing, his back against the shattered glass door. His blood-soaked shirt stuck tightly to his chest. A crimson puddle had formed beneath him.

"He's still alive," said Amanda, waving an open hand at Jake. "Not for long, though. It's bad."

Bethany noticed Amanda's attention was turned elsewhere. She followed a blood trail with her gaze; it led across the street, disappearing behind a parked Mercedes sedan. From her hunched position, Bethany made out a foot partially obscured by the front tire.

"He's behind the car," Amanda whispered. She turned her head, listening to the approaching sirens. "The cops are going to be here any second."

Bethany rushed up the stairs to Jake. "What happened?" she yelled, her face close to his. Jake's eyes fluttered. Recognition dawned. He smiled and started to speak. The words caught in his throat. He coughed up blood.

"Shit!" Bethany snapped. She looked over to see Amanda move around the car, and then turned her attention back to Jake.

"Don't let them get it," Jake said. "It's all there in the brewery. The malthouse floor. Basement. Third quadrant. Millions."

Jake coughed again.

Bethany spoke incredulously, not understanding. "You'll be all right. Just hold on. The police are coming. Hold on." She looked over her shoulder again, yelling, "Amanda!"

"Third quadrant," Jake whispered, his eyes glassing over. "Not them—"

With a rattled breath, Jake fell silent. His head lolled left, the body tipping over. Bethany reached out but stopped herself.

No fingerprints.

She moved quickly down the stairs and across the road. The sirens were close now. They had little chance of escape. Amanda was squatted on the other side of the car. She stood as Bethany approached. Bethany noticed the Luger kicked just out of reach of the splayed hand. She saw the frightened yet defiant eyes of the man on the pavement, the hole in his chest, another life pumping away.

"I have what I need," said Amanda. "Let's go."

"What about—"

But Amanda was already moving away, putting cars between herself and the dying man. Bethany saw the man move toward the Luger and jumped to follow in Amanda's wake. This time she caught up quickly.

"Down that alley," ordered Amanda.

They slid into shadows as a shot echoed down the street. Amanda smiled.

"He wasn't going to be taken alive. The classic Nazi martyr."

Police cars whizzed past, screeching to a halt. Doors opened and slammed shut. Dozens of excited voices yelled in German.

"We need to keep moving. Come on."

They put the chaos behind them, not speaking until they reached a large open field.

"We're still in the city?" asked Bethany.

"Of course," said Amanda. "You don't recognize Bavaria?" She pointed to the large statue several hundred yards away.

Bethany gasped. "This is where they have the Oktoberfest?"

"The Theresienwiese. That's right. An area of prime real estate, kept vacant for the annual beer fest."

"I met Jake here."

Amanda nodded. "Funny how things come full circle."

"What did you mean back there? That you got what you need?"

Amanda looked at her shoe, realizing something. She searched the area from which they had come. The heel of the right shoe, Bethany noticed, was covered in blood.

"Amazing what a shoe pressed against a bullet wound can get someone to say," she said, slipping the shoes off her feet. "I didn't expect the bastard to talk."

"What—"

"Proof. Of everything we expected. He was connected to Stocker. They are moving into action. The son of a bitch was totally defiant. Said it was too late for us to stop them."

"Too late?"

"Yep. It's never fun to be behind the eight ball. I have to tell the boys."

"What if it's just a dying man's bluster?"

"Bluster? What do you mean?"

Amanda tossed her shoes into a trash bin. They entered a U-Bahn station, walking down the steps to the boarding platform. Bethany quietly recounted Jake's dying words, a sadness creeping over her at the loss of another life. But in her gut, something told her that Amanda could not have been more excited.

CHAPTER 18

SUFFERING

From the black circles beneath his eyes, Bethany could see that Michael Persaud had suffered. She was trying to figure out how he fit into this team, understand his role, get a reading on his personality, but one thing was clear: he had taken Albert's death hard. Bethany could see they had been friends, comrades. She could understand how trust between the two had bloomed during their professional relationship. She had experienced the same thing as a cop, losing friends in the line of duty, having everything severed before her eyes, watching a life pulse away in spurts and then a dribble. It had always been nearly too much to bear. She imagined the same was true for Michael.

"Christ!" Michael barked, exhaustion evident in his hoarse voice. Bethany sensed he was at the breaking point, a twig about the snap. "The whole goddamn city is dying around us. First our own. Now this." He turned quickly back to Amanda. "Tell me again what happened."

Amanda repeated the story for the fifth time, focusing on the details she could recall, relying on Bethany when memory failed. Bethany stood beside Francis in the corner of their new Munich apartment, carefully situated away from the windows. She watched him furiously taking notes, reading the occasional questions or comments he jotted in the margin.

How much?

He underlined the question twice, running his tongue across his dry lips. Bethany wondered what the question meant, trying to dig into Francis's mind. Things were moving fast now, the deaths drawing closer and closer together, always nearer to the source of conflict. It was a phenomenon she had witnessed time and again. This was going to be no different.

Who now?

Jake was dead. So was Stocker's hit man. Did Stocker still have the apparatus to go after what Jake claimed was in the brewery? She would never have trusted the operation to just one man. Or perhaps it was something smaller, easily transported. Even just a suitcase packed with diamonds could be worth millions. Certainly enough to jump-start her political ambitions.

Francis tapped his pen against the pad. Amanda had much to say. Bethany, even more. Between them, they painted a horrific picture of pandemonium and death.

Michael was pacing the room now, his eyes frantic. He looked at Bethany. "What else did Jake tell you?"

"I told you everything he said."

"Tell me again!"

Bethany did as commanded, searching for details as she spoke. In just a matter of moments outside Jake's apartment, so much had been seared into her brain. The images were clear behind her eyes. The words played like a recording. She was amazed by the clarity of it all.

"I can't stop seeing him at the end," Bethany said. "Bleeding out. He trusted nobody. Not even me. He had killed to protect the secret. Friends and coworkers. He never saw death coming from the direction it did."

Michael shook his head. "The bastard was after it all the while. A patient son of a bitch, I'll give him that. God only knows how long he was digging around in that brewery. You think he found it?"

"He was quite specific."

"Specific only to the extent he knew what he was talking about," said Francis. "We have no blueprints, no plans. None of us know a thing about that brewery's layout. This is all theory right now."

"I have somebody working on that right now," said Michael.

Amanda glanced at Michael, curious. "Brewery blueprints?"

"Yeah. Whatever we can get. But we're having a tough time looking inconspicuous. The Germans want to know what's going on."

"Maybe we go in blind."

"I've never done that before, Francis. I'm opting for surveillance on the brewery until we have something concrete to work with."

"But someone on the inside—"

"Doubtful. Jake was working alone. The only reason he passed the information to Bethany was because he was dying. A last-ditch effort to keep it out of the Nazis' hands."

"And your man?" Michael asked, looking at Amanda.

"Bethany saw for herself," Amanda said. "The bastard wasn't going to talk."

"You had disarmed him," Bethany said. "And then you told me—"

"I said I got what I needed, yes."

Michael cocked his head. "What does that mean?" he asked. "A confession? Some information?"

"A guarantee," Amanda said.

"You trusted him on this?"

"I have Bethany with me, who has been wanted by the police in various forms since her arrival in Munich. The last thing I wanted to give anyone involved in the investigation was one of my bullets or my fingerprints. I told him to take the honorable way out and do the job himself."

Bethany's ears flushed. She closed her eyes, trying to center on her memories of what had happened. Everything had moved so fast but she could click the clear moments together. This detail was definitely missing. "He promised that?" she asked.

Amanda nodded and smiled. "And the bastard came through with flying colors."

Francis tapped his pencil again. "Surprising he didn't put up a stand against the cops. Take a few with him."

"Not so surprising," Amanda said. "Why draw excess attention to the matter? Stocker's man opts to make it look as clean as possible. Give no direct suggestions of political motives. As far as anyone can tell, it was a robbery gone bad."

"Wrapped in all the recent violence," Michael said, "they might think differently. People are getting nervous."

"They should," said Francis. "The climax is upon us. The death of Stocker's man was an inconvenience to them, but just an inconvenience. They will adjust accordingly."

"Any ideas?"

Francis shrugged. "Only questions. I can't see how the endgame is going to come."

"Jesus, Francis," Bethany said, irritation rising in her voice. "You're supposed to be the genius here! Don't you at least have a theory?"

"I've been writing everything Amanda and you said. I tossed in comments and questions when they popped into my head. Usually things link together. They start making sense. Nothing is clear here. We don't understand their motivation."

"Power is their motivation," Bethany said, aware she was stating the obvious.

"But they are powerless now," Francis said. "They are striving for the means to access that power. What sort of power, I don't know. We have discussed the potential scenarios, but we're months or years before they could take shape. This," he said, waving at the air, "is nothing more than a fucking bank robbery happening in a brewery. We stop the robbery, we stop Stocker."

Michael leaned against the wall. When he spoke, an edge of excitement colored his words. "And when you're dealing with robbery, you're not talking about a nation, a political party, or anything of the sort. Robberies are done by individuals. Small groups at the most. Anything else, and things get confusing."

"Like where will the money go."

Michael stabbed the air with his finger. "Exactly. And if that's the case, if we're dealing with nothing more than a group of two-bit thieves, then we just need to cut off the head."

"Go after Stocker?" Amanda asked.

"It's the best plan, but we can't waste time. Jake and Bethany were cozy. And Stocker was close to Bethany. Now Bethany is with us. Stocker will add it up and not like what she sees."

"But you're talking about taking down a well-known public figure. She can't just disappear without someone taking notice."

"She's going to have to."

"Why not use me?" said Bethany.

All eyes turned to her.

Michael asked the question on everyone's mind: "What do you mean exactly?"

"As a lure. Bring her here or wherever. Whatever it is she feels for me, even if she was using me as part of her plan, she's going to want to see me."

"Why?"

"It's been weeks, for one. She will be curious. And if her group is as small as Francis thinks, she is hurting from that guy's death. Filling the void with a warm body might be an appealing thought."

"It's dangerous," said Amanda.

"She agreed to this a long time ago," said Francis, his tone expressing for the first time a warm respect for Bethany Judge.

"That's right, I did. Don't worry about me. If you think it will work, put me to use."

Michael paced across the room. "Stocker will be suspicious, not curious. But that suspicion will become curiosity. That's what will bring her in."

"And once she's in, then what?"

"Leave that to me," said Michael. His words oozed revenge.

The evolution of events sat heavy in Bethany's stomach. She had difficulty imagining Herta Stocker absconded and killed. In all her years of law enforcement, despite the occasional temptation, she had always kept her hands and conscience clean.

"Nothing rash, right?" she asked. "You'll treat her with dignity?"

"Tell me if she deserves it. Has she earned that from us?"

Bethany fell silent, refusing the obvious answer. After several moments, Michael grunted and turned away.

"Then we're settled," he said, pulling a city map from his pocket and spreading it on the table. "Coax her to the brewery via this street. I'll be somewhere along the way to collect her."

Bethany strode down the stairs and onto the sidewalk, moving quickly in the direction of the professor's apartment. She had to play this carefully. Not once since coming to Munich had she played the aggressor. Herta was certain to note any abrupt personality switch. Despite all urgency, she had to be smart. Get into Stocker's territory and let the professor come to her.

From behind she heard sneakers running on concrete and finally felt a hand on her left elbow, followed by panting breaths and a husky word from Amanda. She was breathless from sprinting, a far different scene than the conditioning she had displayed at Jake's apartment.

"Wait—"

Amanda held up a finger, sucking air through puckered lips.

"I need to get there, Amanda. What is it?" She moved a bit slower. Amanda matched her stride.

"We realized something," she said between swallows of thick saliva. "Not to give away what we know. She could be innocent, you know? Or, if not, she might use anything you say to her advantage."

"I had already thought of that. Everything must be like it was before. Let her take the lead, be the aggressor, but beyond that I hadn't decided on the best tactic. My hope was that something would pop up."

"It's a better plan to not bring her to the brewery. She'll sense something is amiss. Michael can intercept you elsewhere—"

Bethany paused. "You're right," she said. "I can't tell her I know about the brewery. And taking her there—well, I doubt she'd buy the coincidence."

"Is there any place you've been with her? Someplace special?"

"Just that big park in the middle of the city."

"The English garden? That's perfect! Take her there and keep her there. I'll go back and tell Michael."

"Anywhere in particular? It's a big park."

"There is a big beer garden near the U-Bahn. Walk through there and turn right into the park. Head for the Chinese Tower. I'll tell Michael to be somewhere in that area, on a park bench."

"Perfect. I'm on my way."

Amanda wished Bethany luck before hurrying back to the apartment. She sprinted up the stairs, stopping outside the door, her breaths now light and relaxed. The easy part was over. She had played her part well. Faking being out of shape was perhaps over the top, but Bethany had taken the bait, hadn't she? Given her the slightest sense of superiority, or at least less of a feeling of inferiority. And that had been the goal. *Keep her at ease. Make her do your bidding.* Amanda's key slid into the deadlock. She turned the doorknob and entered the warm room, her nose twitching at the musty thickness of death's earliest stage. Stepping carefully past the blood, over the prone, lifeless bodies of Michael and Francis, Amanda grabbed her silenced pistol and the map.

More like *the* map.

The old piece of parchment had everything she could have dreamed of. And how easily the stupid Nazi had given it up, falling so easily for her deception. And then he just killed himself. Almost comical. In reflection, though, what other choice did he have? Not like the professor would have forgiven his failure, not like the police would have refrained from picking his brain about his Nazi ties. And it worked far better in her favor anyway.

Now Bethany would lead the professor to the opposite side of Munich, into the English garden, expecting something that would never happen. And Amanda could go about the work she had been sent to do. Back home in Salt Lake City, millions of people were counting on Amanda's success. As she had promised to the leaders of her Mormon church the day before boarding the plane to Munich, she would not fail.

Michael and Francis, their blank eyes staring at the ceiling, had learned upon their deaths exactly how seriously Amanda took her calling. And now they were face-to-face with eternity. The thought forced a shake of Amanda's head.

A shame they will never know God.

She wiped pity from her mind and slipped back into the hallway. The door locked behind her. In just a few minutes she would reach the brewery. She'd have the treasure and be gone before the stench of decomposition attracted attention to the bodies.

That much, at least, was the plan.

CHAPTER 19

FRITZ WEYERMANN

Clouds often checkered the skies over Bavaria. It was only natural then that nature's design had become the background for the flag of Germany's largest state. Today was another of those beautiful days. Herta Stocker sat at her apartment window, admiring the view, knowing her life was about to change.

It was a shame, certainly, that her trusted assistant had met his untimely demise. Or perhaps it was exactly as the heavens ordained. Either way, she was not one to question fate. She could only thank Christian—posthumously, of course—for his service and move on. Fortunately, he had prepared for her a qualified replacement. This "assistant" was due to arrive late in the afternoon.

Herta had wondered about this young protégé before. What he looked like, his temperament, his loyalty. Christian had spoken highly of the man, but she was less trustful. While he may have deserved death for his only failure, subsequent successes had justified Christian's restraint. And now he seemed invaluable.

Her mind struggled to recall his name. Had Christian ever mentioned it? She thought not. Indeed, she was a whiz with names, committing them to immediate memory in a way that had baffled friends and family. Herta was always at a loss to explain the ability. She described it as a separate room in her mind, fully compartmentalized with faces and their names. But even that did the skill injustice. Her brain worked differently—that was all.

But even the smartest people needed lackeys and strongmen. Christian had been particularly good, if not flawed by ambition. She had tried hard to give him much; he, however, would never have been satisfied as number two. Not when their party had finally won power. But despite his shortcomings, Christian hadn't deserved death, at least not yet. She could have used him a bit longer. Now her timetable depended on unknown and, for the most part, untested loyalists.

She sighed, her eyes straying from the sky to the street, and caught her breath in her throat. Walking over the cobblestone, like a ghost her skin was so pale, was Bethany Judge.

Fresh from a two-week drinking binge and a double homicide. What a vacation you've had, my friend.

There was little reason to flag her down. Things had changed, after all, with the deaths of Christian and Jake. It would be a different operation, flying blind except for the stories from her youth.

Unless, of course, Jake said something to Bethany.

It was doubtful but possible. They had spent two weeks together drinking. Anything could happen under the influence of German beer. Had Jake let a bit of information slip or even boasted of his exploits during an evening's binge? Would Bethany even remember? Probably not, but under the circumstances it seemed a worthwhile concern. She checked her watch. Only 11:07. Plenty of time before the new guy would arrive.

She dressed quickly and pursued Bethany straight up Leopoldstrasse, away from the city center. She was heading into the heart of Schwabing, one of Munich's trendy sections. Herta threaded quickly through the thickening crowd, soon catching sight of Bethany's matted hair among hundreds of pedestrians. It was a tiring effort, and she felt beads of sweat on her brow. That was almost enough for her to abort the effort; she preferred looking stately over harried. This urge to meet Bethany surged inside her, however, and she pushed ahead, catching Bethany just after she had reached Muenchner Freiheit and turned down Martiusstrasse toward the English garden.

"Bethany!" she yelled.

Bethany Judge allowed herself a faint smile before turning to face the professor. The look of surprise, however, was real. She couldn't think of a time in her career when a first pass had yielded success. Not everything, it seemed, would go wrong during this extended trip.

"Frau Professorin," she said in American-accented German.

The professor smiled. "You've learned a little German! That's outstanding! Your stay in Germany has been long. Enjoyable too, I hope."

"Plenty of highs and lows. Today is somewhere in between. I was considering a beer in the English garden. Maybe that would get me out of the middle of the road."

"A beer sounds excellent, if I might accompany you."

This time, Bethany allowed herself a full smile. "I'd be honored."

They continued walking, and the professor chatted incessantly, dancing through topics that normally would have been of little interest. Clothing, the weather, and German soccer were three of the topics Bethany recognized. The rest she shut out. Bethany was, after all, listening to the rambling of a distressed woman.

Take 95 percent as bullshit, and then wait for the good stuff.

And so, when Herta's one-sided conversation stumbled onto the topic of all the recent murders and how they scared her and made her feel unsafe and she asked Bethany, "Have you seen or heard anything?" Bethany knew this was her version of digging for information. That she was so weak in her effort revealed the damage done to her organization. But ultimately, about whom was she asking? Jake or the other guy? She decided not to think too much for an answer. Leave it to Michael and the others. They would get the information from her if they wanted it. Or they would cut the head off the snake.

They arrived at the large beer garden, finding it empty and with no service staff in sight. Bethany flopped her hands to her sides. Truthfully, a beer had sounded great. When wasn't the perfect time for a beer, really? Perhaps keeping the mind sharp was going to be her key to safety and success, but she still frowned with disappointment. Herta patted her on the back.

"Beer before noon isn't a good idea anyway," she said. "Consider it a blessing in disguise."

"You've spent too long in America," said Bethany. "The Germans I've met love their morning brew."

"Ah, the Germans and their feelings. Sometimes I wonder why I care for them so much."

Bethany found it impossible to resist the opportunity. "We all care for our country in one way or another. The question is whether you care enough to get involved."

"You mean politically."

"Sure. Or community stuff, you know. Just being of service."

A twinkle lit Herta's eyes. "It's why I became a professor. My life's work has been to return dignity to the Germans. Regardless of what they say, regardless of how modern and accepted we've become, regardless of how every German denies it, we all suffer a collective guilt from the war. Not the kind of guilt assessed by the Allies, understand, but a guilt for failing at the task."

"For not winning the war?"

"Among others, yes. Germans were presented with a task, and they failed. That is unacceptable. That breeds guilt."

Bethany began walking, lazily looking for Michael or Francis. "I'd say they mask it well."

"Any individual can hide anything under four hundred liters of beer per year. Perhaps you know that better than I."

"Touché."

Herta smiled. "Consider it the casual observation of a friend. Some candied walnuts would be delicious, though."

"And ruin your figure?" Bethany pointed in the direction of an open field, where dozens of nude sunbathers lay about on towels. "Not quite the season, wouldn't you say?"

"They come out of the woodwork whenever the weather warms. Any sunny day is reason to peel away the clothing. Shall we ogle?"

Bethany agreed, somewhat excited by the prospect of sighting some stunning Germans covered in suntan oil, their bodies glistening in the sun. What she discovered was the opposite; the nude sunbathers were mostly older, far beyond worrying about wrinkles and sags. The naked human body was, she learned, a strong argument for the virtues of fashion. Some things were better off not seen.

Which reminded her of Michael and Francis. Bethany led Herta along the paved trails, chatting casually, trying to feign relaxation and not quite succeeding, one thought always lingering in the back of her mind: *Where the hell are they?*

This charade could not last indefinitely. The professor would surmise, eventually, Bethany's ulterior motives. Or she would bore of the conversation and simply walk away. For that matter, perhaps she had her own protection nearby. She might order them to abduct Bethany again. Daylight, she guessed, was her only protection. But even that was in short order by the time they finished their third lap around the park.

"I must be going, my lovely Beer Judge," the professor said suddenly.

"But—"

"No buts. I have an appointment to attend. I had a wonderful stroll. Perhaps we'll see each other again soon?"

Bethany swiveled her head, seeking the support that wasn't coming. She moved too quickly, too nervously, and she knew that. *She might wonder why my demeanor has changed,* but Bethany couldn't quite bring herself under control. The professor was going to slip away, a perfect opportunity to seize her would be lost.

But slowly, it dawned on her. They came to the English garden because Amanda had changed the plan. She had diverted the mission and sent them on this long, leisurely stroll.

Is it possible?

That thought brought the swift realization of how little she knew about the crew to which she had entrusted so much. A memory snapped into place in Bethany's mind, bringing forward the words Amanda had spoken outside Jake's house: "I have what I need."

The recollection of Amanda's voice rang like an alarm bell. Should she keep the professor here? Should she abandon the task Amanda had sent her on? Bethany was not a believer in the double cross. Things like that happened, sure, even to professional cops. But not to her.

"I have to go," Bethany murmured.

The professor wrinkled her brow. "Is everything okay?"

"Fine. I'll see you soon."

Bethany walked slowly away, her pace rising to a fast jog as the betrayal hit home. They would be hours ahead of her, perhaps already finished with whatever they were after. But it might not be too late. Not if she hurried.

"Professor Stocker," he said warmly, extending a hand.

She hesitated, annoyed by the intrusion. People sometimes thought it appropriate to lend her superstar status. Today that would not do. She raised her hand, palm out.

"Not today," she said.

"You don't recognize me?"

She paused, digging into her mental vault of faces and names. Yes, there was something familiar—the round face and olive-tinted skin, the blue eyes that couldn't be replicated, the mouth with cherry-red lips. He was so handsome he should have been memorable.

"Have we met?"

"Not so long ago, yes. You scurried away with the American woman while I stayed in the café. That establishment, sadly, suffered an unfortunate murder."

Herta caught her breath, shocked by her poor recollection. "You're the detective?"

He chuckled and shrugged. "It was an enjoyable role with no strings attached. I did it to improve some skills. Christian told me to come to you if ever ..." His voice trailed off.

The professor fell silent before opening the door, still befuddled by her lack of recognition. She gestured for the man to come upstairs.

"I see now that Christian only handled the best," she said after serving him tea at the kitchen table. "I sometimes wondered."

"My aspiration was to serve you. His mentoring gave me the skills and opportunity to do that."

"Shall I still call you Fritz then?"

He laughed. "Fritz Weyermann! What a name, right? You can use that if you'd like. It's a pleasant nom de guerre."

Herta leaned forward, her voice deadly serious. "Well then, Fritz, I have some work for you. Immediate work that you must successfully resolve. If you fail, I am nothing, the party is nothing, and you are nothing. Do you understand?"

"Completely. Consider it done. What are the specifics?"

She relaxed, smiling. "It began in the 1920s," she said, "and continues today in the basement of a brewery." The long story rolled off her tongue.

CHAPTER 20

BODIES AND BOOTY

Amanda's speed had paid off once. When those gunshots rang out from the direction of Jake's apartment and she had raced ahead, Bethany had been unable to see her jog to a halt in front of Jake and put a silenced pistol round into his chest. And then she'd had enough time to convince the dying German to surrender his brewery blueprints and map.

"I'll finish the job you were to finish," she had said. "Herta wanted it that way." Her tone and composure had been convincing. She had inflicted Jake's fatal wound. Why would the German doubt her? The movement was all secrets and shadows. It made sense that there might be a backup, a guarantee if things went wrong. Without a whimper, he had handed Amanda the information. She hadn't even needed to kill him. Now her speed would pay off again.

But she had been seen, most certainly. To make matters worse, she had been together with Bethany. And hers was a known face. She considered it likely that some meddling German would connect the mental dots. They would search for Bethany and quite likely find her. Americans, after all, couldn't hide forever in Germany, especially those who spoke no German. Yes, she needed to hurry.

She carried three empty duffel bags, knowing quite well they might be too small to hold the entire treasure and too large for her to manage if all three were full. But she had appointed herself the task of acquiring as much as possible. Anything she could carry, she would.

Entry at the brewery's main gate was out of the question. Two guards held a constant vigil, not armed but ever watchful. Assuming she got past without having to kill someone, she would still need to cross two hundred yards in the brewery courtyard with no cover. Perhaps not an impossible task, but it was not worth the risk.

A low wall off Schrenkstrasse offered the best option. With a short rope and a rubber grappling hook, she easily accessed the roof of the brewery's old stable, dropped to the ground within twenty feet of the malthouse doors, and seconds later vanished into the shadows.

The main entrance to the malthouse was unlocked, and for a moment, a flash of fear surged adrenaline through her veins. Was it possible that someone was working in the cellar below? She slipped inside, sliding through the darkness, and took a position behind a massive empty wooden barrel. She breathed easily, maintaining perfect silence, listening for the sounds of footsteps, of people talking, of work in the subcellar. After ten minutes, when no noise came back to greet her, she rose and made haste to the concrete stairs that led to the darkness below. Swallowing deeply, hoping the map did not lie, she put her gloved hands to the walls and began down the seventy-five steps. Only at the bottom would she risk any light.

Damp mustiness rose to meet her nose. As she descended, the smell of wet, germinating barley became overwhelming, if not somewhat pleasant. She couldn't imagine a job down here, swallowed in manmade caverns, a slave to artificial light. She did, however, admire those who did the work. Without them, after all, there would be no Augustiner beer.

When she at last counted the final step, Amanda clicked on her penlight. Machinery surrounded her, including a grain elevator and a large grain transporter sunk into the floor, covered with a metal grate. She stepped into the shadows to her right, flashing light over the grains that covered the floor as far as the eye could see. Amanda knew the story, that the Nazis had used these cellars as a munitions factory during the war. What kind of weapons she didn't know. And it didn't matter now. She circled back around the stairs, past the machinery, and along a walkway that took her to the back of the grain beds that lined the basement. The German had marked the third section. Quickly she hustled past the first and second sections of grain, stopping at the third. Her light caressed the narrow uncovered section of floor, looking for breaks in the tile.

Nothing.

She found a thick-handled brewery broom and swept away several feet of grain but still found nothing. Panic curdled her stomach. She had to force herself to stay calm.

Think rationally! she thought. *Is the work floor the place to have stashed everything? Is there someplace better?*

She flashed the penlight in a circle, to the floor again, and then to the tall arched ceiling and walls, her brain churning. There were walkways connecting each germinating room, far too narrow and far too small to hold anything of interest.

Too small?

She realized then that nobody knew the true size of the treasure. Indeed, everyone had assumed it was substantial in size, and perhaps it was. But perhaps that size had less to do with quantity or cubic feet.

She snapped her head back and forth, dancing light off the walkway in front of her and then the one behind her.

She dashed to the walkway straight ahead. It would be the third one in. Her light hit the uncovered tiles that measured four by eight feet. Immediately she could see that someone had scratched away the grouting.

She reached into a duffel bag, closed her fist around a rubber mallet, and then paused. Tapping the tiles, listening for hollowness, might tell where the treasure was, but the risk of alarming someone was too great. She dropped the hammer and grabbed a crowbar. The floor had to come up.

The first tile creaked slightly and rubbed against its neighbors, but overall, she was struck by how easily it moved. *I'm not the first,* she thought, a lump rising in her throat. This would be the worst scenario—a treasure chest already robbed of its loot. She reached for the tile, lifting it with her left hand while her right hand pressed the flashlight into the darkness. She gasped at the blackness that swallowed the light, sinking her hand into the hole, hopelessness and desperation sweeping over her. She raised another tile, swallowing an anguished moan at the empty pit.

"Too late," she whispered. "I was too slow."

Amanda lifted away the other tiles, stacking them in the fourth germinating room, each empty hole leaving her to wonder what had been there just days or weeks earlier. Perhaps gold, perhaps diamonds, or perhaps silver, but that last thought froze in her mind when she came to tiles that wouldn't lift away.

"What's this?" she said under her breath. She tugged at the tiles, but still they wouldn't budge. Amanda shined light on the grouting, noting they had not yet been touched, and then on the dirt floor beneath where she had already moved tiles.

He never tried these. Maybe they were next.

Amanda's crowbar slipped beneath the tile. She paused for a moment, listening for approaching sounds. Once satisfied, she gave a sharp tug. The tile cracked. Amanda lifted it away and gasped.

Diamonds—all three feet deep and four square feet of diamonds—sparkled in the glow of her tiny flashlight. She barely paused, shuffling them into her duffel bag and cracking open the next tiles, each time revealing more of the same. Her duffel bags sagged beneath the weight. *How much more could possibly have been in the other pits?*

She cracked open the fourth tile, the seemingly empty hole a surprise. *All the better,* she thought, but stuck her hand inside anyway. Her knuckles struck a small metal box. She raised it from the hole and fondled the lock that held it closed.

"I don't have time for this," she said, dropping the box back into the darkness. Hoisting the three duffel bags onto her shoulders, she struggled through the darkness and up the pitch-black stairs, finally gaining freedom fifteen minutes later over the wall at Schrenkstrasse. The streets of Munich were quiet. Windows were dark in the buildings around her. Adrenaline compelled her forward, the weight of the cargo nearly imperceptible, the lights of the Hauptbahnhof drawing nearer as she continued down Landsbergerstrasse.

Inside the train station, nobody took notice of her, nobody asked if she needed any help. She was grateful for that even if she simultaneously resented that aspect of German indifference. Her timing was perfect; a train to the airport arrived the moment she stepped on the platform. Forty minutes later, she was at the airport, and by dawn, she had boarded a plane back to America, her cargo securely in tow, her reputation certain to be secure among her people.

Fritz Weyermann could not help the fact that the sun had already risen. He had needed to meet with Herta Stocker. He had needed to understand his mission and, that accomplished, obtain permission to proceed. And as it stood right now, things were just fine. Standing over the dead guard, he took aim at the second and put a bullet into his skull.

Workers were swarming the brewery yard, and for just a moment, it struck Fritz as ironic that he could have stolen a uniform somewhere and just sneaked inside. *Too late for that*, he thought. He jammed a fresh clip into his pistol, wiped blood from his face, and rushed in the direction of the malthouse.

Forklifts zipped past carrying pallets of beer bottles, kegs, and other containers to someday placate Germany's ceaseless thirst. Fritz grimaced at the sight of many foreign faces: Serbs, Spaniards, even East Germans. Fritz sneered. Even the latter were as non-German as the rest. Their time would come, he knew. Perhaps sooner than they could guess. The fact that none of them noticed him sprinting past revealed just how worthless they were.

He had memorized where he was going and didn't vary from the plan. First, he slipped up to the brewery manager's door—Herr Steingarten according to the nameplate—quietly knocked, and put two silenced bullets through the man who answered the door. Moving quickly, he cut the phone lines and then hurried down the basement stairs. A machine was operating on the first floor. Fritz heard several workers yelling to each other above the sound. These people he would let live. They were not yet in his way.

Once down the seventy-fifth stair, Fritz turned to his right and sprinted over the grain bed, down the third quadrant, and to the back corner where the treasure had remained hidden for decades. Drawing closer, however, he slowed, his mind taking stock of the sight barely visible in the darkness: ripped up tiles, an empty pit, a woman-sized footprint evident among the grains and dirt.

"Who the hell was here?" he rasped, drawing a flashlight from his jacket pocket. The yellow beam revealed nothing but the hurried work of his predecessor. Then a glint of metal deep in a pit caught his eye.

"There you are," he said, kneeling, taking the precious box into his hands. "The one thing not to leave behind. What a fool."

"Who's there?"

The voice rose from the darkness, coming from any possible direction. Without hesitation Fritz clicked off the flashlight and slipped into the shadows, sliding the metal box into a sling pouch he wore inside his jacket, over his shoulder. He ejected the clip from his pistol, inserted fresh rounds, and then jammed the clip back into place. He dashed from his hiding spot without a second thought, hurrying through the walkways in the direction of the stairs that would lead to freedom. Rounding the corner after the first walkway, a rotund brewery employee blocked his way, a bottle of Augustiner Edelstoff in hand. He looked at Fritz with a confused expression. Fritz gave him a bullet through the left eye. The back of the man's head exploded, and he collapsed with a solid thud, his beer bottle shattering into hundreds of shards.

On the floor above, the machinery was still running. No voices could be heard. Fritz paused on the thirty-fifth stair only to glance into the worker assembly area. There he saw what looked and sounded like a Spaniard wildly gesticulating to three other workers, his German broken and accented, but understandable. Something about an intruder. Their manager being dead. Fritz stepped into the opening, allowing them the opportunity to see him. Four quick bullets and thirty seconds later, they all were dead.

The smell told Bethany she was too late. She could guess the identities of the bodies inside and knew she would be wise to leave the scene immediately, but curiosity forced her shoulder and then her foot to slam into the door. Finally, the jamb gave way. The odor was an invisible wall. Francis and Michael, both dead, confirmed her fears.

"Amanda," she whispered.

Time had been short, she knew, for Amanda to have taken such drastic actions. Something must have changed—information, material—and suddenly, the words Amanda had spoken outside Jake's apartment stung with new meaning: "I have what I need."

But what had she needed? Some information? Or maybe something she had taken away from the scene? If that was the case, it would have needed to be small, something she could have hidden from Bethany. Then it was clear, the meaning of the words Jake had spoken in his dying moment: "The brewery. The malthouse. Basement. Third quadrant. Millions. Don't let them get it."

Bethany had allowed this to slip by, believing Jake was speaking about the professor and her followers. But now she knew that was wrong. It had been Amanda after all.

Bethany scanned the room, seeking something that might help her take the next step. Nothing. She was alone in Munich, with death as abundant as beer. She suspected the next days of her stay would produce some serious off-flavors.

* * *

Police surrounded the brewery's gate, their cars blocking Landsbergerstrasse, sirens blaring and lights flashing. Bodies moved about in a frenzy. Bethany arrived at the scene just as the covered bodies of the two guards were wheeled away on stretchers. There was no way for her to make it past the chaos without being stopped or noticed. But there was no way she could not try. Inside that brewery, something big was happening, something to which Bethany had been attached from the beginning. She was not going to quit now. Bethany scanned the main entrance and then the surrounding buildings, looking for a weakness, a way in. She wandered back in the direction of Hackerbrücke, toward the city, and reached the corner of Schrenkstrasse. Here was the Augustiner Bräu café, quiet and empty now except for a waitress and bartender standing in the doorway.

I'll slip in here, Bethany thought. *There must be a way into the brewery. For beer delivery at least.*

But just as she had settled on the idea, she heard a soft thump to her left, up Schrenkstrasse. Bethany craned her neck and saw a man crouched in the shadows. *Did he jump from the roof?* In the same moment Bethany thought the question, the man stood and sprinted up Schrenkstrasse, quickly turning left onto Westendstrasse.

Bethany glanced about. Nobody had noticed this strange character. No police were prowling nearby, watching for suspicious behavior. The fellow must have just climbed over the brewery's wall, jumped down, and dashed away, no questions asked. Without another thought, Bethany lumbered off in pursuit of her quarry.

She made the turn onto Westendstrasse, quickly peering to her right down Ligsalzstrasse. She caught sight of the man several hundred yards ahead, now walking. Bethany moved quickly, following him three blocks down and turning left on Gollierstrasse. Another three blocks and she was only two hundred feet behind, now crossing a large field. Bethany slowed, feeling oddly like she knew the place. She looked to her right and saw the statue of Bavaria looming over the field.

"The Theresienwiese!" she whispered, drawing even closer to the man with a few quick steps.

They were halfway across the field, crossing Mathias-Pschorr-Strasse, when Bethany made the final sprint to overtake him. Just then, however, a voice off to their right shouted an alarm.

"Fritz! *Achtung!*"

Fritz turned to face his attacker at the moment Bethany sprang forward. Bethany felt the hard steel of a pistol slide between her left arm and ribcage, the percussion from a silenced shot forcing air from her lungs. She jammed a fist into Fritz's face, shattering his nose. He reeled back, nose bleeding. Bethany gasped, recognizing the man's face.

"Officer Weyermann?" she said, drawing back her bloodied hand.

Fritz shook his head, clearing the cobwebs. "Damn you, Judge!" he yelled. "Why the hell are you still in this country? You're sticking your damn nose in places you don't belong. Don't you know there were some murders at the Augustiner Bräu today? Can't you see I'm busy?"

"Yes, sir. I was just over there and saw the police activity."

"At the brewery?"

"I was, yes. And I saw you come over the wall, which is why I followed."

"You saw me come over—"

From over Bethany's shoulder, a familiar voice chimed in. "She always was too curious, Fritz."

Bethany spun around. "Herta?"

She laughed. "We've been entwined since the beginning, my dearest Beer Judge. Why would you be surprised that we meet now?"

Fritz pushed Bethany aside, his left hand pressed into his bleeding nose. "What would you like me to do?"

"Do nothing." She looked at Bethany. "Do you have any idea what has been happening?"

"I've known nothing," she said. "Except the feeling of being caught in something outside my control."

Herta laughed. "I know that feeling well. Which is why I strive to be in control of all things at all times. Even you, my friend, though you might not like to hear that right now. Much of your suffering has come indirectly from my hands."

"I've wondered."

"Yes, of course. Your friends. Those who would have stopped me. Does it surprise you to know that your ally, Amanda, is already returning to America with millions of dollars' worth of stolen diamonds? Stolen twice, I should mention! First by the Nazis. Now by her."

"That's why she killed them—"

"Her partners? She killed them for many reasons, I'm sure. Diamonds alone are never enough. Not for the smart women."

"You mean she killed the people at the brewery? In order to snatch the jewels?"

Fritz sniffed and raised his chin. "That was me."

Herta smiled. "Conceited about your handiwork, are you?"

"I take pride in my job. And I'm not going to let some American woman get credit for my accomplishments."

"But I don't understand," Bethany said. "If she already took the diamonds, why even go in? And why kill innocent people?"

"You missed what I already said. That diamonds are never enough for women. In my case, the something else lies in a small metal box. Isn't that correct, Fritz?"

"Yes, it is." He reached into the pouch, withdrawing the metal box and placing it in her hands.

"For decades this technology has waited. Perfected before the war by our brilliant German scientists, this weapon had the power to secure German victory. But they kept it from the führer, those traitors of the fatherland. Hid it in the dungeons of a munitions factory. And now it rests in my hands. His rightful heir. Yes, the cycle has come full circle."

Bethany swallowed hard. "You're telling me there's some kind of weapon in that little box?"

"A weapon of unimaginable magnitude! The world will cower at our feet!"

The smile on Fritz's face spread as Herta spoke.

"What do you mean?" Bethany asked. "What sort of weapon could be placed in a box that small?"

"Just think of the things all humans need. That should answer your question."

"What humans need? Like shelter, food, water—"

Herta jabbed a triumphant finger toward her face.

"Water? The weapon contaminates water?"

"That's far too primitive. Think of it merely as having the ability to allocate appropriately."

"I don't understand—"

"And you shouldn't!" Fritz yelled, suddenly waving his pistol in Bethany's face.

"Be calm, Fritz. She's been our friend. She has sacrificed so much to secure our victory."

"Unwittingly," said Bethany.

"Yes, I will grant you that. You would have never volunteered your friend to be murdered."

Bethany's face paled. "Louis?"

"I'm sorry," Herta said, frowning. "You didn't know? Did we perpetrate the ruse so well? Oh my, Christian was a talented man."

Bethany said nothing. Fritz's smile widened. Herta scanned the horizon, suddenly nervous.

"We should move ourselves to a less conspicuous location," she said.

"How do you know there's anything in that box?"

"I'm sorry. What did you say?"

"The box," Bethany said. "It's locked. It could be empty."

"That's impossible!" Fritz said. "It was undisturbed. The lock was unbroken."

Herta simply giggled. "Don't let her get inside your head. She's not concerned with what we possess. She's acting selfish after realizing how much she has lost and how badly she was used. Now, Bethany," she continued, moving closer and focusing her eyes, "this is when we say adieu for good. It is time for you to gather your things. It is time for you to fly home to Buffalo."

"But I'm not—"

"There's nothing left for you here. We have what we need, my dearest Beer Judge. Go home."

"This can't be how—"

The professor grabbed Bethany's chin, her voice sharp. "Bethany, listen to me! Just go home! It's over. Go before it's too late."

CHAPTER 21

THE ROAD BEYOND HOME

It couldn't have all been untrue, couldn't have all been fabricated, but when Bethany traveled to Garmisch to receive police clearance to leave the country, she discovered that Detective Fritz Weyermann had removed his name from the investigation long ago and that Weyermann had subsequently disappeared.

"Perhaps this is why you did not know," said the officer behind the desk, sensing Bethany's exasperation. "The detective had failed to inform you. Of course, his apparent disappearance may not have received the attention it deserved. I shall report this to my superiors."

Bethany thought for a moment to share what she knew. It could be enough to stop a disaster. It might uncover a dangerous political group. And it might trap her in Germany for another six months. No, she decided, the situation was a German problem. One that she had been mixed up with for far too long. Herta had been right: it was time to go home. She could practically taste the buffalo wings. *What types of beers would I want to pair with that?* A pale ale or IPA would ramp up the spice, while a malty beer would tone it down. Both sounded good—why only choose one?

Outside her Munich hotel, the taxi driver had waited patiently.

"Sorry I'm late," said Bethany, sliding into the backseat.

"Not a problem," the driver said, tapping the meter. It had been running for the last ten minutes.

Bethany nodded, accepting the expense. "How far do we have to go?" she asked.

"About twenty kilometers. The traffic should be light, though. I'd be worried if we were driving early in the morning, when people are on their way to work. Afternoon is good."

"That's fine. Good, good. Whenever you get me there, I'm happy. Just so I make the flight."

The taxi driver said nothing, touching the gas pedal with his foot, easing the car into traffic. Soon they were on the Autobahn, zipping between cars, the rhythmic motion rocking Bethany toward sleep.

She had been so fatigued that she had practically forgotten how exhausted she felt. It had become almost normal. But in the well-kept car, with the wind shut behind tinted glass and the plush leather seats molding to her body, Bethany felt comfort for the first time in months. Tension and anxiety melted away. She heard the radio come on, felt thankful to the driver for keeping the volume low, and drifted into her thoughts.

"What's that?" she snapped, sitting up.

"Just an airplane taking off. We're by the airport."

Bethany rubbed her eyes. "I must have fallen asleep."

"You did, yes," said the driver as he swung a sharp curve and parked beside the curb.

Bethany frowned at the price on the meter but paid without complaint, leaving a handsome tip. The driver climbed from the car and helped his occupant out.

"You have all your papers, miss? Correct documents? Airline ticket?"

"Everything is here," said Bethany, patting her bag. "Thanks for your concern."

The driver grabbed her arm, looking toward the door. His mouth grew tight, his eyes sinister. "It's just that security may be a little tighter than usual today, you understand. Something is happening in Berlin."

"Berlin? What's happening there?"

"She said you would know."

"She? Who is—"

"And she said to say thank you for your help and for you not to worry. Everything is under control."

"This is the professor you're speaking of? Herta Stocker?"

The taxi driver slid his hand to Bethany's elbow, leading her toward the door, trying to calm her. "Do not be alarmed. They have the situation exactly where they want it."

At that moment, Bethany realized the driver could offer her nothing. Just simple assurances. She glanced toward the voluminous airport, the nervous sweat already trickling down her spine. With a quick skip she was through the main door and running through the hallways. She heard the taxi driver yelling from behind her: "You have plenty of time to catch your plane!"

Of course I do. I just want a TV.

Bethany fought to be patient while waiting to clear security. She had to appear calm and controlled. If not, she'd arouse suspicions and quite likely be detained. But it was impossible to stem the sweat that beaded on her forehead. It made her nervous, made her eyes twitch and dart. She needed to get it together. She was next in line.

The female security guard casually checked her ticket and passport and languidly drifted her gaze over Bethany's face. "Lane four," she said.

Bethany stripped her shoes and belt, rifled her pockets for anything that might set off the alarm, and placed everything in the plastic bin. She cleared the body scan, waited for her belongings to slide down the conveyor belt, collected them, and then hustled toward the gate. She found an open bar, perched on a stool below the television, and reflexively ordered a Dunkel. The bartender poured it quickly, just a half liter, and Bethany took a long gulp without examining the color or enjoying the malty nose. The alcohol worked quickly. She exhaled, relaxing, allowing the pleasure to ease through her limbs.

The television showed a soccer game. Bethany waved to the bartender and pointed at the screen. "News?"

The bartender inhaled deeply, both bored and annoyed. He grabbed a control and languidly pushed the buttons, changing channels. What looked like a news station appeared on the screen. The anchors spoke quickly in German.

"Anything in English?" asked Bethany.

The bartender sighed at the inconvenience. After a dozen more clicks, he landed on a major news station. Bethany nodded a thank-you and settled into her stool, looking for something, anything that would reveal the professor's plans.

After one hour and five half liters, Bethany had caught up on the US stock market and the latest tabloid news. Nothing about Berlin. Maybe the German news station would have been a better choice after all. She shot a cold eye at the bartender. The asshole would have never offered to translate.

A perky female voice called all passengers to board their flight to JFK. Bethany set a thin stack of euros on the table, waved the bartender a drunken farewell, and staggered to the gate. She boarded the plane and passed out before they taxied away, her inebriated snores loud and obnoxious the entire flight home.

Bethany first awakened to the murmurs of her in-flight neighbors. A general sense of uneasiness pervaded the tightly packed space. The overhead speakers clicked, and the captain's voice filled the cabin.

"Sorry for the inconvenience, folks. Air traffic control had asked us to remain in this holding pattern for the last thirty minutes. We were given permission to land just a moment ago. Please stay seated."

A buzz of happy murmurs burst forth until someone shushed loudly, commanding silence.

"…enough fuel to land at JFK."

"Did he say we have enough fuel?" Bethany's neighbor whispered.

Bethany nodded, trying to hear the rest of the captain's announcement.

"...should expect tighter security upon landing," he continued. "We might be on board for a while before they let us deplane, so I ask in advance for patience on everyone's part."

"Is there something wrong with the plane?" yelled a woman from the back end of the plane.

"Are we being quarantined?" shouted a man.

Bethany felt a knot in her throat and tried swallowing but found it too uncomfortable. She was the reason, she figured. For some reason, they were going to arrest her upon arrival. Perhaps they considered her a terror suspect.

A stewardess spoke into the microphone. "Please be calm, everyone. Stay seated and stay calm. The pilot will address the cabin in just another moment."

There was sudden rapt silence again, filled only with the muted sound of air rushing past the plane. Finally, chimes rang and lights came on, signaling the passengers to fasten their seat belts. The plane rolled left and began its descent.

The pilot clicked on the intercom again. "We'll be on the ground in fifteen minutes. And I'm sorry to have alarmed anyone. The delay has had nothing to do with this plane or anyone on board."

Bethany sighed audibly.

"There has been, however, an incident today. It was international in nature, and the reports are still sketchy. As I understand it, there was a massive explosion in downtown Berlin. Thousands are reported dead and injured."

The pilot left the rest unsaid. The passengers remained silent, none reading books or magazines, none fingering their cell phones, none whispering to one another. Each stared into space, knowing the world had changed once more but not knowing exactly how. None, of course, but Bethany Judge, who felt the warm sting of tears on her cheeks when the plane's wheels touched ground.

Bethany returned to Buffalo, where for two weeks she heard nothing but rumor and innuendo about what the newscasters were calling "the Berlin Incident." The explosion at the Reichstag had been reminiscent of Adolf Hitler's burning of the same building on February 27, 1933, but the situation had grown steadily worse. Air pollution from the fire had killed tens of thousands of people within five hundred miles downwind of Berlin. The city's water was grossly polluted and poisonous; signs reading "unsuited for human consumption" were posted over water fountains in and around the city. Trace elements of those same poisons had shown up in water supplies around the globe. Specialists claimed the world was on the brink of a global catastrophe if the problem wasn't soon brought under control.

One afternoon, as Bethany paired a homemade beef on weck sandwich with an ice-cold American lager, she saw good news on the local television station.

"It seems," said an international crime specialist into a stack of microphones, "that the threat of a future attack, the thing we have all feared since this despicable event occurred, was eliminated at the moment of the initial explosion. Evidence—and I am not at liberty right now to go into detail now beyond the following points— indicates the attack was conducted by the influential leader of a radical neonationalistic group and a large group of her adherents. The fact that the leader of that group—a Professor Herta Stocker— unequivocally perished in the initial explosion suggests to us that the timing of this explosion was premature."

"Was she trying to blackmail parliament?" shouted a reporter.

"I can't speculate on that. Though we can't be certain the threat was eliminated entirely, we can assume that the leadership of this organization is significantly reduced. The only remaining question is whether this weapon, whatever it was, was singular in its existence. Indeed, we have no scientists thus far that can identify the nature of the explosive, define its destructive capacity, or pinpoint its origin.

We have many guesses—some date back decades—but I emphasize that they are only guesses at this time."

"Decades?" yelled another reporter. "Can you be more specific?"

The man waved off the question, and the television station cut back to local news.

A fitting end, Bethany thought, satisfied that the professor had received her comeuppance but sad that her actions had been so tragic for others. Could Bethany have stopped her? Somehow she doubted it. She had been too worn down to fight anymore. The professor would have crushed her like a worm.

She stuffed the sandwich in her mouth, chewed thoroughly, and chased it down with the watery beer. *Even the large breweries make brew that hits the spot when the time is right*, she thought. Who needed to go to Germany for beer anyway? The American craft brewing scene was the place she needed to explore!

Bethany stopped, her eyes bulging. Among her junk mail and bills was a single postcard, a picture of the Mormon Tabernacle Church gracing the front. On the back, a simple inscription: "A shame, the water over there and everything. You'll just have to drink more beer! Why don't you come on out and visit sometime? If you thought that was good, you'll love this."

And the signature: "Amanda."

Bethany reached for her beer, swallowing deeply, draining the glass. She poured another and, over the next few hours, many, many more. She would need to get ready for this—her mind and her liver—to find the loose end that got away.

"We shall be seeing each other soon, Amanda. And perhaps I'll even meet these dead parents of yours. Any other surprises? I suspect so. Yes, things were never quite right from the beginning. I managed to miss it all, but not this time. No, not this time."

Please post an
Amazon review!
Prost!
Tom